PENGUIN MODERN CLASSICS
Still Bleeding from the Wound

ASHOKAMITRAN, born in 1931 in Secunderabad, is one of the most distinguished contemporary Indian writers. In a prolific career that began in 1955, he has written over 250 short stories along with two dozen novels and novellas, in addition to a steady output of columns, essays and book reviews, earning him a central place in post-Independence Tamil literature. His work has been translated into many Indian and European languages. Five major novels as well as four collections of short fiction from his oeuvre are available in English translation. His years of rich and diverse contribution to Tamil literature have brought him many honours, including the Sahitya Akademi Award (1996). Ashokamitran lives and works in Chennai.

N. KALYAN RAMAN has published seven books of Tamil fiction in translation, including four of Ashokamitran's. His translation of contemporary Tamil poems has been published in several notable anthologies. He lives and works in Chennai.

BY THE SAME AUTHOR

Fourteen Years with Boss
The Ghosts of Meenambakkam
Manasarovar

ASHOKAMITRAN

Still Bleeding from the Wound

Translated from the Tamil by
N. Kalyan Raman

PENGUIN BOOKS
An imprint of Penguin Random House

PENGUIN BOOKS

USA | Canada | UK | Ireland | Australia
New Zealand | India | South Africa | China | Singapore

Penguin Books is part of the Penguin Random House group of companies
whose addresses can be found at global.penguinrandomhouse.com

Published by Penguin Random House India Pvt. Ltd
4th Floor, Capital Tower 1, MG Road,
Gurugram 122 002, Haryana, India

| Penguin
| Random House
| India

First published in English by Penguin Books India 2016

10 9 8 7 6 5 4 3 2

ISBN 9780143423287

Typeset in Dante MT Std by Manipal Digital Systems, Manipal

Printed at Repro India Limited

www.penguin.co.in

This is a legitimate digitally printed version of the book and therefore might not
have certain extra finishing on the cover.

Contents

Contents

Translator's Note

Ashokamitran, unarguably, ranks among the great writers who have emerged in post-Independence India. Now eighty-four, he has tirelessly pursued his craft for over sixty years, contributing a prolific output of narrative fiction as well as essays and commentary on a wide range of topics. He writes nearly always in Tamil, a language he shares with 70 million native speakers in Tamil Nadu and around the world.

Although Tamil boasts of an unbroken literary tradition of over two millennia, modern literature, narrative prose fiction in particular, didn't make its advent till 1879, less than 150 years ago. In fact, truly 'modernist' writing in Tamil, giving the individual—any individual—an unprecedented centrality and agency, only began in the first half of the twentieth century. Subramania Bharathi, great poet and freedom fighter, was the pioneer of this tradition, creating a new vision of Tamil modernity. In his own way, Ashokamitran, who began writing in the 1950s, has sustained and extended this vision through his fiction, exploring human reality in an impressive range of contexts, framed inexorably by the confusions and conflicts of a reluctantly modernizing, traditional society.

Ashokamitran may have been led to this mode of exploration by the trajectory of his personal life. He is from an entirely urban background, an uncommon circumstance among Tamil writers of his generation. The son of a railway official in Secunderabad, he moved to Chennai (then Madras) in 1952, at the age of twenty-one. Soon thereafter, he found employment in the story department of Gemini Studios, a major film-production company of the time, where he worked for fourteen years. In 1966, he quit his job to become a full-time writer, a difficult but courageous decision for a person of his background and means. His work since then has earned him a pre-eminent place in the world of contemporary Tamil letters, as well as widespread national and international attention.

Any reader of Ashokamitran's fiction will immediately discern that the writer's main focus is on exploring the human predicament. His art prioritizes the experiential reality of individuals over the abstractions of history, culture, family and work, which suggests that he is moved less by ideology or intellect than by an imagination that is more forceful and illuminating than either.

Ashokamitran's narrative technique can be termed as a kind of 'documentary realism'. He describes the surface of events, apparently choosing the details with great care, but never spelling out what they might mean. In this quiet and unobtrusive way, he brings startling epiphanies and dazzling insights about the human world to the reader. It has also been observed that Ashokamitran's characters tend to be 'ordinary' people of humble circumstance, and through his nuanced account of their struggle—not always successful—to survive with dignity in hostile environments, the reader learns, more clearly than ever before, what it means to be human in these times, in this world.

Ashokamitran employs a simple language and spare prose style to suit his narrative technique. The reality he portrays is vivid and accessible, even when he is describing the inner monologue of an anguished person. His tone is normally wry and detached, punctuated not infrequently by his talent for highlighting the absurdity and humour inherent in commonplace situations.

All these markers of Ashokamitran's art are easily discerned in this collection. Written over a period of forty years (1961–2000), the twenty stories in this volume are among the best in his oeuvre, and represent all the major contexts that keep recurring in Ashokamitran's work: his boyhood in Secunderabad; his stint in Gemini Studios; the tribulations of lower middle-class families; and the muted rage of the working class. Given his profound concern for 'ordinary' individuals in a hostile world, it is not surprising that more than half of these stories are about women, of various ages and circumstances, and how they cope with their generic condition.

Though the stories in this collection are but a small fraction of his output, the reader will observe that certain characters appear more than once, as indeed they do in the larger body of his work. The author returns again and again to Chandrasekharan, the well brought-up adolescent boy constantly bewildered by life and forever in danger of losing his innocence; the film director, Prakash Rao, obliquely a debauchee, with his inept sense of decency; and Manickaraj, the oppressed working-class man in Madras, full of bravado, hankering for release, and frequently wrong-headed. These chosen few, and there could be more, sometimes assume different names while retaining the basic contours of their real-world context and, of course, their shifting natures. Ashokamitran has said that looking back on his work, he wonders if he has been writing one long story over the years. These engaging characters, endowed with the privilege of returning time and again in different situations and under different names, are perhaps signposts to the unity of his work and what it stands for.

Given the spare prose style employed by him, some believe that Ashokamitran's stories are more easily 'translatable' than the work of those whose language is more complex and descriptive. As someone who has considerable experience in translating the writer, I don't find this to be true. Ashokamitran uses details and simple language to convey complex realities, and unless one translates with a sure sense of what he has left unsaid, it is difficult to succeed in producing a narrative that can equal the original in literary impact. In that sense, it is certainly a challenge for the translator to navigate the intricate pathways of Ashokamitran's unique craft.

I would like to thank my editors at Penguin Books India: Tarini Uppal, for her support and gentle guidance through the making of this book, and Shatarupa Ghoshal, for her fine editing which has contributed significantly to the quality of the translation. Any errors that remain are, of course, mine.

Chennai   N. Kalyan Raman
February 2016

Spinning Wheel

'**N**immi!'

Pankajam's call resounded all over the house.

'Nimmi!'

Amma's reply from the kitchen was terse: 'She is having a bath.'

Pankajam shut her husband's drawer forcefully. The ink bottle kept precariously on the edge of the table toppled over. She quickly reached out and caught it before it fell. As though it had been waiting for just such an exertion, her pulse rate shot up, almost audibly. She closed her eyes. For a moment, the room itself seemed to spin around her. Pankajam grabbed the table for support and steadied herself. It would take at least half an hour for the palpitations to die down.

Amma was cutting some greens. Pankajam could see that she was anticipating an earthquake.

Pankajam went and stood beside her mother. Then she asked in as steady a voice as she could manage, 'Amma, why is our Nimmi like this?'

Fortunately, Amma didn't offer a reply. She continued to chop the greens even more attentively.

'Amma . . .'

Amma raised her head and looked at her. Pankajam sat down next to her.

'Amma, won't you please tell Nimmi not to poke around in his drawer?'

'Are you sure it was Nimmi?'

'Who else is going to open his drawer, Amma? Even this morning he arranged everything neatly before he left. And she has messed it up already.'

'Why would she mess it up?'

Pankajam hesitated for a moment. Then she told her mother gently, 'Amma, she steals small change.'

Amma stopped chopping for a moment. When she resumed, a teardrop fell on the pile of cut greens.

Pankajam grasped her mother's shoulder. 'Do you think I brought you here after Appa's death only to make you weep?'

For a few minutes the only sound was of chopping.

Nimmi came out freshly bathed. She gave her mother and Pankajam no more than a glance before she went to the front room.

Pankajam whispered in her mother's ear: 'Amma, I'll go and find out what she has to say. If we let her go on like this, it will become difficult for all of us. Please don't cry. I won't do anything on my own.'

Pankajam got up and went to the front room. Dressed in a skirt and blouse, Nimmi was standing before the mirror.

Pankajam asked her very calmly, 'Nimmi, why did you open your athimber's drawer today?'

Nimmi simply stood there, without replying.

'Why are you always opening it and taking money?'

'I don't steal and all.'

'Whoever said you were a thief? Why do you keep opening his drawer when nobody's around?'

'I didn't open anything.'

'Then how can there be less money in the coin box now, if you didn't open it?'

'If there is less money, why should it mean I took it? You lock up everything all the time, don't you?'

'Is that why you open his drawer, because it's never locked?'

'I don't know anything. Go!'

Pankajam held her temper in check. She went to the corner of the room where Nimmi's school books were stacked.

'Stay away from my books,' Nimmi warned her.

'Let me just see what you have here.'

Nimmi sprang towards her sister, but not before Pankajam had got hold of Nimmi's school bag.

'Don't touch that! Don't touch that!' Nimmi pulled at the bag with both hands, but Pankajam was ready for this.

3

'I won't take anything, I promise. Let me just see what there is.'

'Let go! Let go! There's no need for you to touch my things.'

Pankajam was firm. She reached into the bag and took out Nimmi's geometry box.

Nimmi let go of the bag and grabbed Pankajam's wrist. Pankajam struggled and broke free of Nimmi's grasp. She opened the tin box. Pencil, pen, eraser and compass—all scattered to the floor. Along with them, a one-rupee note and a few coins tumbled out.

Amma came running from the kitchen.

'Didn't I tell you, Amma? See this!' said Pankajam. Amma looked at Nimmi's face. Nimmi glared at Pankajam. Pankajam turned to her and froze in terror. She had never imagined that a young girl's face could express so much hostility.

'What's all this, Nimmi?' It was Amma who eased the tension of that moment.

'None of your business! Go away!' replied Nimmi.

'Why don't you ask me if you need money?' said Pankajam.

'Oh, yes? And if I did, you'd give it to me?'

'When have I not given you what you've asked for?'

Nimmi picked up the coins from the floor and flung them at Pankajam. 'Go away. Just take them and leave.'

'Nimmi, this is horrible,' said Pankajam.

'What is *not* horrible? Am I any good? Everyone's always after me!' Nimmi started bawling. Amma hugged Nimmi's shaking body while Pankajam walked away.

When Pankajam returned to the room some time later, Amma had gone to the kitchen. Nimmi was sitting alone in a corner, hugging her knees. Pankajam felt sorry for her. Even when Appa was laid up in bed for a year, Nimmi had been a lively little girl, active and vibrant. In the two months since Nimmi came to live with her, Pankajam had never seen her enjoying a hearty laugh.

Nimmi's books and coins were still lying scattered on the floor. Pankajam hesitated for a moment, then picked up the books and put them away neatly in Nimmi's school bag. She put the coins back inside the geometry box and shoved it into the school bag as well. After stowing the bag in the cupboard, she told Nimmi, 'All right, get up and eat. You have school today.'

Nimmi showed no sign of having heard her. Pankajam went and sat beside Nimmi. 'Get up,' she said. 'You've missed school for so many days already. Get up.'

Nimmi looked away.

'You mustn't be so adamant at such a young age, Nimmi. If you miss Appa, so do I. Do you think I don't feel sad? I too want you to study hard and come up in life, just as much as Appa did. Just wait for a few years. Can't you understand that we cannot always live as we wish to? Look at the baby, she is wailing. How can I go and attend to her if you don't stop crying? I didn't say what I did simply to hurt you. I have to account for every little thing to Athimber. If you need anything, anything at all, just ask me. But don't open his drawer on the sly, 'ma. It's not a good practice to open somebody else's drawer and take money. People will only mistrust you. Get up. Go and eat a little bit, go to school.'

Nimmi got up. That was enough to satisfy Pankajam for the moment.

The baby kept crying. Amma was well within reach but she made no effort to attend to the child.

Pankajam couldn't ignore Amma's restlessness any longer. It was already half past five, and Nimmi had still not come home. Pankajam too was feeling uneasy.

'When he comes back from work, will you give him a cup of coffee? I'll go and look for her,' she told Amma.

Her mother looked blankly at her. Pankajam continued bravely: 'There's some fresh decoction in the small tumbler. I'd make the coffee myself if he came back now, but it looks like he's got held up today. I'll go up to Nimmi's school and be right back.'

Before she put on her chappals, Pankajam went to check on the baby, who was asleep in the front room. Although the child was almost a year old, she was abnormally thin. She might wake up any moment but

Pankajam could attend to her only after she returned. These days, she could not expect her mother to do much for the baby

Outside, the traffic was quite intimidating. At any time, there were plenty of buses plying on that road. Now it was choked with all kinds of vehicles and pedestrians. Clusters of men travelled on the footboards of buses, hanging on precariously by their fingertips.

Rather than wait for a bus, Pankajam hailed a cycle rickshaw. The school was empty. Classes got over at half past three. The only voices that could be heard were in the headmistress's chamber. She went there.

The headmistress and two other teachers had several large sheets spread on the table and were entering various bits of information in the little boxes on them. One of the teachers asked Pankajam, 'Whom do you want to see?'

'My sister hasn't come home yet.'

'Which class?'

'Eighth standard. B section.'

'Eight-B. It's your class, teacher.'

'Oh, hasn't she reached home yet?' the other teacher asked Pankajam, 'But we even cancelled the last games period today! What's her name?'

'Nirmala. K. Nirmala.'

'Nirmala?' Now even the headmistress began to pay attention.

'This is the girl who lost her father recently . . . '

'Yes. That's right. I am her sister.'

Both the teachers got up and came to Pankajam. One of them told her, 'She must have reached by now. I saw her playing in the school grounds after we had let them off. Are you her own sister?'

'Yes. She was born many years after me. I was already married when she joined this school. That's why I've had no occasion to visit the school so far. I'll go home and see if she's come back.'

Before Pankajam could take the first step towards the door, the teacher said, 'There have been complaints about Nirmala here. You should be strict with her.'

Pankajam was shocked. 'What complaints?'

'Oh, she is studious all right. But it seems you give her a lot of pocket money at home.'

'Does she bring money to school?'

'If she only brought small change, there'd be nothing to worry about. But one day she treated four of her classmates to Limca.'

'What did you say she bought them?'

'Cold drinks. Each bottle costs a rupee and a quarter.'

'It was her birthday . . .'

'Her birthday can't be a daily affair, can it?'

Pankajam was seized by a fit of trembling. The seizures had become more frequent since Appa passed away. She walked out and got into the waiting rickshaw. It would be dusk soon: time for lighting the lamps at home. Not only was her sister missing, but she, Pankajam, had to scold her for many other things as well. Who was there to discipline her? If Pankajam did, wouldn't it have the opposite effect, making the situation still worse?

Pankajam's feelings of anxiety about Nimmi's whereabouts were eclipsed by a more serious worry: how was she going to handle Nimmi from now on? When she saw three girls in skirts and blouses walking together on the street, Pankajam's immediate worry reared its head again: Nimmi was not among them. Since the traffic was heavy, the rickshaw moved along slowly, ringing its bell and weaving its way through pedestrians. Pankajam could not, therefore, scan the passers-by properly. If her husband was home by now, her burden would grow heavier still.

As it turned out, her husband had reached home. Fortunately, nothing had happened yet to make him fly into a rage. When Pankajam entered the house after paying the rickshaw-wallah, she could sense that he didn't yet know why she had gone out that evening. But Nimmi had still not returned.

Amma had the baby on her lap and was giving her milk; she looked up at Pankajam. Pankajam felt consoled and annoyed at the same time. If Amma had looked after Appa with a little more care and attention, he wouldn't have died so soon. But what was the point of blaming Amma? Appa never got himself proper medical care. To get proper medical treatment, one had to make regular visits to the doctor, get all the tests done, and take all the prescribed medication regularly. For that, one must spend a lot of money; one must *have* a lot of money. If Appa had had a lot of money, it wouldn't have been put to proper use anyway. A man who gave his ten-year-old one or two rupees daily as pocket money, how would he have a lot of money? And even if he did, what was the use?

But she couldn't avoid saying something to Amma. Pankajam asked her, 'Nimmi is not in school. Could she have gone over to a friend's place? Do you know?'

Amma said, 'You look after the baby. I'll go and find out.'

'Where will you look for her, Amma? We could ask him to inquire with the police.'

'Let me go and look for her first.' Amma stood up, determined to have her way. 'Give me a rupee in change.'

'Will one rupee be enough? Shouldn't we tell him something?'

'I'll go and look in the house where we used to live. I only have ten-rupee notes with me.'

Amma left immediately. Her puja box adorned a corner of the kitchen. This box had come to Amma from her mother. Every day she offered a flower and a namaskaram—her sole prayer and worship—to the miniature idols inside that box. Pankajam looked at the box. She didn't know at that juncture how she might pray for her sister's return.

'Why is the whole house dark? Isn't Amma at home?' her husband asked, walking into the room.

Pankajam had the child in her lap and didn't get up.

'Where has your mother gone?' he asked.

'To her old house.'

'Looking for your sister, is it?'

Pankajam was startled. Had Amma told him when she wasn't around?

'You needn't search for her there. She is in this neighbourhood, right in the next street.'

'Did you see her?'

'I saw her there on my way back from the office.'

'Why didn't you tell us, then?'

'Did you ask me?'

Pankajam hugged the child and got to her feet. 'Just hold the baby for a minute. I'll go and bring her.'

'There's no need for you to go. She'll come on her own.'

Pankajam thought she was going to cry. He said, 'Your mother has no other child, son or daughter, who can support her. She has no brothers either. So she's come to live with you. Even if my family don't like it, I can tell them she has nowhere else to go. In fact, that *is* what I tell them. But it looks like your sister's going to spoil everything.'

When Nimmi finally returned home that night, Pankajam didn't ask her anything. Even when Amma came back an hour after that, Pankajam didn't ask Nimmi what the matter was, whether something had happened to keep her out so late. It was only when she saw her mother pack her trunk and bedding the next day that she realized she ought to have talked it out with her the previous night. Amma wanted to go back to their old house.

'Amma, how will you cope, living all alone? Why didn't you say anything to me before you made up your mind?'

'It's not like that, Pankajam. After all, I am not going far away, am I? It takes only half an hour to get there by bus. Luckily, there's a small place vacant right now in that building. It'll do for us, Nimmi and me. It's a familiar place, so it won't be difficult for us to manage.'

'You should have told me this morning. I would've had a word with him about this! What will he think if you leave abruptly like this? What will the others think? No, Amma. What terrible thing has happened here that you must go away in such a hurry?'

'Oh, nothing at all. But shouldn't we make sure that nothing happens in the future as well? Don't worry yourself about anything.'

'How can I not worry, Amma? Don't think I am blaming Nimmi, but her habits and behaviour are not at all proper. It was different when Appa was alive. But if there's no one around to take her to task, I can't imagine where it will lead. Here at least we can get her to show a little fear and respect for your son-in-law. Do you know what she was up to last evening? She had gone off with a couple of boys from the next street to learn to ride a cycle. She's nearing puberty, and if she goes off to the park with any old loafer, do you think she'll come to any good?'

'Your father had promised to buy her a bicycle this year. He kept talking about it.'

'It'd be all right if Appa was alive, Amma. All this talk is necessary only because he is no more. I don't think it's right for you to stay alone with her.'

'But how long will you feel like that? Are you sure you'll always think that way about our living together?'

Pankajam made no reply.

'No, Pankajam. Now that we are going back to the same place, there won't be any problems. If we can stay put there for another two, three years, she'll complete her SSLC. Then we'll see.'

Pankajam wanted to ask, 'Do you think your daughter will ever get that far?' If boys went astray, one could set them right so that they eventually succeeded in life. Was it possible with a girl?

'At any rate, I think it'd only be proper if you waited till he came back, and told him yourself,' said Pankajam.

Amma was silent. But she didn't stop packing her things.

'Amma, won't you listen to me?'

'No, Pankajam. We'll be at someone's mercy. He'll also say: why are you leaving, stay back here. And if he did, I would. But sooner or later something else will crop up. It's only right that we go where we belong.'

'All right. When do you plan to leave?'

'Only in the afternoon.'

'When Nimmi comes here should I send her to you?'

'No, she will come there directly after school.'

'So, mother and daughter have planned all this in advance?'

Amma lowered her head. Pankajam was furious. Then she felt pangs of remorse. How sad that even her mother felt she had to hide things from her!

Amma didn't take all her things. Clothes, bedding, and a few cooking utensils and vessels—that was all. Amma went to the street and hailed a rickshaw herself. When she left, she didn't even have a kiss for Pankajam's baby.

It was a baby born after a long wait, and they had even performed a ceremony in joyful anticipation of its arrival. Since her mother's house was in the same city, Pankajam had continued to live with her husband almost until the time of delivery, and then returned within a month of the baby's arrival. Amma had shuttled between the two houses thereafter. That must have been when Appa's health took a turn for the worse. Amma couldn't take proper care of her daughter or her grandchild. Appa too was in a bad way, and had no one to attend to him. When he was admitted in the hospital, Amma had done hectic rounds of duty at all three places for a month. Maybe Appa had decided not to linger simply to grant Amma a reprieve from that grind.

Pankajam's precious baby was lying on the floor, all skin and bones. She couldn't even turn over on to her stomach yet. Being on her back all the time had caused blisters to form on it. They said that some babies tended to develop slower than normal. Because the baby lay immobile all the time, even her husband couldn't play with her.

It's good for a baby to grow without being indulged. It was because of everyone's pampering that Nimmi had become so stubborn; stole money. I hope she will stop with that.

Amma's absence wasn't very hard on Pankajam. Because the baby was not very active, Pankajam could do her household chores without much distraction. She had a lot of free time now.

Leisure brought its own consequences. Pankajam went without sleep not only during the day, but also at night. When she closed her eyes, the image of Nimmi's glowering, hate-filled face, still wet from a bath, swam into view.

Nimmi hadn't been particularly fond of Pankajam even when their father was alive. Being a girl child of elderly parents must have instilled a feeling of helplessness in Nimmi. A girl young enough to have been Pankajam's daughter was her sister. By the time Pankajam had a child of her own, her hair had already started to grey.

Pankajam could have had complaints about other people, but she couldn't fault her husband on any ground. He never gave credence to the embarrassing and cruel things that his family and friends said about Pankajam. Just when he was beginning to accept that they would never have a child, there were signs that this stick-thin baby might be born after all. It was a normal delivery. But from the time she was born, the baby lay in the same spot, an inert doll that moved only her hands and legs.

Pankajam got up from the bed and switched on the light. It was not yet two o'clock. The baby was sleeping peacefully. A little away, her husband slept on the bed, a sheet covering him from head to toe.

Pankajam turned off the light and went to the bathroom. Earlier, they would leave the bathroom light on all night to double as a night light, which forced her husband to sleep with his face covered. When the baby's feeding habits stabilized a little, they stopped leaving the bathroom light on. But now her husband was unable to sleep without covering his face.

Pankajam sat down next to her bed. If her mother had been around, she would have got up and asked Pankajam what was wrong. Not that Amma had been a great help in looking after the baby. She had forgotten many things. Even simple tasks like giving the baby an oil bath had been hard for her. She must have brought up Nimmi just as ineptly.

Pankajam looked at the baby's face. She was sleeping with one corner of the mouth turned down slightly, just like Appa used to. Nimmi had teased him about it once, in front of Pankajam. Appa had been extremely indulgent with her regardless of how much she teased him. That was perhaps why, after he passed away, Nimmi reacted with extreme hostility whenever someone assumed his position to discipline her.

Pankajam's husband stirred a little in his sleep, then sat up in bed suddenly, as though startled. 'Was it you who left the bathroom light on?' he asked Pankajam.

'I forgot. I'll turn it off right now.' Pankajam stood up.

'Didn't you sleep at all, then?'

He got up from the bed and walked towards Pankajam. He was alarmed when he saw her face. 'Aiyo, why is your face looking so strange?'

'Strange? In what way?'

'You look really strange! What happened? Did Amma come here today?'

'No, she didn't. Amma hasn't been here since she left that day.'

'Are you brooding about that?'

Pankajam lay down.

He said: 'I didn't say anything to your mother. I don't have any serious objection to her living with us. No matter where she chooses to live, she can't avoid inconveniencing someone or the other. Still, your mother needn't have taken umbrage and left suddenly in a huff. I didn't even say anything to her that day!'

'No, you didn't say anything. But I had given Nimmi a piece of my mind, and that blew up into a big row.'

'I thought so. It was the day she didn't come home, wasn't it?'

He turned off the light and went to bed. Pankajam couldn't shut her eyes. Panic gripped her when she did. It would be such a relief if her baby woke up and cried. It was these little interruptions that helped one forget major worries.

When the next day dawned, the many small distractions and chores around the house filled all her hours. Once her husband left for office in the morning, Pankajam finished her work in the kitchen. Then she packed her husband's lunch and kept it ready for the man who delivered the tiffin carrier to his office. When it was time, she ate her own meal listlessly. After sending off her husband's lunch, she picked up the baby, locked the door and set out.

The house looked the same now as it had when her father was alive. As she approached the doorstep, memories of her father being carried away for his cremation rose vividly in her mind. The landlord's people had let them keep Appa's body in the downstairs hallway. In that narrow passage, there hadn't even been enough room for any of them to stay beside Appa and weep out their grief. When the bedsit was finally vacated, carrying Amma and Appa's possessions out of the house had been a difficult task. And now Amma had gone back into that house through the same narrow hallway. She had packed herself into a tiny room at the rear.

Amma was napping on the floor when Pankajam arrived. She was able to sleep during the day.

'Amma!' Pankajam called out softly.

Amma woke up immediately. 'When did you come?' And then: 'Have you eaten? Will you eat here?'

'No, Amma. I set out only after lunch. Has Nimmi gone to school?'

'Yes. I wanted to come there myself today. If I had known you were coming, I would've asked you to bring a few things with you. Are you all right? Just leave the baby over there on the mat.'

Pankajam sat down on the floor. 'There was a letter for you from the insurance people. You have to sign another form and send it to them.'

'Do you have it with you?'

'Here it is.'

Amma took the letter from Pankajam. 'Who opened the front door for you? Did you see the landlord?'

'No. The door was open. I came here directly.'

'It seems he has to get some work done in your husband's office. He mentioned it to me yesterday. Have you sent lunch for maapillai?'

'I have. I started only after the cycle-man came and left.'

'Did you get a bus quickly?'

'I did, but it was a little crowded.'

'Buses are crowded at all hours these days.'

'Did you reach here safely the other day? Did all the luggage arrive in shape? Isn't it a bit cold here? I should have brought both blankets.'

'Oh, we can bring them any time,' said Amma.

Pankajam felt as if she had exhausted everything she had to say. Fortunately, Amma had one or two things left to talk about.

'If sastrigal comes to your house, ask him to come here from this month on. Did he come by?'

'No. I'll tell him if he does. Or I'll send word to him.'

'Tell him only if he comes by. If he doesn't, I'll send Nimmi over with the message.'

Pankajam's voice was firm now. 'Don't send Nimmi on such errands,' she said sharply.

Amma was silent.

'Nimmi's behaviour is worrying, Amma.'

Amma clucked her tongue. 'Fatherless child. She is not even aware of her own problems.'

'So what if Appa is no more? Aren't we all here for her?'

'But *she* must feel that way, isn't it?'

Pankajam didn't wish to delve further into Nimmi's behaviour and hurt her mother's feelings. She wondered about one thing, though. Her grandmother had also suffered the same fate as her mother. But the house had teemed with people then. Relatives and acquaintances, so many of them, had gathered in their house for ten or fifteen days, grieved loudly, wailed, wept, had their coffee and left. When Appa passed away, there were ten mourners on the first day; four on the second. Within a week, Amma had to attend to many things herself. It has hardly been four months, and Amma acts as though she has been a widow for a very long time!

Amma fetched the ration card from behind a framed picture on the wall. She told Pankajam, 'Next time, can you bring the kerosene tin? We had to buy some as soon as we came here. Do you know where I've stored it? In a stainless steel vessel!'

'Amma! Amma!' Nimmi breezed in. As soon as she saw Pankajam though, she froze in the doorway, her spirits flagging visibly.

Pankajam pretended not to notice; she spoke to Nimmi in her normal, friendly tone: 'Do you know, you'd left your dictionary and colouring box behind? I've brought them for you. I also mended your skirt and brought that with me. How's school? Even yesterday, some of your friends came home looking for you. I told them that you live here now. How is that wound on your leg? Has it healed now? I hope you are changing the plaster regularly.'

Nimmi didn't respond to any of this; she kept her school bag in a corner of the room and went out again, calling, 'Amma!'

Pankajam got up and followed her out of the room.

Amma was speaking to the tenants in the upstairs portion. When Appa was bedridden, they had been extremely helpful. On seeing Pankajam, the lady gave her a bright smile and said, 'Come, Pankajam! I didn't know you were here. Amma told me just now. How have you been?'

Pankajam felt mildly angry. It was because they were such caring people that Amma must have decided to come back here.

'Look at this!' she protested to the lady. 'Amma doesn't even need her daughter; she's come back to you people.'

'So what? She should have thought of everything before she decided to move. Those who were to leave this world have left; and those still alive need a place to stay, don't they? In this city, is it ever easy to move house? You have to change your milk-card and ration card. Letters won't be delivered properly. There's Nimmi's school as well. She can walk to school from here. Luckily, you didn't have her transferred to some other school.'

Pankajam told her mother, 'Shall I leave now? If I leave now, I can reach home in time.'

'Wait a minute,' said Amma. 'Nimmi, go and light the stove.'

But Nimmi didn't go. Mother and daughters had to leave together. Pankajam took Nimmi's hand as they were coming down the stairs. Nimmi snatched it away.

Amma made coffee for Pankajam using the decoction left over from the morning. Pankajam fed the baby. When she was about to leave, Amma said, 'Wait. The landlord's people have just plucked drumsticks from the tree. I'll get you three or four.'

'What will I do with four drumsticks? One or two are enough,' said Pankajam.

As soon as Amma left the room, Pankajam asked Nimmi, 'Still angry with me?'

'Who am I to be angry with you?'

'Why do you say that? It's only with me that you can really show your anger.'

Pankajam said this in a palpably affectionate tone, but it didn't seem to have sounded that way to Nimmi.

'When Appa was alive, you took away everything we had, one thing after another! Must you rob us even after he is dead?'

'What are you saying, Nimmi? I haven't come here to take anything away.'

'What have you spared that you can take away now? Haven't you already taken everything and hoarded it in your house? When you had everything you wanted, you threw us out.'

'Is this how a little girl should talk? Who taught you to speak this way?'

'I'm only telling you what's going on. Who needs to teach me that?'

'Does Amma also talk like this?'

'What does Amma know? She only knows how to lavish things on you whenever you turn up.'

Amma came back with half a dozen drumsticks and offered four to Pankajam. Nimmi kept staring at Pankajam.

'How much for these, Amma?' asked Pankajam.

'Oh, they didn't mention anything.'

'Amma, I don't want them. Nimmi's complaining that you give me everything, do everything for me. It's only fair, what she's saying.'

'What are you trying to say?'

'I am talking about what we should have discussed a long time ago. When Nimmi grows up, we'll have to make arrangements for her to marry and set up house, won't we? People shouldn't say at that time that you gave everything away to your elder daughter.'

'Who's saying anything now, Pankajam? It'll be many years before we even have to think about Nimmi's wedding. What are you trying to tell me, Pankajam? I'm so weary, everything has been so painful.'

'I'm not saying this to hurt you, Amma. After all, who do I have as my own family except you and Nimmi? But we shouldn't end up where we can't bear to see each other, isn't it? But that would be impossible if Nimmi starts doubting my intentions. You've done a lot for me. From now on, I should do what I can for you and Nimmi.'

Pankajam picked up her baby and left. She was very agitated. She was even afraid that she might become dizzy and collapse.

She had to wait for the bus, and it afforded her enough time to calm herself. Even if Nimmi's suspicions were inappropriate right now, it couldn't be said that they were completely unfair. A woman's status was determined solely by how much she took with her to her husband's house. Pankajam's husband might not hanker after anything, but could they expect everyone to be like him? Was it this fear that made Nimmi think of her as a rival?

Pankajam removed the cloth covering her baby and looked at her face. This baby was indeed born after a long wait, but why couldn't she have been male? Whom would she hate when she grew up? She too might become a vessel for jealousy, hatred and fear. She will lie like a doll where you set her down, all blinking innocence, only till she is a year old. When she grows up, she will nurture in herself all the evil propensities of mankind. She will hurt herself, and also hurt others. Still, people yearned for babies. They even got married so that this kind of existence could go on and on.

For the second time that day, Pankajam's husband was acutely alarmed on seeing her face.

'What happened to you? Who asked you to visit your mother's place?' he scolded her. When he saw her sitting awake all night without sleeping, he was terrified. He took her to a doctor the next morning.

There was a crowd at the clinic. More than half the patients who had come to consult the doctor were women. Barring one or two, the others were quite ordinary. Average material comfort, average looks, confusion or dullness etched on their faces, a veneer of artificial calm and poise from having to sit among strangers in a new, unfamiliar setting. The sleekness of the waiting room was hardly suited to the shabbiness of their condition. The doctor's know-it-all air, superficial questions, partial and imprecise information from the patients being forced to answer such questions. What can 'a child born many years after marriage' possibly convey? How many different things can be inferred from 'the child has not had normal development'? Then Appa's death, her short stay with Amma, her living alone now . . .

It proved to be of no use. Unless being drowsy with sleep all day after swallowing pills counted as a benefit. Amma and Nimmi had come to live with them temporarily. Amma looked after the kitchen and her child. Nimmi ran errands, helped around the house, and then attended school. She grew taller by the day, wore a half-sari once in a while and poked about the house. She must have certainly started pilfering money again.

Pankajam had only intermittent periods of lucidity. During those phases, dread and anxiety held her in their grip. Whatever she set eyes on made her feel as if she was in great peril. Whenever she looked at Nimmi, she only saw a face still wet and dripping after a bath. Her child's mouth itself had morphed into Appa's face. Amma appeared faceless. When she saw any two people together, they seemed ready to tear into each other. However, before all this could reach an intolerable stage, there were three pills: green, red, white.

Nothing happened immediately after she took the medication. But within fifteen minutes, a cave would appear in front of her. Entirely without her volition, she would enter it. The floor of the cave would change abruptly into a steep incline. She would keep going deeper, and when she knew that she could no longer turn back, the cave would suddenly turn into a well. Pankajam would continue her descent into the bottomless hole. Her fall, too, would be endless. Hurtling headlong into that abyss, she would suddenly grab hold of something within reach. Perhaps a leather strap, the sort that standees hold on to in a bus. But how could this leather strap be cylindrical? And so thin? But, she was not on a bus, and this was no leather strap. It was a drumstick! Somebody had put away this drumstick safely inside the drawer. There was one thing about drumsticks. They never rotted. They dried up. If you planted a drumstick seed, the plant came up. But did you plant a drumstick seed or a cutting? You had to plant a cutting. This baby was pretty much like a small, tender drumstick. Eat lots of drumstick with your food. You'll have lots of babies. Babies like drumsticks, one after another.

Pankajam asked for her medication at the right time and took it without fail. In the mornings and evenings, her husband took care of it. Amma was supposed to give her the pills in the afternoon, a very minor responsibility. A simple task, really. One red pill and one white pill. But Amma was always confused. There were also bottles with blue and yellow pills on the bedside table. And another bottle of different white pills. Which two did she have to give Pankajam? Pankajam's husband explained everything to her every day, but that same afternoon, Amma would sit there perplexed, all the bottles around her. She didn't wish to mess around with medicines when she was confused; so she chose to give none at all.

Pankajam would sense Amma's confusion. There was only one kind of red pill. There was no room for doubt there. Of the two white pills, the bigger one was supposed to be taken in the afternoon. Pankajam explained this to her mother and took the medication from her. Amma would give her what she wanted with great reluctance. It was the red pill which brought on the cave. Nowadays Pankajam lost consciousness as soon as she began her descent into that cave-turned-well. It felt good to be unconscious. When you are not conscious at all, how can you tell what is good or what is bad?

The number of pills prescribed by the doctor began to decrease. Now Pankajam had to see the doctor only once every fortnight. The reception room at the doctor's clinic was beginning to lose its sheen: she could see cobwebs hanging here and there in the corners. Even the crowd that came to see him had changed. Only half the patients present were regulars. There were quite a few new patients. Plenty of girls who were not yet twenty. Etched on their faces were the usual confusion and dread, and that vacant look.

The doctor still had his know-it-all air. Still the same shoddy, half-baked information. Questions that were far removed from her real situation. Replies to those questions. How is she now? How does one reply to 'now' and 'how'? What can the doctor gauge from just one or two sentences? Words were totally useless as guideposts to reality. But treatment was based entirely on those useless words. Not only treatment, but the whole world, it seemed: father, mother, husband, sister, mother-in-law, relatives, neighbours, even strangers she had never set eyes on. As Pankajam attained clarity by degrees, her anxiety also grew. She must put an end to this 'crazy' treatment as soon as possible.

Every now and then she felt the urge to giggle when she saw the doctor's cheerful disposition. He was satisfied that his medicines were bringing about improvement in Pankajam's condition, and he declared it openly. He spoke to Pankajam in a friendly manner. He smiled. Her husband, too, felt more confident now and shook the doctor's hand.

Everyone at home was happy that morning. Amma gave her son-in-law a second cup of coffee. He called for Nimmi and when she ran to him, he gave her money from his drawer and asked her to fetch the ironed clothes from the laundry. She took the coins and hurried out. Ten minutes later, she came back carrying the bundle. He said something funny to her. She laughed uncontrollably, as though she would burst if she suppressed her laughter. In the midst of all this, the baby emitted a feeble cry. Both Pankajam's husband and Nimmi went to the baby. Pankajam sat in a corner of the same room. They grew happier still on seeing the baby. The one-year-old child had at last turned over on to its stomach, all on its own!

'Let me do the cooking today,' Pankajam told Amma. Amma chopped the greens. Pankajam had a bath and then put the cooker on the stove. Her hand shook a little when she garnished the sambar. Except for that tremor, she finished cooking without incident.

Amma fed the baby tiny morsels of mashed rice. Nimmi, who was off to school in a new half-sari, pinched the baby's cheeks and gave it a fond kiss before leaving.

Even the man who took the lunch to her husband's office had been dispatched. It was leisure time at home. Amma had gone to sleep on the floor, with her head resting on a small, raised plank. Pankajam swung between clarity and stupor. When she made up her mind not to give in to the stupor, it disappeared. She kept her eyes wide open. She went to the well at the back, picked up the baby's clothes from the washing line and folded them neatly. The baby had learnt to play and was trying to crawl. She smiled at Pankajam.

Amma had brought back only a few household articles with her. They were stacked neatly along the walls or under the bench. The kitchen was clean. Pankajam went to her husband's table. These days, Nimmi sat at that very table and did her lessons. Pankajam opened the drawer and looked inside. Pen, scissors, bank passbook, diary, large wallet, five or six large envelopes and a few letters—everything was neatly arranged inside the drawer. There was a round black enamel box. Its lid was in place, undisturbed. Her husband usually kept his small change in that box. No one must have opened it today, and even if they had, they must have shut it properly.

Suddenly, after god knows how many years, Pankajam remembered the first line of a song she had learnt in the distant past. She felt like giggling. Everywhere you turned in that small house, you could see a kind of order. It hadn't been that neat even when she had run the house on her own. Her husband laughed and joked now. It was not even a year since Appa had passed away, but Amma slept peacefully in her son-in-law's house in the daytime. Nimmi seemed to enjoy going to school. Nowadays, she asked for and got a rupee as pocket money every day. Her husband didn't shy from giving it, either. This was the same man who had once told her that Nimmi would disrupt their domestic harmony and spoil good relations between them. How quickly people changed! Pankajam remembered the whole song now. She had been no older than Nimmi when she learned that song. During her schooldays, she had never so much as laid eyes on a whole rupee. Never even thought of learning to ride a bicycle. Or had the gall to pick up and use things that didn't belong to her. People changed with time. It was just that she could no longer put up with these changes.

Pankajam felt that her falling ill was good in a way. Right then, she had a strong urge to go off somewhere and sing heartily, in a full-throated voice.

From the original Maruthal (1981)

Tiger-Artiste

Our tiffin recess was from one to two in the afternoon. They say that earlier it used to extend up to half past two. Our office too opened for business only at eleven in the morning. If one had one's morning brunch at home at around ten-thirty and eventually reached office at half past eleven, leaving for snacks shortly thereafter, at one o'clock, would have been impossible. That was why our cafeteria attracted a real crowd only at two o'clock. The management advanced the opening hour from eleven to ten-thirty, and last month they issued orders to begin work at ten. So, tiffin recess was scheduled from one to two. Closing hour too was extended from five to six in the evening.

However, our work remained the same as ever. Those in the production department—carpenters, electricians and laboratory technicians—have always worked an eight-hour shift. It's the same with people in the accounts department. Whether or not any work gets done, they have to keep writing accounts through the year. Then the telephone operators—there is no recess or holiday for telephones. Therefore, only those who are not in any of these departments have the chance to relax from time to time during office hours—for days, weeks or even months together. I recall one period when our studio didn't produce any film for a year and a half. You could draw your salary without doing any work for a year and a half, put your feet up on the desk and sleep during office hours, let your hair turn grey, gain fat around your belly and make room for diabetes, and since your thoughts are aimless, develop a darting, shifty look in your eyes and bring in plenty of prattle in your speech. Then, when some real work comes your way after eighteen months, you might feel elated at the end of this period of forced inactivity. At the same time you might also stumble because you've lost the habit of working. It was during this period, when we were anticipating the imminent arrival of the thrill and awkwardness, that he appeared before us one afternoon, just when we were enjoying a round of betel nut and tobacco after our tiffin recess.

'What can we do for you, 'pa?' Sharma asked him. There was a time when Sharma was seen only in trousers. After working as a sub-inspector of police, he had written and published plays and short stories, earned a name for himself and became a key person in our studio's story department. In those golden days, he had gone scouting for outdoor locations on his motorcycle, with our boss perched on its pillion. Now he wore a veshti and had become addicted to chewing tobacco. Only the square set of his shoulders hinted that he had a physique that was once shaped by a regimen of hard exercise.

It was a small room, crammed with three antique desks of differing sizes. Sharma, seated behind the largest, could be deemed the room's presiding officer. There was one extra chair besides the three we sat on. All our chairs were antiques of different styles. In the extra chair, one leg was shorter than the others. Whenever someone tried to sit on it, it would tilt dangerously to one side, churning the person's gut for a moment.

Our visitor stood in front of us, gripping the back of that treacherous chair.

'What do you want, 'pa?' Sharma asked him.

'I came to your house on Saturday, saar.'

'But I wasn't in town last Saturday!' said Sharma.

'I came in the morning, saar. You were at home, repairing an umbrella.'

'Oh, it was you! Velayudham, right?'

'No, saar. Kader. "Tagar Foight" Kader.'

'So, you'd come, then?'

'Yes, saar. Vellai told me, saar. Look up ayya in his house.'

'Who is Vellai?'

'Vellai, saar. Agent Vellai.'

Sharma seemed to understand now. Vellai was the agent who collected men and women by the hundreds and brought them to our studio whenever we had to film big crowds. Apart from being part of the crowd, no acting was required of them. Each person was given food for the day and two rupees as wages. Vellai took a rupee as commission.

'We are not shooting any crowd scene now, 'pa,' said Sharma.

'I know, saar. He said if I look you up, you will give me role, saar.'

'Who said that?'

'Like I told you, saar. Vellai, saar.'

Sharma looked at us. We stared at this man, our visitor. He was quite short. He must have had a well-muscled body once, but he was so thin now that his shoulder bones were sticking out. His prominent jawbone made his dark cheeks look abnormally sunken. Most of the men Vellai brought in were in a similar condition. Even if we filmed the splendour and prosperity of Ramarajya, the kingdom of Lord Rama, the citizens looked as though they were famine-struck.

'I'll send word to you through Vellai,' said Sharma.

We leaned back in our chairs. The interview was over.

'Yes, saar,' he said. Then his voice grew thin. 'If you give me something right away, it would help, saar.'

'But we haven't even started shooting, 'pa. Don't you know, they shoot all the crowd scenes only at the end?'

'Don't mean that, saar. Please give me some role.'

'What role can we give you, 'pa? Our casting assistant is over there. Give him all your details and go.'

I was the casting assistant. I had noted down in my register the particulars—name, age, height and address—of thousands of individuals like our visitor. From those notes, if we dropped a postcard to four of them, three would come back with a stamp saying 'addressee has moved'. Then Vellai was our sole recourse.

But he didn't turn in my direction. He seemed quite certain that Sharma was the most important person among the three of us.

'I can get something only if you put in a word, saar.'

'Do you know how to swim?' asked Sharma.

'Swim?' the man asked Sharma in turn. Then he said, 'A little, saar.'

'A little won't do. We have to shoot a scene where a man dives into a river from a cliff and swims away. You won't be able to do that.'

'I can do tagar foight, saar. They call me "Tagar Foight" Kader.'

'What is that, "tagar foight"?'

'"Tagar foight", saar. Tagar. Don't you know tagar?'

All of us were paying attention by now. It made no sense at all.

He said, 'Puli, saar. Puli. Puli foight.'

'Oh, tiger fight, is it? Tiger fight. You fight with tigers, do you?'

'No, saar. I wear costume like puli. People call tagar foight, right?'

'Oh, you wear a tiger costume! Why would we need a fellow in a tiger costume for a film? You wear a tiger costume, do you? Okay, okay, when Vellai comes here, I'll definitely send word if we find anything for you.'

'I do very good tagar foight, saar. It will be like real tiger, saar.'

'If we want a real tiger, we'll get a real tiger, won't we?'

'No, saar. What I do will be exactly like real tiger. Shall I show you, saar?'

'No, no. There's no need.'

'Just watch, saar. Where would big man like you get to see "tagar-dance"?'

'Why, the streets are full of people doing tiger dance every year during Muharram and Ramzan processions.'

'My act is very different, saar. It'll be like real tiger.' He took out a 'tiger's head' from somewhere. Only then did we realize that he had brought a cloth bag with him. The 'tiger's head' was only the head's outer skin. A second later, he had pulled it over his face like a mask and tugged the mask near the chin for a tight fit, turning into someone with his own eyes and a panther's face. He scanned the room quickly for one or two seconds.

'Besh,' said Sharma appreciatively. We were staring intently at Kader.

He raised his arms above his head and relaxed his body. Then he bent down with his hands on the floor and stood like a four-legged animal, turning his face from side to side.

'Besh,' said Sharma again.

Like a cat, he raised just the middle of his back, contorted and shook his body. Then he opened his maw. We were stunned. We had never before heard such a terrifying roar at close proximity.

He roared once more and then swung only his behind this way and that. The next moment, he leaped on to the empty chair in the room and crouched on its narrow seat, with all four 'paws' drawn in. The chair shook noisily. I cried out: 'Aiyo!'

Kader jumped on to my desk in a four-legged leap, and then, in the blink of an eye, was on Sharma's desk. Several papers, books and a packet of betel preparation were strewn haphazardly on it. His feet didn't touch even a single object. He crouched once again on the desk, glowered at Sharma and let out a blood-curdling roar. From the table, he leaped up straight towards the ceiling.

'Oh!' all of us shouted in sheer terror.

It was an old building. At a height of ten feet, a ledge, two inches wide, ran along the walls on all sides. A little above the ledge was a small window in the wall on one side of the room, a single bar across it, which served as a ventilator. It was thickly covered with dust, filth and cobwebs.

He sprang on all four limbs, jumping higher than a man's height, and fit himself on that two-inch ledge above our heads for a second. Then he held the bar of the ventilator with his hands and roared again like a tiger.

'Careful, 'pa! Careful!' Sharma shouted. At that height, the ceiling fan was whirring madly beside his face. There were scarcely a few inches between him and those fan blades.

From that height, he sprang directly on to a chair and then to the floor.

We were in a state of shock, our fear still undiminished. His eyes flashed like a tiger's inside the panther's mask. The panther opened its maw one more time and let out a roar. The next moment his body went slack, he got up and stood on his feet.

Even Sharma couldn't manage to say, 'Besh!' Kader had taken off his panther mask.

All of us were completely dumbstruck. Kader was the one who gathered his wits first.

'I'll certainly see what I can do, 'pa,' said Sharma. His tone had changed drastically. Kader paid him obeisance with folded hands.

'Where do you live?' Sharma asked him.

'Mirsahibpet,' he answered, mentioning a door number and the name of a lane. I noted them down. Then he said hesitantly: 'I don't know for how long I'll be staying there.'

'Why?' asked Sharma.

'No, saar,' he began, and then fell suddenly at Sharma's feet.

'Get up, 'pa. Get up, 'pa, Kader,' pleaded Sharma, who was extremely perturbed.

Kader stood up and wiped his eyes. 'My wife has asked me not to come anywhere near our home, saar,' he told Sharma. This was the same man who had been a tiger a few minutes ago.

'So many months since I earned anything, saar. What will she do? Four children, saar. So small, all of them.' He was crying now.

Something occurred to Sharma and he asked Kader, 'Have you eaten today?'

He said, 'No, saar.' There was no need to confirm that he had gone hungry not just that day, but many days before that.

Sharma put his hand into his pocket. We foraged in ours as well. The change added up to two rupees. Sharma said, 'Here, take this. Go to our cafeteria and have a good meal.'

He said, 'No, saar.'

'What do you mean "no"? Go and eat first,' said Sharma.

'Get me some role, ayya,' Kader begged through his tears.

I had never seen Sharma so angry before. 'If you refuse to accept money, how will it ever come to you? Even if it's a beaten coin, it's still Lakshmi, 'pa!'

Kader wiped his tears and took the money. 'Giving you a role is not in my hands, but I'll do what I can,' said Sharma gently. 'Go, go and eat something first!' Then he turned to me and said, 'Take him to the cafeteria and make him eat.'

I got up at once.

He said, 'No, saar. I'll go and eat. I'll go myself and eat.' Then he bowed to us again and left the room.

We were silent for a while. Sharma spoke aloud to himself: 'What can we do for this fellow? We are filming a king-and-queen story now, aren't we?'

But he did keep Kader in mind. When the story department met again two weeks later, he managed to obtain their approval for filming a sequence where the hero sneaked into the enemy's fortress in the guise of a tiger. When the hero performed the 'tiger dance', Kader could play his 'dupe'. We could get him at least a hundred rupees.

I dropped him a postcard. It came back in four days: 'Addressee not found.'

Sharma took Vellai along and looked for Kader. We also inquired everywhere in our attempt to track him down. The day for filming the scene where the hero entered the enemy's fortress drew closer and closer. Kader couldn't be traced.

But even if we had found him, it wouldn't have done much good. A film released that month featured a scene in which the hero did a kavadi dance with folk music playing in the background. That scene was drawing unmanageably large crowds all over Tamil Nadu.

It was decided that the hero in our film would do a karagam dance.

From the original Pulikkalaignan (1973)

In the Reception Room

As soon as she came into view, he became busy with work which had not existed till a moment before. Though he did not look up during the three minutes it took her to slowly cross the hundred yards between the entrance and the reception room, he was keenly aware of her growing proximity, and kept his eyes lowered in anticipation of the encounter which he was sure to find embarrassing. Once she reached his desk, having floundered a little at the steps to the entrance of the reception office, he could no longer keep at what he was doing, or, in truth, what he was not doing. When she gave him a diffident smile, he assumed as stern an expression as he could and asked her brusquely, 'What can we do for you?'

'I would like to meet your boss.'

'He is not in right now.'

As though he was no longer obliged to attend to her, he opened a drawer, brought out a file and began to turn the pages busily. She stood there looking at him. He closed the file, looked up again and asked, 'Anything else?'

'When is he likely to return?'

'I have no idea. You should have called before you came over. Here, this is our telephone number. Please call our boss's secretary during working hours, and take an appointment. There is nothing I can do. Only his personal secretary will know when you can see him, or if he would agree to even give you an appointment.' He extended a slip of paper with the telephone number on it.

She accepted it graciously and told him after a minute's pause, 'I already have this number. You gave it to me the last time.'

'Then you should've called before you came. It would have saved you a lot of trouble. You needn't have come all the way here in this heat.'

She smiled as though she had caught the real meaning behind his words of sympathy and concern. Yet her smile held no derision. She said, 'I called twice, but I couldn't get through to his secretary.'

There were three telephones in that busy office. Unless one had a phone at one's disposal, one couldn't get through to anyone there that easily. Still, he asked her in a combative tone, 'Did you try and call today?'

'No.'

'Then what can we do?'

The lack of outrage in her bearing made him squirm.

'Could you please inform the secretary that I was here?'

He didn't reply. Instead, he gave her a slip of paper and said, 'Please put down your name. I'll send it across.'

Since she had nothing with which to write, he handed her a pen. She bent over the counter, so far that her nose nearly touched the surface, steadied the tremors of her gnarled fingers with great effort, and wrote down in large capital letters—MRS ABRAHAM, HONORARY MAGISTRATE. He noted the time of her arrival on the slip and sent it in through an office boy. Then he told her, 'Please sit down over there. It'll be some time before we get a reply.'

She smiled to express her gratitude and moved away towards the cane chairs arranged at one end of the veranda. Several people, who sat there with nothing particular to do, got up and left when they saw her. Even though she was very old, and obviously very poor, she carried herself in a manner that evoked feelings of respect in those who saw her. She sat in the cane chair with an air of serenity, as though she had no grievance at all against the world.

The secretary called. But he did not refer to her. He asked for a car to be sent immediately.

'Sir, there is a lady here . . .' he tried.

It was useless. The secretary brooked no interruption and hung up before he could say anything further. Hardly a minute later, he passed briskly through the reception room and went out.

'Mrs Abraham,' he called to her. 'Our secretary has just gone out.'

'Did he get my note?' She rose quickly and came to him.

'He must have left his room before it was delivered there. He is out on some important business.'

'He doesn't know that I am here then?'

'That is probably the case.'

'Oh.'

For the first time, disappointment clouded her features. Her smile had vanished.

'Do you think it will be quite a while before he comes back?'

'I don't know, Amma. It could be an hour for all I know.' He realized that he had called her Amma only after he had completed the sentence.

She lingered shyly near the counter for a brief while. Then she asked softly, 'Could I have a glass of water?'

'Oh, certainly.'

She stood there as she took the glass from him and drank slowly from it. Then she said, 'I'll wait. Please inform him as soon as he comes back.' Even after she had said this to him, she remained standing at the counter.

The day was hotter than usual. Mostly cars and buses went by at that hour. The office had a boundary wall with separate gates for the entry and exit of vehicles. A curved driveway connected the two gates. The space between the driveway and the boundary wall had been landscaped into a manicured lawn. Since the wall was very high, the road was visible only through the gates. The bell in the church across the road began to toll; he counted up to twelve.

There was no breeze even though the electric fan was whirring madly above his head. The lawn in front of him lay parched. Not one of the squirrels which were always darting back and forth over the lawn could be seen that day. But the lady kept standing near the counter, resting her arm on it with a low light in her eyes which spoke of thoughts far removed from the blazing day around her. He wished she would go and sit down somewhere rather than stand right in front of him.

She had come many times before. She had her letter ready, or she wrote it after she got there. They were all addressed to his boss, and the envelope was always sealed. Even though he sent those envelopes directly to his boss's office, he knew what the letters were about. They would have sought a little help, a small amount of money. The boss had never once sent for her. But on many occasions, replies to her letters had come in the form of envelopes. She would open them right there. They contained money. But this did not always happen. There were times when her letters went unanswered. In that event, she was asked to come again, or to telephone later. Mostly she was asked to call later.

The envelopes with cash or any other information always came from the secretary, never from the boss.

Perhaps the boss had no direct acquaintance with her; perhaps he was giving her money solely on the basis of her letters of supplication. Though he sent the money to her, the boss never met her. Perhaps he found it uncomfortable to dole out charity in person and he wished to avoid it. Moreover, money sent through a third party was not likely to cause the recipient much embarrassment. But now, the boss was not in; neither was his secretary. He yearned for the boss to return to the office soon so he could send the lady away. She stood so still that he wondered if she was breathing at all.

'Why don't you sit down? Please.'

She didn't hear him. He bit his lip in annoyance, then said to her again. 'Please, do sit down.'

'Uh?'

'I was saying that you can sit down and wait. It might take as long as half an hour for any of them to return.'

'Yes. I should not disturb you.'

'No, I didn't mean to say that.'

She stood there diffidently, as though she was not sure what she should do next. He finally overcame his reluctance and asked the question he had been holding back for a long time, 'Shall I send for some coffee?'

'Pardon me?'

'Coffee?'

'Why?'

'I thought you wouldn't mind a cup. That's the only thing we can get quickly around here.'

She smiled. He was afraid that he had hurt her feelings.

'All right, I'll have some. May God keep you well.'

Greatly relieved, he sent a boy to bring them coffee.

'Are you really an honorary magistrate?' he asked her.

'Yes, but that was a long time ago.'

'What does Mr Abraham do?'

'Who, my husband? It's been fifteen years since he passed away.'

'You don't have any children?'

'I have two sons and a daughter. You want to know why they don't look after me? They are all adults now. A lot of things change when children grow up. I don't want to blame anyone. Poor things, they are themselves not all that well off. They have their own children, brothers-in-law, sisters-in-law, mothers-in-law. Moreover, I have been in this situation only for the past three years. I have never looked to my children for money or help. It's very hard to do something you have never done before.'

'I don't know what's taking them so long to send the coffee.'

'It's all right. I have to wait anyway, don't I? Now there is no one to look after me. And I have stopped worrying about finding someone. In fact, I find it less difficult to walk these three or four miles to come here than to worry my head about who in the world is likely to look after me.'

The coffee had still not arrived. He told her, 'If you could just sit down over there, I can finish my job. I have a lot of accounts to go over.'

'I shall certainly do that. Poor boy, I should not disturb you. I am not very well these days. When you have no money, many other hardships come along with it.'

She went over to where the chairs were. She drew one up to a small table and rested her head on her forearms. When the coffee came, she had to be woken up.

He noticed the sudden increase in the bustle of people on the road and realized it was past one. That was also the time when he usually left for his lunch. The secretary's car came in through the gate just then. He waited for a couple of minutes and then told the secretary on the intercom, 'Sir, Mrs Abraham is waiting in the reception room.'

'What does she want?'

'She says she wants to meet the boss.'

'Tell her to call later.'

He hung up and turned to look at the lady. She was fast asleep. He telephoned the secretary again.

'Sir, I am calling from the reception. She has been waiting for a long time. It looks like she needs some immediate assistance.'

'The boss hasn't come in today and he will be out for the next two days. Tell her to give us a call tomorrow, or better still, the day after. Or she can write to us.'

She was still asleep. All his friends would have assembled in the cafeteria by now. Even the person who would relieve him at the reception desk had arrived, on time—the rarest of events. The lady was in a deep slumber.

'Mrs Abraham . . . Mrs Abraham,' he called to her softly. Then he went over to her. Though the skin of her face was dry and criss-crossed with many wrinkles, she herself seemed to be at peace. He touched her gently on the arm and tried to wake her. 'Mrs Abraham.'

This time she woke up. She stared at him blankly for a moment and then sat upright in her chair.

'I am told that the boss will be out for another two days. We can't do anything without his permission. There's no point in your waiting.'

'Is that so?'

'His secretary says that if you give us a letter, he will make sure it reaches the boss as early as possible.'

'Letter?'

Yes. I'll give you a sheet of paper right away. You can write the letter here itself and hand it over to me.'

It didn't appear as though she had heard him. He waited for her to reply, but she rose and started to leave.

'Aren't you going to write the letter? It'll save you the trouble of coming all the way here again. If there is a reply, it will be conveyed to you at your address.'

'No. It's all right.'

She descended the steps slowly and began to proceed in the direction of the 'OUT' gate.

He went up to her and said, 'Amma, if it is all right with you, please take a bus home.'

She stared at the rupee note he was holding out. It seemed she accepted it merely to avoid the embarrassment of declining another person's offer of assistance.

He wasn't hurt that she had not thanked him. He returned to his seat and watched her walk towards the exit gate on unsteady legs, the rupee note held between her fingers. There was over a hundred yards' distance between the reception room and the exit gate. As she crossed the gate, the note seemed to slip from her hand and fall to the ground. At that moment, she walked past the gate and went out of his view. It appeared to him as though some passer-by bent to pick up the note. Because the reception room was at such a distance, he couldn't see any of this clearly.

From the original Varaverparaiyil (1964)

Cap

'Bring me a cup of tea.'
    'Another one?'
'Yes.'
'Right away, sir. May I have the bill back?'
'Did you give me a bill?'
'Yes. I kept it on the table, next to your cup.'
'I didn't see it.'
'Here. It must have fallen off the table. Tea will do?'
'Yes . . . um . . . no. A special kind of biscuit used to be available here. I think it was your own product. Do you have biscuits?'
'We do, but they're common biscuits from the bakery, sir. Which one are you talking about?'
'It had multiple layers, but it was a single biscuit. Cheap too. We used to get it here.'
'Where? Here?'
'Yes, here.'
'How long ago?'
'Must be fifteen, twenty years.'
'Twenty years?'

'Yes, twenty years ago.'

'I wasn't even born then. We sell only common bakery biscuits here; or else, biscuits in packets. Shall I bring some?'

'No, thanks. Just the tea.'

Not twenty years ago; twenty-two, to be exact. Over the years, the restaurant's layout was not all that had changed. The employees and the fare had changed, too. Its name alone hadn't changed and it was still a restaurant. They had placed small display cupboards across what was once a large hall and partitioned the space into several sections. Once seated, you couldn't see the people sitting in the adjacent section. Through the glass in those cupboards, you could see only the items displayed inside. Earlier, only one cupboard had held varieties of cakes and biscuits; now they were displayed in all of them. And not just locally made confections but also many packets of biscuits produced by big companies. Porcelain items were on display too: cups, saucers, bowls and jars. However, the biscuit which used to be available earlier was no longer sold here.

He sipped from the second cup of tea in a leisurely manner. He had been wandering around the town for more than two hours. Driven by a strange impulse, he had roamed every road and street on foot, and was now overcome with exhaustion like never before. Many houses, shops and buildings familiar to him had become unrecognizable. On seeing this Irani hotel, which still retained its name at least, he had felt an urge to enter. It was only after he had been in the restaurant for fifteen minutes that he remembered the biscuit.

This was how many things from the past—in truth, thousands of things—were rising to the uppermost layer of his consciousness. As far as he could tell, he hadn't thought about them even once in these twenty years. But now, people didn't surface in his memory as easily as places did. He couldn't recall a single name properly, nor, barring one or two, could he clearly remember faces. The ones he saw in this restaurant were not familiar either.

How could they be? To recognize faces after a long gap, you need special powers of imagination. You need the ability to divine the changes that have been wrought in others, just like the ones in your own face. But was he even aware of the changes that had taken place in him?

Why was he wandering about in this town after so many years?

His visit had not been intentional. It was a coincidence that he found himself here today. Instead of waiting at the railway station for four hours, he had chosen to come into the town. Soon enough, what he had initially undertaken as a means to pass the time assumed a different character. Now his feet travelled purposefully towards every road and street. His arrival at this restaurant after wandering all over the city was not accidental.

As he stepped out of the restaurant after paying the bill, he was startled to see his own shadow. It had shrunk to a point. Even that natural phenomenon seemed to signal something to him. The town's soil didn't relish even the touch of his shadow. It must be due to a devious conspiracy on the town's part that he was suddenly restless.

There couldn't have been a spot in that town left untouched by his shadow. Whenever he accompanied his father, his father would point at something and tell him, 'This is the hospital where you were born', 'This is the house we were living in when you were born', 'We were living here when you had a tumour in your stomach as a two-year-old', 'For many years, we bought our provisions from this store'. Had there been sunlight in the labour ward of the hospital where he was born, he would have cast a shadow immediately after his birth. However, labour wards were not normally filled with sunlight; even the ambient light there was somewhat dim. Would a man cast a shadow only when there was light? I don't cast a shadow even now, when there's so much light. Why?

A bus stopped in front of him, dropped some passengers, picked up a few more and left. That bus would have taken him to the railway station. He could have spent the remaining two hours relaxing on the platform. Though his body was pleading for some rest at that point, he started walking in the opposite direction. Twenty-two years ago there had been no buses in this town; horse carts were the quickest means of transport. There were horse carts here even today. He spotted buses now and again, and also a couple of taxis. Somehow, he didn't think they would be of any use to him. There was no apparent reason why he had to strain his tired legs further. Nevertheless, something made him roam the streets for longer.

He walked yet again down a road which he had ambled through twice already that morning. The left side of the road was lined with grand old bungalows. A large ground stretched out for about a mile along the right. One couldn't call it a secluded road; nor was it an important thoroughfare. But even that road seemed to differ from the image that rose from his memories of the past. A pillar had been erected in the middle of the ground: a monument to commemorate someone, perhaps. Military parades used to be held in that ground every now and then. The ground must have belonged to the army. The monument too was probably army related. There are monuments commemorating the two world wars in all the big cities of the world: 'To the Unknown Soldier'. Of what use are names in an army? They are a minor nuisance, to be avoided by any means. Therefore, everything in the army is in numbers and signs, and monuments too are erected for unknown soldiers. But what if names must be mentioned? How many names can we possibly write on a monument? And what an outsize monument we would need to inscribe the names of the dead in their millions! Would the size of the Himalayas be enough? Though killing so many people is entirely feasible, erecting a monument for them is not; therefore, economically, a pillar. It might well turn out that this is not even a monument for the dead. There was a victory pillar in Chittoor, in Daulatabad, in Warangal. There used to be one in Hampi too. On the vast parade ground, the only change in the past twenty years was this monument. But it had transformed the entire landscape.

The road led him to a crossroads from where he headed for the town. When he had arrived at that junction earlier that morning, he had set off towards the town immediately. The second time, he hesitated momentarily and looked around before turning back. Now, although he had turned towards the town without the slightest hesitation, he felt as though something was dragging him back; he was simply unable to advance further. The turmoil and numbing pain that one experiences when one has just let slip a great, once-in-a-lifetime opportunity seemed to have engulfed him. He turned back and walked to the crossroads once again. In the distance, the pillar appeared like a lone tree on the landscape.

The sun was searing hot. The hour of his impending departure from the town was nearing. He was standing in a locality that was almost on the edge of town. There was a cinema house near the crossroads. As far as he knew, it screened only English films. Even those who worked there seemed to walk with their noses in the air. There were five or six bungalows next to the cinema, ancient bungalows with gardens cultivated so thick as to hide the buildings from view. Then . . . then . . .

He couldn't remember. Of the four directions that led away from the junction, why should he worry his brain only about this one? What was the matter with his brain anyway? That organ which ordinarily spewed out a hundred bits of information and memories every second— why was it lying low now, as if jailed? Had he returned here in this head-splitting heat, with little time to spare, only to subject his brain to this ordeal?

He stood there in a helpless, half-comprehending state, unable to decide what to do next. His train was due to depart in a short while from this town. Even if he walked slowly to the railway station, he could reach in forty-five minutes. But he had twice that amount of time on his hands. Was that why he was dithering, he wondered.

But what was the reason for his hesitation at this particular spot? Should he go a little further and find out?

He walked past the cinema house. There was no show at that hour. All the doors were open. From the road, he could see chairs installed in neat rows. They had been renovated. In fact, they were not so new, merely different from the ones he had seen earlier. He must have watched no more than three or four English films in that town. It was his father who had taken him along. Had he gone alone, he wouldn't have understood even one-fourth of any film; probably nothing at all.

He passed the bungalows, one after another, seeing them for the first time today. Only one bungalow had the same gate as he remembered it. The others had changed, and been enlarged. These were new buildings. In a large empty ground, they had laid the foundation for several buildings.

After passing the last bungalow, he stopped. There was a small alley along its side. Next to the alley was Montgomery's Hotel.

Now he understood why he had been drawn in that direction. Montgomery's Hotel.

There was a world of difference between Montgomery's Hotel and all the other hotels he had visited. Although they shared the common appellation of 'hotel', in the establishments he had known, anyone could walk in and sit down at one of the tables laid out in a couple of rooms there. In due course, a man with unruly hair and a filthy shirt would come by, and they could ask him to bring them something to eat. However, during the time that he had lived in that town, people like him couldn't even have *imagined* stepping into Montgomery's Hotel. Nor were they clear about who the hotel was meant for. Posters were put up all over town every month about a dance being held there on a particular day. On that day, he saw a lot of sattakkaris—Anglo-Indian girls—going towards Montgomery's Hotel. You had to be either an Anglo-Indian girl or a British soldier.

Suddenly he remembered it all. Until now, to him, those twenty-two years had been totally erased, without even the smallest trace. Only a few memories of the town where he was born, where he had lived for a few years and roamed all over, had lingered like pale shadows. He had not cherished those memories enough for them to have emerged even once in his dreams through countless nights. In his mind, the years he had spent in that town were completely wiped out, as if they had never existed. Montgomery's Hotel in particular was buried quite deep. That was why, though he had come very near it thrice today, it never surfaced in his consciousness. Why had he made himself forget it so completely?

He stopped at Montgomery's outer gate and peeped inside. This was the only place that was still the same, without any alterations. Apart from renovation efforts to counter the changes wrought by the passage of time, no other modification had been made: the place was largely left untouched. It felt exactly like the time he and his father had walked in that area one evening long ago.

Two Tommies had emerged from Montgomery's and stepped on to the road. Their normally flushed faces had turned even redder by then. Their eyeballs seemed ready to pop from their sockets and fall to the ground. Their heavy boots, the soles studded with dozens of hobnails, made so much noise that even the tar road trembled. Tak-kadak. Tak-kadak. The men had marched straight towards his father. Appa grasped his hand and stepped back even further. Both Tommies moved closer and stood next to them like two man-mountains. Appa stood still, not knowing what to do. One of the Tommies knocked his cap off his head. It fell in the middle of the road and rolled along for a short distance. Appa hastened to pick it up, but the other Tommy leaped in and kicked the cap. It rose like a ball and landed in a different spot. This time, Appa didn't rush forward. The first Tommy ran to the spot where the cap had landed and he too gave it a mighty kick. For the next few minutes, he and the other Tommy played football in the middle of the road with Appa's cap. Two butlers who worked in Montgomery's Hotel stood near the gate, enjoying the spectacle. When the Tommies deliberately kicked the cap in Appa's direction and it dashed against him, the two butlers burst out laughing. When the Tommies grew tired of the game, they took turns stamping on Appa's cap over and over again, squashing and battering it out of shape, before they walked away whistling. By the time Appa picked up what had been his cap, the butlers had gone inside.

He wiped his face. Exactly like on that evening long ago, the locality was quiet, without much human traffic. The world war had come to an end; the country gained independence; the white soldiers returned home; several provinces of India were divided into linguistic states and three general elections were held; two wars were fought;

one day, at two in the afternoon, Nehru passed away; the sea erupted into a tidal wave that flooded and destroyed Dhanushkodi town; a few women and children in India wept when President Kennedy was assassinated; the horns on Madras's suburban trains began to sound different; the rulers of Russia and the Queen of England paid formal visits to the country and went back home. Yet, despite all those events, Montgomery's Hotel appeared to have remained almost the same as it was before.

He had to walk several furlongs to pass the gate and reach the building. On the way, he noticed that pretty flowers had bloomed on a few plants.

He crossed the foyer and stepped inside the building. It was hard for him to imagine that old-style bungalow functioning as a restaurant. They had furnished the spacious hall with large sofas. As no natural light entered, the place was dark. It was odd for a room that was not air-conditioned to be so dark. Those two Tommies must have walked out from this dark interior.

The hall was empty.

A young man dressed in a jacket and tie greeted him and showed him to a sofa. 'What would you like to eat?'

'What's there for lunch?'

The tie-clad young man had to search high and low for the menu card before he found it and handed it to him. The card was filthy and frayed from being handled by hundreds of hands. A list of items and rates was printed on it, but every entry had been struck out and revised with a pen.

Even as he was studying the menu card, the tie-clad young man asked him, 'Would you like a drink?'

He remembered that prohibition was not in force in that town.

'I don't like anything here,' he said. It was a place that had been unimaginable to him as a young boy. Now, he had entered it, seated himself and told them to their face, 'I don't like anything here.'

The young man blinked, uncomprehending.

'Can you bring me just a coffee?'

'Sure. But wouldn't you like to eat something?'

'I told you, didn't I? I don't like anything here.'

The tie-clad youth called a waiter and told him in a gentle voice to bring coffee. Then he went over to something that looked like a bureau and flicked a switch. It was a phonograph with cylindrical records which had been popular before gramophone records were invented. Played in soft tempo as on a piano but punctuated with scratches, a European melody wafted from that bureau.

He felt as though the hall's interior had suddenly turned bright. The place was overflowing with soldiers and Anglo-Indian girls. Holding hands, they danced in time to the music from that broken phonograph. The Tommy who had knocked Appa's cap off his head was dancing with a very young girl who couldn't have been older than twenty. Snatching that girl away was the only proper punishment for the Tommy. He stood up from his seat. The Tommy, the girl, the dancing crowd— everything vanished in an instant. Only the music from the phonograph was still playing.

To the waiter who brought him his coffee, he said, 'I am not a sattakarichi, do you understand?'

The waiter stood there bewildered. The tie-clad youth came over, asking politely, 'What do you want?'

'Do you know my father?'

'Excuse me. What are you asking about?'

'Nothing.'

He drank his coffee. What would they know about his father? Even if those butlers were somehow alive today and still working here, how could they have remembered him? I didn't either. How neatly, how completely had forgetfulness blanketed everything! Why did I have to disturb it?

When he left the town later that day, he departed without any hope or wish to return there again. However, the sounds from that antediluvian phonograph would delay the onset of his sleep every night for a long, long time.

From the original Thoppi (1975)

Free at Last

'Was it Prakash Rao who went out in that car?' Chander asked her again.

'I too thought it was someone else but it was him all right,' said Sujatha.

Chander sat down in the steel folding chair, facing a different direction this time. He had smelled a rat during their last visit to that cinema studio. His suspicion was confirmed: the studio's programme manager Prakash Rao had been deceiving them, sending word to them that he was out when he was actually in the studio. Deception was probably not the right word. He was fobbing them off. This time, too, he had told them that he was not there and sent them away; only later did he actually set out.

'Shall we leave?' asked Sujatha.

'Well, what else can we do? Why do I take you seriously and run around like this, I wonder,' said Chander.

'All right, let's go.'

Sujatha stood up. She was not in the least disheartened. Looking at her, even Chander felt momentary pity. Her sari was so badly frayed that there were large rents in a couple of places. He knew, because he had himself ironed it unevenly earlier that afternoon. But she wore it with great skill, never allowing it to become shabby and creased. She was also able to sit still in the same spot for more than half an hour. Even this time, like always, it was largely at her instigation that he had set out to meet Prakash Rao. Rao was Sujatha's chittappa's son, a first cousin. Now Sujatha had found out for herself about his lack of integrity.

'Okay. Come, let's go,' Chander too stood up.

The studio receptionist in that room was writing something at his desk. Sujatha told the receptionist: 'Please inform Mr Prakash Rao that we had come to see him.'

Just then Chander exclaimed, 'Look over there!' Sujatha turned to look. A car was entering the studio.

As the car drove past, Prakash Rao, who was sitting inside, turned in their direction. He had noticed that Sujatha and Chander had spotted him.

Sujatha promptly told the receptionist, 'Tell him now that we are here.'

'Let him go to his cabin first,' said the receptionist.

But it became unnecessary. Prakash Rao himself called the receptionist and asked him to send them in. Sujatha and Chander went to his cabin.

Nearly the entire space was taken up by a huge executive table and two smaller ones. Cane chairs were wedged haphazardly in the little area that remained. There were piles of papers, document bundles and files everywhere.

Unwashed coffee cups lay in a corner on the floor. Two other men shared the cabin with Rao. The two telephones on his desk rang incessantly, sometimes at the same time.

'Come, Sujatha,' he welcomed them heartily.

Sujatha gave him a fond smile. 'You remember I spoke to you about a friend? This is the gentleman, Chander.'

'Come, sit down.' Prakash Rao pointed to two cane chairs. Sujatha's chair faced Prakash Rao, while Chander's faced the door. After sitting on the chair, Chander twisted his spine as much as possible to sit in a position facing Prakash Rao. Since his chair had a deep seat, this was somewhat difficult.

'This must be the person you had mentioned when you came home,' Prakash Rao opened the conversation.

'Yes, yes. We studied together at the drama institute in Delhi. He stood first in our batch. A very good actor.'

'Ah . . . ah,' said Prakash Rao.

'We are jointly conducting drama classes here in Madras. Everything is going smoothly enough, and we've even got a grant from the government. But someone who doesn't know the first thing about theatre has been appointed as chairman. It has become very difficult for us. For two years now this Mrs SSP has been harassing us.'

'What does that lady do?' asked Prakash Rao.

'We take care of all the tasks, big and small, required to run that place. But she doesn't say a good word about us anywhere. When experts visit from abroad, we are never properly introduced to them. We give the training, but some local good-for-nothing is brought in as "visiting professor" and we have to cope with his antics.'

Chander wondered why Sujatha was narrating all this. These didn't sound like atrocities even to him. But Prakash Rao commiserated with her: 'It must be very hard for you. Working under such a person can be a real torture.'

'That's the right word: torture,' said Sujatha. 'I told Chander that we should explore other avenues instead of getting bogged down with this drama. He is a very fine actor. A great talent. If he had entered films a few years ago, he would've reached the top by now.'

Prakash Rao paid Chander only the slightest attention. Not solely out of indifference, thought Chander.

'We came here last Monday and then again on Friday. It looks like you were out on both occasions.'

'Yes, yes,' Prakash Rao replied hastily.

All three were silent for a while. The two men who shared Prakash Rao's cabin were absorbed in their work. A boy came in and said, 'Saar, they are packing up on Stage Three.'

'Have they scheduled any work for tomorrow, or are they going to dismantle the set? Ask them!'

'Subramaniam said he'll come and talk to you himself, saar,' said the boy.

An obese man entered the room. Unmindful of Sujatha's presence, he greeted Prakash Rao with gruff male camaraderie, 'What's up with you, rey!' he asked in Telugu.

Prakash side-stepped this neatly and asked him, 'Subramaniam, are you going to continue tomorrow, or is everything over?'

'Our producer and partner are going tonight to Machilipatnam to try and raise some money. Everything will be on hold till they come back.'

'I heard the accountant sent for you and you never showed up.'

Subramaniam was nonchalant. 'That cheque I gave you, I believe it bounced,' he said. 'That's why I wanted to avoid him.'

'If it happens again, you won't be allowed to shoot here.'

'Suit yourself,' said Subramaniam. 'If not this studio, there are nine others to choose from.'

By now Chander's back was aching. He sank deeper into the chair and settled himself comfortably, as comfortably as that awkward chair allowed him to. He would have gone out of the room, but that fat Subramaniam was standing near the door.

Prakash Rao and Subramaniam looked at Sujatha. 'Your director—is he still here, or has he left?' Prakash Rao asked Subramaniam.

'The first person to leave the studio after the shooting was our honourable director,' replied Subramaniam. Then he asked, 'Why, what's the matter?'

'I actually called these two to meet him.'

Chander was not amused enough to laugh out loud.

'Do they want a role? In this film? It's nearly over, and even if there is something, it would be a very small role. Who wants it?'

'This gentleman.' Indicating Sujatha, Rao added, 'She is my cousin. My uncle's daughter. These two are colleagues.'

'Where?'

Prakash Rao's reply was totally inaccurate. Chander started to correct him, but stopped himself.

Subramaniam asked Chander, 'Do many people come for these lessons that you are giving?'

'At least twenty a year.'

'When do you take these classes?'

'From six to eight-thirty in the evening. Four days a week.'

'Your salaries . . . regular . . .'

'What's that?'

'No, I wondered if they pay you regularly every month.'

'Oh, we get paid promptly on the first of every month. The school gets a grant from the government.'

After giving it some thought, Subramaniam told Chander, 'Saar, think of me as your blood brother. Decent people like you should not enter this wretched film industry. Just stick to your present job, saar. That will be the best thing for you.'

Chander and Sujatha remained motionless in their seats.

All of a sudden both telephones rang simultaneously. It galvanized Prakash Rao into action. He put one handset to his ear and said, 'Hello,' and then nodded to one of his colleagues in the room, 'This is for you.' He had to shove aside everything that was in the way to get to the other phone. Sujatha sat in her chair, leaning far to one side. However, before he could answer, the ringing ceased. 'Idiots!' he swore under his breath.

'Why don't you try and fix him up in your studio production?' Subramaniam suggested to Prakash Rao.

'I don't think it will work out. Nowadays, our director firmly rejects anyone we recommend.'

'What do you expect? You gather all the worthless extras you can find in this town and make them stand in front of him. There is no respect for you any more . . . Excuse me, saar,' Subramaniam concluded with an apology to Chander.

Someone came along just then and called Subramaniam away. Prakash Rao ordered coffee for Sujatha and Chander. A boy arrived with a coffee kettle, kept it on the floor and took away the dirty cups. He would probably wash those very same cups and bring them back. Chander didn't want the coffee.

'Give me a couple of your photographs. I'll let you know in ten days,' Prakash Rao assured them.

Sujatha took out two photographs of Chander from her handbag and gave them to Prakash Rao. He opened one of the drawers at his desk to put them away. Chander was able to peep inside the drawer: it was crammed with photos of many other hopefuls. It occurred to him that deception might not have been the sole reason why Prakash Rao had sent them away twice.

When they came out of the studio, Chander asked Sujatha, 'Shall we have coffee?'

'But we had coffee just now!'

'I feel like having another one.'

They sat in the family room at the restaurant. Chander drank the single cup of coffee they ordered. Sujatha paid the bill. A thick envelope fell out of her handbag.

'What does the astrologer have to say?' asked Chander.

Sujatha handed him the envelope. She had written to the astrologer asking about Chander's future, and not for the first time either. She had faith in astrology; at the same time, she had faith in her cousin too.

They had no classes that day. Sujatha walked with Chander to the corner of the lane where he lived and then took a bus to her hostel. Chander's family knew about Sujatha. His mother often told him, 'Why don't you marry her first, and then go out with her?' That required real courage, Chander thought. Without a steady job or income, one could be brave enough or foolhardy enough to take a chance on many things, but marriage was always a daunting proposition.

There were four envelopes in the mail for Chander that day. Of the four, only one was a letter. The other three were invitations to theatre-related functions, at two of which ministers were slated to participate. The third event would take place at the residence of a consul-general. They served first-rate foreign liquor in those places. Chander would be expected to give a small talk on the traditions of south Indian theatre. They would listen keenly to his talk and ply him with free liquor, but they would never get him a real assignment. He had no option but to continue dealing with that half-baked connoisseur of the arts, SSP's petty intrigues and mental turbulence. It was because of Chander that SSP disliked Sujatha too. It wouldn't take him long to tell her off, but the moment he did that he and poor Sujatha would be forced to leave the institute. Antagonizing SSP wouldn't mean the end of their lives, but after that, they wouldn't get even a five-rupee job in any government-supported drama school. At that juncture, Chander and Sujatha could neither do nor get any other type of job.

There was an advantage to conducting drama classes for a living. You could sleep during the day. Chander woke from his afternoon nap and went over to Sujatha's hostel. She was not in. From there he went to the building adjacent to the Kali temple, where the classes were held. During the day, a kindergarten school functioned in that building. The school had a management council; SSP was the chairperson of that council too.

Sujatha didn't turn up to take her class that evening. Chander stood in for her in addition to conducting his own class. He was teaching the students how to drop a handkerchief in case they were called upon to enact such a scene in a play. The handkerchief had started to get very dirty.

Sujatha walked in at a quarter past eight. She was very excited. 'Chander, let's leave immediately. Prakash has sent for you.'

'You went to see him?'

'I got his message at five o'clock. I rushed quickly to the studio, but he had already left, and he came back only at half past seven.'

'You're sure he had actually gone out?'

'This time he was really not there. I believe some director has asked him to bring you along. Please go to the studio right away.'

'But it is already nearing half past eight!'

'If you put it off till tomorrow, they'll find someone else.'

'If this deal is going to fall through overnight, it might be too late even now.'

Sujatha stood silent. Then she said, 'I'll ring up Prakash Rao and check again, if that's what you want.'

Chander stuck out his lip. Since SSP was not expected that day, they could end their classes right then. The school had no telephone. Only the fourth house after the temple had a phone. SSP lived there.

As they passed the temple on the way to the house, Chander prayed, 'O Kali, let SSP not be at home now.' Sujatha's prayer may have been: 'Amma, please grant that Prakash remains in the studio, in his cabin.'

SSP was not at home. Prakash Rao was in the studio, and miraculously, in his cabin. Sujatha noticed SSP's servant hovering and sent him off to bring water. Prakash Rao told them to wait at the bus stop nearby; he would pick them up in about fifteen minutes. When the call was over, Chander and Sujatha came out.

'I didn't even shave properly today,' Chander muttered to himself. It was quite dark near the bus stop. Sujatha took a small round box from her handbag and gave it to Chander. He used the powder puff lightly on his face.

A car stopped nearby. Prakash Rao was driving. 'Come on, get in.'

Sujatha said, 'You think I should come too? Why don't the two of you go ahead?'

'I'll drop you at your hostel.'

Sujatha had to get in. While they were on their way, Prakash Rao said, 'Let's just meet the director first.'

'All right, who is this man?'

Rao told them. Siddhartha, as he was called, was known to be a talented filmmaker. He also had a reputation of another kind. When a film of his was under production, the girl playing the female lead would behave as though she was under a spell, abandoning hearth, home, husband and mother for Siddhartha, who became everything to her. People cited this too as a contributory reason for the outstanding performances in his films. The car stopped in front of a high-rise building. Siddhartha's apartment was in the second block, on the third floor.

Prakash Rao pressed the doorbell. The director opened the door himself. 'Oh, you've arrived! Good. Good. Come in,' he said.

'She is my uncle's daughter, Sujatha. He is Mr Chander, the stage actor I told you about.'

'Come in. Let's get comfortable first.'

Once they had settled in the living room, Siddhartha told Prakash Rao, 'All right. Tell me.'

Prakash Rao pointed to Chander and said, 'I told you about this gentleman here.'

Siddhartha looked at Chander. 'Um, what is he doing these days?'

'Well, he has a diploma in acting from the drama institute in Delhi. Though he has yet to act in films, he has performed in many plays. He conducts drama classes here in Madras.'

'Which one? SSP's?'

Chander wanted to protest: 'No, SSP has merely been nominated as the school's chairperson by the government. She doesn't own or run the school.' But nobody was interested in listening to these nuances, nor did they understand them. 'Yes,' he replied succinctly.

'I see. And this lady?'

Prakash Rao said, 'My uncle's daughter. She works with Mr Chander.'

'What kind of work?'

'I work in the same drama school. As an instructor, like Mr Chander.'

'So, you also have a diploma in acting?'

'Yes.'

Siddhartha looked intently at Sujatha for a minute. Then he asked her, 'Aren't you Miss Sujatha Ananda Rao?'

Eyes widening in surprise, Sujatha replied, 'Yes.'

'You acted in the NSD production of *Mrichchhakatika*, didn't you?'

'Yes . . .'

'You played Vasantasena, right?'

'Yes.'

'My God! Did you know that I've been looking for you everywhere since then?'

'Looking for me?'

'Yes! That year I was in Delhi for the National Awards function. I had to return to Hyderabad the very next day, after your play at NSD. By the time I made inquiries at your institute, your batch had already left.'

'That was our last month in Delhi. The diploma course is only for a year.'

'When I asked for the girl who played the lead in *Mrichchhakatika*, they said they had produced this play seven or eight times with as many Vasantasenas. I got your name only after I checked with several other girls. Tell me, would you have any objection to acting in films?'

Sujatha appeared bashful. Prakash Rao said, 'We came here for Mr Chander. In fact, Sujatha wasn't even supposed to come along with us.'

'Well, it's great that she has come! I've been looking everywhere for her for two years now. Miss Ananda Rao, the film I have in mind is not aimed at the box office. It is based on Sarat Chandra's *Chandranath*. The moment I saw you, I knew that you would be perfect for the role of Sarayu, and I've been looking for you ever since.'

'Chander also performed in *Mrichchhakatika*. He was Charudatta.'

'Oh, of course. Of course I remember. But right now, I'm talking about *Chandranath*.'

'Her parents will never agree to let her act in films,' said Prakash Rao.

'Do they live here?'

'No. In their home town.'

'Where is Miss Ananda Rao staying, then? At your place?'

'No, no. She lives in a hostel for women.'

'If her parents let her live in a hostel and mix with loafers who say they want to learn acting, they won't object to her being in films. Don't get me wrong, Miss Ananda Rao. An opportunity like this comes only once in a lifetime. I give you my word. This film will take only three months to complete; at the most, four. Did you know, Prakash, the financier for this film is Nandalal Baliga of Jayashree Talkies? He is one of the biggest parties in India today. Once the film is done, immediate release, that's it. Four months is all it would take. After that, Miss Ananda Rao, you'll be free to go back to cinema or drama or a kitchen nook, wherever you'd like to go.'

Prakash Rao was embarrassed. Chander was agitated. Sujatha didn't seem to like Siddhartha's pitch very much, and he had sensed it.

Siddhartha said, 'I don't want you to say yes or no right now. Think it over for a couple of days. Let me put it this way. You must be quite keen to act; why else would you go to Delhi and get yourself a diploma and all that? I am giving you the chance to play the lead right away. No one else would cast a fresh, unknown girl as the heroine on a mere hunch like this. But I have faith in you. It'll be all right if you let me know in a couple of days.'

All of them fell silent as though the discussion was over for the evening. Prakash Rao was the first to say, 'Okay, I'll come and see you tomorrow.' He stood up to leave, followed by Chander and Sujatha. Sujatha gave him a pointed look, which prompted Prakash Rao to speak again. 'Our visit was only for Mr Chander,' he said.

Siddhartha said, 'Let's see. There is only one hero for this subject. Chalam is going to do Chandranath. The other roles won't suit Mr Chander. Never mind about this film. I'll certainly use him in my next.'

They climbed down the stairs and walked to the car. Sujatha asked, 'Shall we drive to the beach first before going back home?'

Prakash didn't reply immediately. Then he said, 'All right.'

At ten o'clock in the night, they found the beach deserted with only its row of sodium lamps lit. There was a slight chill in the air. But for the occasional rumble in the distance, the sea mostly held its peace. Near the shoreline, however, the breakers rose and collapsed noisily on the wet sand, meeting oblivion again and again.

'I suggest you look up this man as often as you can,' Prakash Rao told Chander.

Chander didn't even smile. The list of people he had to look up often was already very long.

Sujatha asked him, 'What do you think?'

'Let's see when he makes his next film,' Chander replied.

'No, I didn't mean that. I meant his offer to me!'

'His offer to you? Why, take it up if you want to.'

'Well, what does Chander think?' asked Prakash Rao.

'Nothing,' said Sujatha. 'Shall we go back?'

When the car was near the Mount Road roundabout, Prakash Rao said, 'Which way?'

'Go to the Flower Bazaar Police Station,' said Sujatha.

As the car approached Flower Bazaar, Sujatha said, 'Drop us here. I'll give you a ring tomorrow.'

'I thought I'd drop you at your hostel,' said Prakash Rao.

'It's all right, I'll manage. If I can't, I'll spend the night at Chander's place. He lives with his mother and sisters.'

Prakash left without argument. Chander was walking at a pace too brisk for a stroll. Sujatha half ran to catch up with him and suggested, 'Come, let's eat something in Buhari's.'

'I don't have money for Buhari's and all,' said Chander.

'But I do. Please, let's go.'

Sujatha led the way. As she passed the restaurant's entrance, its bright neon lights revealed that her sari had begun to tear. Most of her saris were in a similar condition. It had probably been a long time since she last bought herself new clothes. From her salary of two hundred rupees, she paid a hundred and ten as hostel charges, sent forty rupees home, bought two large boxes of Surf detergent, and with the money left over she treated Chander whenever they went to a restaurant. Occasionally, she asked him to iron her sari; he did it once or twice a month at the most.

Chander felt all right for about five minutes. Then his head began to throb.

Sujatha told the waiter, 'Biscuit, samosa and tea.' Then she asked Chander, 'Why are you angry with me?'

'Nothing.'

'Why are you pulling such a long face, then?'

'What can I do? Maybe some faces look like this, always.'

'I was quite hopeful.'

'Sure, it's turned out well enough. Siddhartha has taken a great liking to you.'

'But I don't like his offer at all.'

'Don't say that. In just three months, you could become a big star. '

'I don't have any great desire to become a big star.'

Just then the waiter brought tea and biscuits in a big tray, rattling the cups and saucers noisily. Chander didn't eat anything; Sujatha couldn't. They drank the tea half-heartedly. Sujatha left a ten-paisa tip and followed Chander out. He walked past Kandaswamy Temple and turned into a nearby lane. It was quiet except the milk booth on the corner, which was still open. Cows and their calves sat happily in the middle of the lane, chewing cud.

Sujatha called out, 'Chander!'

He stopped in his tracks. 'What's the matter with you, yelling in the middle of the road? Aren't you an educated person?'

'What's come over you? I have absolutely no intention of working in films . . .'

'A man likes you. He has been searching for you, yearning for you, for years. Are you going to deny him too? Well, I should have known. You are not Vasantasena for nothing!'

'Don't talk like a little child! We went there today only for your sake . . .'

'I was only an excuse. Your cousin probably wanted to take you all along. He is your cousin, after all! But even he must have felt a little shy about taking a girl there alone, without an escort.'

'Chhi! Your mind has become a sewer.'

He walked on briskly without saying anything. She ran after him again. 'Chander!'

Before he could respond, three cyclists came speeding down the road; their cycles had no lamps, nor did they ring their bells. Sujatha stopped abruptly, and Chander leaped to one side to let them pass. Once the cyclists had raced ahead, he walked past five or six houses, and then knocked on a door. He went in and immediately told his sister to latch the door. But she had seen Sujatha.

'Has Sujatha akka come with you?'

'No akka-thakka. Just close the door.'

'But she is here! Come in, akka.'

Chander grabbed his sister and pushed her aside. He shut the door, latched it and waited there for a few seconds. There was no knock on the door.

'Why did you shut the door on Sujatha? I am going to call Amma!'

'Just mind your business and go your way quietly. If you don't, I'll break your teeth!' His sister went inside, muttering something in the dark. Chander undid the latch without making a sound. He opened the door very gently, yet it creaked. It was deserted outside.

He stepped out and stood in the lane. Though it was dark he could see clearly. Cows, calves, homeless persons curled up on both sides along the walls; a rubbish bin; the milk booth on the corner; a lamp post and, coiled around it, the glowing end of a thick coir-rope where smokers lit their bidis and cigarettes; a street dog. Sujatha was probably walking on the main road by now. She would not look for a taxi. She would go straight past Raja Annamalai Hall and reach Fort Station. There was a train even as late as eleven-fifteen. The watchman at her hostel would open the gate for her. Once inside her room, she would undress for the night and lie down on her bed. Only after lying down would she weep her heart out, with nothing to stem the flow.

Chander's palpitations died down and his breathing grew easy. Once again he had made Sujatha cry in public.

SSP's harassment of her was not even a hundredth of how poorly Chander had treated her! If she had been by herself, without him around, SSP might have been truly kind and supportive to Sujatha. Without him in the picture, accepting this recent offer that had come her way wouldn't seem like a great crime to her. After having been with him all this while, she wouldn't have had to stand late one night in the middle of a dark lane and have a door shut on her face. She was not there any more, she had left.

Chander was breathing freely. He normally choked when someone was sweeping the floor at home, panted while climbing several flights of stairs at once, and became short-winded when he ironed clothes. Even so, he had voluntarily offered to iron her saris. But over the last six months, he could do so only once in a while. Sujatha was aware of this problem and seldom asked for his help. Now she would never ask him again. She would never come back to him, or forgive him for making her cry yet again. She might even agree to act in that champion seducer Siddhartha's film. Now Chander would have to cope with SSP's horrors all by himself. Sujatha leaving him was indeed a great loss.

Or was it? Chander had his doubts. It was true that she had sacrificed a lot for him over the last three years. But had he contributed nothing at all? If she hadn't dragged him along, would he have sat on Prakash Rao's rickety chair, climbed three floors till he was completely out of breath, and allowed himself to be treated like dirt by a director who had eyes only for anything in a sari? If he really thought about it, what had he done or thought all these days apart from what Sujatha wanted him to?

Chander entered the house and latched the door. He realized that their quarrel was a very good thing for both of them. If they didn't part ways now, they would forever be teaching people how to drop handkerchiefs. They might even have to marry. That would really be the end; nothing could be salvaged after that. Thank God there was no longer any need to worry about that.

Another thought occurred to Chander. He wouldn't have to iron saris any more.

From the original Ini Vendiyathilai (1968)

Still Bleeding from the Wound

'You! Move on up!'

Dhanapal was pushed from behind. He could only shift his feet a little. Among the many passengers standing densely packed in the front section, one man carried an umbrella tucked under his arm, affording Dhanapal some leeway—a small gap had opened up in the crowd trying to steer clear of the umbrella's sharp point.

Now the conductor banged hard on the roof of the bus. 'Move on. Move on. There's plenty of space over there. Move up. Move up.'

There didn't appear to be a lot of room that people could move into. Even so, a flurry of tiny movements was observed among those who were standing. Suddenly, the man who stood in front of Dhanapal shouted, 'Why do you keep pushing me?'

When Dhanapal did not reply, the man turned around. He saw the can Dhanapal was holding and immediately glanced down at his own veshti. Of his own accord, he took a few steps towards the front section.

Dhanapal, whose breath had caught in his throat, started breathing again. Fortunately, the man had not noticed the small green spot on his veshti. Dhanapal stood very carefully in the same spot, bending and twisting in order to avoid touching anyone with the can.

All that caution was to no avail. When the bus halted at the next stop, another seven or eight people got on, increasing the congestion among those standing. Dhanapal realized that his can was staining the clothes of many more passengers. Some time later, when the bus stopped again for a few seconds, he hurriedly wiped the rim of the tin can with his left hand as best as he could. However, he ended up smearing the overhead bar in several places with the paint when he gripped it once more.

The bus did not start immediately. The conductor couldn't persuade the passengers riding precariously on the footboard to get off. They couldn't climb in either.

'Let's move. It's baking inside.' The voice belonged to a man who was trapped among the passengers crowding the middle section. The passengers were indeed baking, but they were able to take it in their stride. Meanwhile, Dhanapal's can had grazed a man in a pair of shorts. When the man looked back abruptly, Dhanapal stood still, without betraying his fear.

'What's this?' the man demanded.

Dhanapal did not reply.

The man asked him again: 'What's this? A paint can?'

'Yes.'

'Are you out of your mind? Why did you board this crowded bus where you'd knock your paint can against everybody?'

'I am trying to make sure that doesn't happen.'

'What do you mean? You've tipped it over me and ruined my clothes, haven't you?'

As he saw anger far in excess of his outburst spreading over the man's features, Dhanapal loosened his grip on the overhead bar. Just then the bus came to life and surged forward. Jolted by the speed, Dhanapal leaned backwards, on to the people who were standing behind him. The paint can and brush in his hand slipped to the floor, but even in that mêlée, he reached down immediately and grabbed the paint can. Fortunately, it had not tipped over.

An old man, who was seated next to where Dhanapal was standing, noticed his plight. Shifting slightly in his seat, he told Dhanapal, 'Sit down here.'

It was a two-seater which already held as many passengers. Dhanapal would get no more than a few inches of space and if the old man did not hold him, he would surely slide down.

Dhanapal tried to manage as he remained standing. But the old man took Dhanapal's can from him.

'No need, sir,' protested Dhanapal

'I'll keep it safely down here.' The old man put the can down between his feet. 'Sit down here,' he said.

'No need, sir. It'll be inconvenient for all three of us.'

Meanwhile, the passenger seated next to the old man stood up. 'I am getting down at the next stop,' he announced. Now Dhanapal had no way of declining the old man's offer.

After he had sat down comfortably, Dhanapal pulled out his handkerchief and wiped his hands. Then, with the same handkerchief, he wiped the paint can's exterior. Finally, he rolled the handkerchief around the paint brush and held it in his left hand. The old man watched all this intently, while Dhanapal avoided eye contact with him.

'How far are you going?' asked the old man.

'Chintadiripettai.'

'Going there for a paint job?'

'No. I'm going home.'

'Is this paint yours?'

'No. It belonged to a group. We finished a job today. They themselves gave it to me.'

'That's a lot of paint—maybe ten or fifteen rupees' worth?'

Dhanapal looked at the can. 'Maybe,' he said. 'But a lot of lead has been mixed into it.'

'What?'

'This is not paint from the original can. It's mixed with plenty of white lead oil.'

'Even then, it seems like a lot.'

'I get paid very low rates, sir.'

'How much do you get?'

'Normally, for a painting job these days, people charge ten or even twelve rupees per day. I get only eight.'

'If you work for eight rupees, don't the others get mad at you?'

'They do. I could charge ten if I did this work on a daily basis.'

'Can't you find work every day?'

'No, sir; I can't. And even if I did, I couldn't go.'

'Why?'

'On the occasional holiday, I can work during the daytime. But otherwise, I can work only for two or three hours in the evening. That too, only for people known to me.'

'You should work for a contractor, then.'

'That's not possible, sir.'

'Why?'

Dhanapal hesitated. 'I am a student, sir. At the polytechnic institute here.'

'So, you work and study?' There was admiration in the old man's voice.

'I couldn't study if I didn't work.'

The old man did not inquire any further.

Perhaps to avoid hurting me, thought Dhanapal. He continued: 'My parents can't afford to pay for my studies. They are farmers, in a village. What they earn is not enough even for the family.'

'Where do you stay?'

'With relatives. But I have to eat out. That's why I work for at least ten to fifteen days in a month. I pay them thirteen rupees for letting me stay with them. Occasionally, if I can, I send some money home.'

'Can you earn that much?'

'I can't. That's why I don't spend more than a rupee and a half daily on food. If I could somehow finish my studies and find myself a proper job, everything can be sorted out.'

'Can't you eat where you stay, and pay them a little money?'

'That won't work.'

'Why?'

'I am neither a guest nor am I someone they need to oblige.'

'How did you settle on thirteen rupees?'

'I hand over the whole amount to the house owner. Even now, I don't really have to go home. But I got fifteen rupees today. I can give it to the landlord right away.'

The bus went past Anna Statue and stopped near the entrance to Simpsons. The old man got down. The crowd in the bus had also thinned.

Dhanapal got down near the Chintadiripettai market. After the bus left, he put his hand into his trouser pocket. The fifteen rupees he had kept there was missing. He ran behind the bus, but it had travelled very far by then. The sun was directly overhead. There was no shade available for a pedestrian unless he stepped inside a shop or a house.

Dhanapal crossed the road and waited at the bus stop. He had worked all night without going home. The men were trying to complete that multi-storeyed building by working day and night. Tasks like plastering the walls and polishing the mosaic floor were being done in the bright light of a naked bulb, along with painting. Though the job was mostly indoors, the floor was still wet; he couldn't sleep properly even for two hours. Towards dawn, Dhanapal had lain down on the sand piled in the open yard outside and caught some sleep. He had promised to pay the house owner's wife that day. Ever since he started handling money, he had never once failed to keep his word.

A lot of buses plied up and down that road. Dhanapal waited, careful not to lose himself in any extreme emotion. But he couldn't prevent the pangs of hunger from growing and gnawing at his stomach as time wore on.

The bus he was waiting for arrived an hour later. Fortunately, it had the same conductor. This must be the last trip before there was a change of personnel for the afternoon shift.

'Don't stand on the steps. Get inside,' said the conductor. The bus was near empty. There were no standees. Dhanapal remained standing on the footboard.

'Are you coming in? If not, get off.'

'I lost my money here.'

The conductor became alert.

'I got down here on your previous trip. I lost my money.'

From his seat, a man inquired: 'Your pocket was picked?'

'No, it wasn't a pickpocket. I must have dropped it here, in the bus.' Dhanapal climbed aboard and started looking under every seat.

The conductor asked: 'You travelled on this bus?'

'Yes. I have the ticket here.'

The conductor took the ticket from him and examined it. He started looking too. Everyone on the bus started searching the floor. The driver had turned off the engine by now. The conductor turned over and sifted through all the used tickets and scraps of paper lying on the floor of the bus.

'Did you lose a purse?'

'No. Just two notes. A ten-rupee note and a five-rupee note.'

The driver remarked: 'Who knows where you let them slip!'

'No, no. I had the money when I got on the bus.'

'Was there a pickpocket next to you?'

'How would I know? The bus was very crowded.'

'Did you give me a note?' asked the conductor.

'No, only change. I had kept the rupee notes in my pocket.'

'Look . . . look . . . it's getting late.'

Dhanapal had searched the entire bus to no avail. Opinions about pickpockets in Madras were exchanged among the passengers. A lone passenger protested: 'His money is not here; why are you still holding us up?'

The conductor asked Dhanapal: 'Did you sit at all?'

'Yes. There was an old man sitting next to me.'

'When it comes to picking pockets, what's young and old? Haven't the old coots become shameless about everything these days?'

There was some dissent in the bus over this remark. Sympathy for the boy who lost his money had mostly vanished by then.

Dhanapal reluctantly got off the bus. The bus resumed its journey. Dhanapal carried the paint can to a hardware shop. He could get only three rupees for the paint he had brought in. He safely stowed the brush away, rolled up in an old newspaper. If he didn't clean it properly with kerosene in the next couple of hours, the brush would dry up and be ruined.

Around the Kannagi statue, there were several obstacles for pedestrians. The city had begun digging the ground for a pedestrian subway. Dhanapal noticed a lone figure walking past in the half-dark of twilight. It seemed familiar, as though he had seen it somewhere. The figure walked on, passing near the hedgerows. Dhanapal crossed the road in one swift motion. He raced towards the hedgerows and caught the person by the arm, stopping him. 'Thieving old man!'

'What? What?'

'You acted like such a do-gooder, making me sit next to you. Where is my money, da?'

'What? What?'

Within no time, five or six people collected there.

'Worthless old bastard! Picking the pockets of little boys—is that any way to make a living?'

The moment Dhanapal caught hold of the old man's shirt and called him a pickpocket, the crowd acquired a degree of briskness. Kicks and blows were rained abundantly on the old man, who dropped to the ground. One man had ripped his shirt open. Another had pulled his veshti off. Only a small packet was left on the old man's waist.

'Thieving scoundrel! Let's roll him over!'

'Hold him! Don't let him go!'

'He has already passed the purse to his partner!'

'Where is the purse, da?'

'This thieving gang, will they confess for the asking? Hit him on the face a few times, that'll do the job!'

'When was it stolen?'

'When was it stolen?'

'Was it just now?'

'Where is the purse, you old scoundrel! Pretending to be a gent, are you?'

'Call the police!'

'Why call them? Drag this fellow to the station!'

'Not a purse,' said Dhanapal.

'What are you saying?'

'I didn't lose a purse. I had the money in notes.'

'He took your notes, did he? Just now?'

'Not just now.'

'Not just now?'

'Around three months ago. He sat next to me on a bus and stole my money.'

A sudden change came over the crowd. When a police constable sauntered over to inquire—'What's the trouble here?'—only Dhanapal and the old man squatting on the ground were left.

'Why the commotion? What's the matter?'

It was the old man who replied: 'We are talking to each other, that's all.'

Relieved, the policeman went away. Dhanapal helped the old man to his feet. Walking a few steps, they came into the light. The old man's veshti was tied in a haphazard manner and blood trickled down from a couple of cuts on his face.

'Why did you beat me? Who are you?' asked the old man.

Dhanapal turned away from him, seething with rancour. The old man narrowed his eyes and looked at Dhanapal.

'Aren't you the painter boy?'

Not wanting to talk to the old man, Dhanapal started to walk away. Now the old man caught him by the arm and asked him, 'Aren't you the boy who travelled with me on the bus one day?'

'Yes. You acted like you were very concerned, and then you stole my money.'

'I stole your money?'

'Yes.'

The old man positioned himself under the bright light. Looking directly at Dhanapal's face, he said, 'I am not that kind of man, 'pa.'

'Who do you think you are bluffing?'

The old man wiped the blood on his face. 'Is that why you had a crowd beat me up, because you thought I had taken your money? I don't know anything about it, 'pa.'

Dhanapal stood still, not saying a word. Even the sounds of the city and the sea seemed to have died down.

'I've thought about you many times since that day. But I never imagined that you would call me a thief and beat me up.'

'Who knows what really happened! My money is gone.'

'I didn't take it. I don't know anything about it.' The old man put on his tattered shirt.

Dhanapal looked intently at his face. There wasn't a trace of anger on it.

'Believe me, 'pa. I didn't take your money. I know nothing about it.'

Slowly, very slowly, the old man walked away.

From the original Pun Umizh Kurudhi (1978)

She Was the Only One

It was over. Finally, after strenuous effort, they removed the Ramar Pattabhishekam portrait from a high wall in one of the rooms using a ladder left behind by some workmen who had come to whitewash the house many years ago. A few more hours, and they would finish packing.

Prabhushankar looked up at the ceiling. The house had a tiled roof, but it was at a height of nearly thirty feet. They needed two ladders and a couple of men just to clear the cobwebs. Therefore, the house was cleaned only when the railway authorities sent workers to whitewash it once a year. Even then, the workers tackled the job in unseemly haste, doing whatever was conveniently at hand, and left quickly. Afterwards, one still found a whole mess of cobwebs near the roof, left untouched.

A portion of those cobwebs could very well have been there for twenty or thirty years. Prabhushankar tried to work it out. His father had come to that town thirty years ago as a young boy who hadn't even grown a proper moustache. After spending his life in many different places and facing numerous hardships, he had lived the last few years of his life in this house with its high roof, and died here too. For all one knew, some of the cobwebs had been hanging there for all thirty of those years.

Because of that absurdly high ceiling, they couldn't install a swing in their house or string a washing line indoors or hang a cradle for babies. Even the brightest lamps couldn't dispel the feeling of being perpetually in the dark. On the day Appa died, he had been afraid to even glance at the ceiling. But in the month and a half since, it seemed as though Prabhushankar had aged fifteen years and become twice as old. He faced such a mountain of tasks that he had no time in which to mourn or experience fear. The tasks were complex and completely new to him; and he had to perform them by himself. He was no longer afraid to look at the roof. The real terror, he knew, lay beyond the roof, outside the house, maybe even beyond this town. He would be leaving in two days. Genuine dread would set in only after that.

What did he have left to do during those two days? As a final task, he had carted more than half the furniture and other assorted items from his house to Allauddin Khan Auction Company, had them auctioned last Sunday and collected the money. Three cots, a large crib, two big cupboards and a gramophone set with eighty records—he had received one hundred and twenty rupees for the lot. Allauddin Khan had kept twelve rupees for himself. The buffalo sold for fifty rupees. Poor Appa! He had paid five hundred rupees for the animal. If someone untethered it, that expensive beast would go straight back to its previous owner's house. They had suffered so many crises because the animal often ran away like that! The buffalo had mellowed a lot since Appa's death though. Just when it had become quiet and manageable, and begun to show fondness for the people in this house, they'd had to let it go. That poor buffalo must be feeling forlorn too.

Many of their things had been taken away, and what remained lay scattered on the floor, giving the house a widowed look. What was widowhood? It was a hateful condition, but one that had to be endured nonetheless; a situation where you had to put up with an attitude that said, 'All right, all right, live if you want to, but leave us alone.' Because he was about to go away from that house, it looked to him like a woman bereaved. When the next tenants came to live there, it might be transformed again into something radiant and dazzling. Newly occupied, any house looks neat and fresh for the first few days. That's why you must never live in any one house for too long; certainly, not like they had done, residing in the same house and in the same town for so many years.

Prabhushankar felt the urge to go around the town one last time. It was not really a very big place. If he'd had his bicycle, he could have easily circled it once and been back in an hour. Ever since he was old enough to remember, this town had remained the same. The houses and other buildings had aged somewhat. A few roads had been newly resurfaced, but the posh neighbourhoods, lonely and deserted, were still unchanged. Perhaps many others were also leaving town, like he was.

It was no longer rare to come across locked-up mansions. On Oxford Street, there were just ten bungalows along the half-mile stretch between the spot where he was standing and the clock tower, of which four were vacant.

Who were the people who had erected these mansions? When had they built them? How many people had they intended to accommodate? Barring one or two, almost all the houses were alike: a high compound wall, two massive iron gates linked by an arched driveway, and at least two outhouses. In some, even the kitchen was housed in a separate building. Perhaps the white lords and mistresses of the time couldn't stand the smoke and the aromas of cooking. A more pertinent reason, though, was their probable disdain for the kitchen staff.

Prabhushankar didn't know what the insides of those bungalows looked like, but he knew their gardens rather well. The buffalo in their house had trespassed into the gardens of all those bungalows as though it had consciously planned the visits. While searching for the animal, he had needed to enter the gate of the bungalows, overcoming his shyness and fear. They had no buffalo now, there was no need, but the fear had not left him.

Prabhushankar wanted to visit at least one of those bungalows. If he didn't do it now, he would never get another chance. Why not try Dr Ramchander's house?

Though the gate bore a nameplate that said Dr Ramchander, the man had passed away many years ago. Prabhushankar's father had told him about the doctor. Ramchander had belonged to a wealthy family. His father, Dewan Bahadur Araavamudhu, had sent him to college in England. On his return to India, the boy had married a Parsi girl. The Parsis were fair-skinned people who always dressed in spotless white. Every one of them seemed to move sideways when they walked. When they died, they kept the corpse somewhere out in the open, so it was convenient for the birds to feed on it. He didn't know anything else about their way of living. Ramchander and the lady had fought all the time; mostly over food matters, according to Appa. Ramchander had lived in that huge mansion with his wife and daughter, and one or two servants. One night, the couple had a big row. Dr Ramchander swallowed poison and killed himself. The Parsi woman still lived in that house; Prabhushankar had seen her from a distance.

Prabhushankar thought that since the Parsi woman was a widow, her bungalow too must have changed like his own house. Changed, yes, but that bungalow still looked beautiful. Small flowerpots had been suspended from the ceiling in many spots along the outer veranda. The house was surrounded by a well-laid garden. The upper halves of the main door and the windows were all made of glass, and although nothing in the house was visible from the street, one could see whether the lights were on. Even though it was forenoon then, the lights inside the house were on.

Would he get to see that Parsi woman once more before he left town for good? A man had walked out on his family for her sake; then, finding her world intolerable, he had committed suicide. And this was a *doctor* who had studied in *England*. The Parsi woman must have been a very special person, Prabhushankar thought.

As if to grant his final wishes during the last few days he would spend in that town, the Parsi lady stood in the garden, looking on as a workman tapped away at something with a hammer.

Did a man take his own life for this woman's sake?

She was tall and very fair. Her hair was gathered in two plaits and she wore a long dress that came down to her ankles like a raincoat. She looked very beautiful.

He stood on the road in front of the bungalow and gazed at her. She didn't look like a widow. Perhaps widows looked different in every community.

She had spotted him. She smiled gently and nodded as if to ask, 'What do you want?' She had also walked over to the gate by then.

Prabhushankar wondered if he should run away. He had learned that in such situations on normal days, it was smarter to flee the scene rather than stay back, replying to questions. He had no suitable answer for her, nor would she gain anything from his reply. He could run away. But he was going to leave that town in a couple of days anyway, so why run now?

'Why are you standing here? Do you want anything?' she asked him.

'I study in the school next to that clock tower.'

'Yes. I've seen you around often. What do you want? Why don't you come in?'

'Our buffalo has come to your house many times.'

'Is it here now?'

'No.'

'Is that right? Would you like to bring it here, then?' she asked, laughing.

In the meantime, the workman who had been tapping away with the hammer came to her and said, 'It's set right now.' On seeing Prabhushankar, he exclaimed in Urdu, 'It's you! No buffalo came here today.'

'You won't have our buffalo coming here any more,' said Prabhushankar.

'Why?' asked the Parsi lady.

'We are leaving this town.'

'Why? Whatever for?' The Parsi lady opened the gate. 'Come, come in. Have some tea with us before you leave.'

She didn't seem so tall now. Her nose was slightly crooked. There were a couple of grey strands in her hair.

'I have a boy too,' she said.

'A son? I've only seen your daughter.'

'My daughter lives here, my son is studying in Poona. He must be slightly older than you.'

They had reached the veranda by then. She indicated a cane chair and said, 'Sit down.'

'No, I should be going. My family will start looking for me.'

'Yes. You said you were leaving town; so you'll have lots of work to do. But have some tea before you rush off.'

She called for tea. A servant girl answered from inside, 'Yes, 'ma.'

'But why are you going away?'

'My father passed away, so we are leaving.'

'Do you really have to leave town because your father is no more?'

'I don't know. The elders in my family have arranged it.'

'It's a great loss, certainly, to lose your father. But there's no loss that cannot be endured. My daughter went around with a morose expression on her face for a few days. Now, she's all right. Only Naushir, my son, still pines for his father though he was only three when my husband died.'

As if she had suddenly remembered, she asked him, 'Where do you live?'

'At the end of this road, in Railway Quarters.' He gave his address. She could not recognize it.

'Are there many houses like yours over there? I've never been to that part of town.'

'Yes. Not too many people pass that way. There's a small workshop beyond our house. It's meant for unemployed old men who need to make a living. It's only those grandpas who normally go past our house.'

'I don't go out of the house much.'

'There aren't too many houses in our neighbourhood, but the place is really pretty to look at. There are two big banyan trees, with plenty of aerial roots hanging from the branches. You can swing on them. There are lots of other trees too. And a huge playing field. There's a hillock further away. Lots of scorpions and snakes there.'

'There are many snakes right here in this compound. Sometimes, they even enter the house.'

'Three snakes came into our house recently, one after another. That's why my father died, they tell me.'

'Did your father die of snakebite?'

'No. They say: when snakes come into your house, death is sure to follow.'

'Is that so? I don't think so at all. The people who told you that couldn't have been sure of that. Anyway, whether they were right or wrong, your father *has* passed away.'

Prabhushankar felt like crying.

'Don't cry. You still have your mother, don't you?'

Stifling his sobs, Prabhushankar replied, 'Hmm. Hmm.'

'What's there to worry about, then? If your father's dead, it's not the end of the world.'

Prabhushankar didn't reply.

'Maybe, you can't say that of *all* fathers,' the Parsi lady conceded. 'As for me, I found it really hard to get on without my mother. My father is still alive, but he flies into a rage whenever he sees me. I don't feel like talking to him at all. So we hardly speak to each other.'

'My father talked a lot. Whenever I went out with him, he spoke to me about a lot of things.'

'I've never gone out much. Never even had a proper look at this town. I don't know your neighbourhood at all. Have you gone around this town a lot?'

'Um . . . but I don't know some localities. I haven't been to the Ranigunj side much.'

'That's where my father's shop is.'

'Shop? What shop?'

'Motor car showroom.'

Prabhushankar kept silent. He hardly knew anything about motor cars. The maid brought piping hot tea; the cup fairly floated in the tea which had spilled over into the saucer. In her other hand she held a plate filled with small eats. She stood there for a moment, as if she was wondering, 'Where do I set this down?'

The Parsi lady said, 'Keep it here,' and indicated the parapet wall of the veranda. To Prabhushankar she said, 'There's no meat in any of this. Go ahead and eat.'

Prabhushankar reluctantly picked up a piece and put it into his mouth. Despite her reassurances, he felt like retching. Her husband, Ramchander, must have suffered like this. How great his agony must have been for him to make up his mind to die! This Parsi woman did look like a widow now. The house also wore the same bleak air.

But the tea was tasty. Who should take the credit for it? The servant girl, naturally. Would the daughter of a motor car dealer know how to make tea?

'It would've been nice if my son was here. He comes over only during vacations. But you just told me that you are leaving this town for good.'

'Yes.'

'Why? If your father's gone, has everything else also gone with him? Do you have to leave this town? Don't you like it here?'

'I like this place a lot. Even so, I haven't gone around very much.' He then blurted out the question he had been holding back for a long time: 'Why did Dr Ramchander die?'

She didn't understand at first. 'Who are you talking about? My husband?'

He nodded yes.

'Why do you ask? You couldn't have met him.'

'Perhaps. It was such a long time ago.'

Both were silent for a while. 'I think your father must have told you something. Ramchander died of a ruptured appendix due to his ulcer.'

'Do you get that after you drink poison?'

'Get what?'

'That thing. Whatever you said it was.'

'What? Ulcer? No, not at all. You can get an ulcer in many ways. Why do you ask?'

'No. Simply.'

'Why did you ask about poison?'

Prabhushankar once again felt like running away. He ought to have fled the moment he first saw her. He got up to leave.

'Don't be afraid. I'm not going to do you any harm.'

'I must go. I must go.'

'I can't bind you hand and foot and keep you here, can I? I could do that to your buffalo, though.'

'I'll be leaving now.'

'If you ever come back to this town, be sure to look me up. I'll be right here, I am not going anywhere.'

Prabhushankar had gone to that street. He had paid a visit to that house, which was an impenetrable mystery for many years. He had also talked to that mysterious woman. When the meeting had been so unexpected and so comfortable, he could have asked her directly: Did Dr Ramchander really drink poison and kill himself? She talked of something called ulcer. What was ulcer? A Parsi delicacy, perhaps.

A man might have taken his own life because of her, but she was the only one who told him that it was not the end of the world when your father passed away. Everyone else had merely tried to console him with their talk of this and that; she alone had said that death was not such a big thing. She hadn't been around that town a lot. But she liked it here, just like he did.

If possible, some day, I must take this Parsi woman around this town and show her the sights, thought Prabhushankar. That he was going to be in this town only for two more days hardly mattered to him any more.

From the original Aval Oruthithan (1980)

Debt

Nadamuni Mama was already in the habit of snoozing in the afternoon when I began working in the studio. Though we were not really his nephews, all of us called him Nadamuni Mama. Every afternoon he slept, reclining comfortably in his cane chair, loud snores issuing from his open mouth. This often left me nauseous as I had to work sitting in the same room.

There was a time when Nadamuni Mama had gone without sleep for days on end. It was when the owner of our studio produced a spectacular Tamil film, which not only broke fresh ground in the way it was made, but also broke all previous records for the size of a film's budget. (I had watched a matinee show of the film as a small boy in shorts, playing truant from school.) Work on that film had continued round the clock for years.

Those days, Nadamuni was among the three or four people who were very valuable to the boss. On any work-related matter, the boss was wont to say: 'We must ask Nadamuni'; or, 'Do as Nadamuni tells you to'; or, 'Tell us, Nadamuni, would it work if we shot the sequence this way?' Nadamuni Mama would go home in the studio car for half an hour every day—for a bath and a change of clothes. The rest of his daily needs—meals, tiffin, morning and afternoon coffee, cup of Horlicks at night, and sleep— were taken care of in the studio itself. At the time, our boss ran the studio cafeteria as a separate department of the studio. While the whole city had to make do with a small quantity of the reddish flat rice given as 'ration', unlimited quantities of rice as white as jasmine was served in our cafeteria. Even the coffee beans for our coffee were bought wholesale by our buyers at planters' auctions.

While our boss had arranged for all of Nadamuni Mama's needs to be fulfilled at the studio, others stayed back of their own accord. They went home briefly after work and returned to the studio for dinner. They would often wistfully recall the pongal served early in the morning, dripping with ghee and garnished with a heap of cashew nuts, and share their reminiscences with me. All this had changed drastically by the time I started my job there.

So had Nadamuni Mama's status.

Our boss was no longer a novice: he had no need for advice and affirmation on every little thing from the likes of Nadamuni Mama. Now his decisions were quick and completely autonomous, and people like Nadamuni were required only for implementing them. Since Nadamuni was blessed with talented assistants, even his supervisory duties were light and undemanding. So Nadamuni began napping in the afternoon, right there in the studio. Though my work had little to do with his editing department, they had placed my desk in his room to economize on office space. From the rise and ebb of Nadamuni's snores, I had the privilege of imagining the difficult situations he experienced in his dreams and the dangerous apparitions he was forced to fight all alone.

When awake, Nadamuni Mama seemed to have aged far beyond his years. He might indeed have been very old. His furrowed cheeks and grey hair made him look like a youthful impostor, a Tamil film hero who had stolen into his girlfriend's house for a tryst disguised as an old family retainer. In contrast, his wife showed no visible signs of decline. They had six children, including two grown daughters. Nadamuni Mama's brother-in-law, along with his wife and child, also lived in Nadamuni's house. Everyone at the studio would greet this brother-in-law warmly—'Hello, *Raja!*'—and chat him up. His real name also happened to be Raja. He chewed paan constantly and talked an endless stream of bravado. He said he was engaged in some business. He would barge in twice or thrice a week and wake our sleeping Nadamuni, and hiss at him inaudibly in Telugu. Nadamuni would be in a daze for a couple of minutes, and after pretending to feel through his pockets for money that wasn't there, he would ask me if I had a couple of rupees he could borrow.

The money I loaned him was immediately given to Raja. It was common knowledge that Nadamuni's wife counted and gave him only his bus fare for the day.

However, when Nadamuni Mama returned home from work, he never took the bus: he walked. Most days, he and I walked home together. When the boss still thought he was indispensable, Nadamuni's name had figured in the credits of every film in big, bold letters. They even announced once that he was going to direct a film. Nadamuni never uttered a word to me about these past laurels. Instead, he spoke at length on diverse topics and events. For example: the Taittiriyopanishad; the way Sundaram Iyer, the proprietor of City Motor Company, had turned up regularly at the bus station during peak hours to issue tickets for the additional buses he operated over and above the day's schedule, all for the lofty cause of getting people to their place of work on time (bus transport in Madras city was not yet a government enterprise); the conflagration which burnt down a Congress Exhibition in Royapettah; the sirens going off in Madras warning its citizens of an imminent Japanese air raid even as flood waters swirled and rose in his native village. He talked of these things not only to me, but to just about everyone he knew. You would never guess from his conversation that he was employed in a film studio, let alone as the head of a talented and creative team in the editing department.

Long after his professional role had become unimportant to him (and to everyone else), Nadamuni suddenly featured in the limelight once again. The studio had arranged for a distributor to exhibit one of our biggest films across north India. The distributor was from a very wealthy family, engaged in business for many generations. They themselves had dispatched all the raw stock—the 'positive' film—required to make exhibition prints of our film. (In those days, there were no controls nor shortages in the availability of raw stock.)

Nadamuni, who had strayed into the processing lab one day entirely by accident, discovered that all the reels sent by the distributor were 'master positive'. The lab superintendent was on a month's leave at the time. In his absence, the other workers at the lab might have taken out prints even if they knew that the raw stock was 'master positive', and sent them to the distributor. From the 'master positive' print, the distributor could have made a 'dupe negative' and from that, any number of exhibition prints. He could then have screened the film in a large number of towns and pocketed all the money. Moreover, he could have smuggled the prints out to foreign countries where Indian films were in great demand. A gigantic swindle! It was as absurd as losing something produced after years of arduous labour, in the face of many risks and at the expense of vast sums of money, through sheer carelessness. For those five or six days, when the scale of the disaster-that-might-have-been sank in, Nadamuni was the most important person in our studio. The boss himself visited Nadamuni Mama in his room and spent a few minutes talking with him. One day, they even drove him home in the studio car like in the earlier days. Nadamuni Mama, too, seemed like his old lively self again. Then the commotion died down. The lab superintendent returned from leave and resumed his duties. The boss left on a tour of north India, first to Delhi to receive an award from the government, and then to finalize the cast for our next Hindi film.

And Nadamuni Mama resumed his afternoon naps.

His snores were particularly revolting that day. If I felt revulsion over anything, it invariably resulted in nausea. I made an effort to carry on with my work, but the sound of that relentless snoring expressed something different with each new respiratory cycle; it simply didn't allow my mind to focus on anything else. Not even a year had passed since I joined the studio. But that day I lamented the fate of people who had to pass their workday afternoons in the oblivion of sleep and dreaded such a prospect in my own life. I stood up, pushed my chair backwards with disproportionately loud scraping sounds, and strode out of the room. Nadamuni Mama's response was a profound and heartfelt sigh from the netherworld of sleep.

'Why would a man like him come to see me any more?' he inquired dramatically of his dreamworld companions.

'What was that?' I turned to him.

But sleep had already reclaimed him.

I returned to my chair. He had babbled in his sleep, but I couldn't grasp precisely what he meant. When he woke up, I told him: 'You were talking in your sleep today.'

'Is that so? What did I say? What did I say?'

'Nothing I could make out. It sounded like "What can I do?" or something like that.'

'Is that right?'

Nadamuni Mama was silent for a few minutes. Then he said, 'Come on, let's go and have a cup of coffee.'

On our way to the cafeteria, I could see that he was trying very hard to recollect something. People who were schooled in the discipline of film editing had this extraordinary ability: they could reconstruct, from snatches of a lengthy conversation lasting as long as half an hour, an orderly sequence that made complete sense.

'Did I say, "Raja, don't bother me"?' Nadamuni Mama wondered.

'No,' I replied.

The coffee was awful. We returned to our room without finishing it. I put my papers back on the desk and was about to begin work when Nadamuni Mama asked me, 'Could you do me a small favour?'

I was terribly annoyed. 'Certainly, sir,' I replied and waited. Nadamuni Mama was once again lost in thought. I had a lot of work to do. I was saddled with two bosses. They should never have dumped me in this man's room. They could have at least served decent coffee this afternoon.

'Raja is putting me under an awful lot of pressure,' Nadamuni Mama told me.

'You, sir?'

'Yes. I didn't know what I was letting myself in for when I borrowed five hundred rupees from him. His sister doesn't know about it. And now he wants me to pay up this minute.'

'But sir, isn't Raja the one who keeps borrowing from you?'

'Oh, that was only the interest on the loan. Don't worry. I have kept an account of all the money I owe you. I will settle the whole amount in one go.'

'No, sir. That's not what I meant.'

'For a week now, he has been pressurizing me to return the whole five hundred. He's even threatened to tell my wife and take it from her. She does have the money, but how will I ever sort things out with her after that? You've seen her, haven't you?'

'Indeed I have, sir. I've been to your house twice.'

'Would you happen to have five hundred rupees?'

I made no reply. A man who earned a salary of seven hundred rupees had the gall to ask someone like me with a monthly income of less than one hundred and fifty!

'You know Prakasam, don't you?'

Prakasam was an actor who was paid a monthly retainer by our studio. He managed to play the second lead in just about one film a year. There were rumours that he had recently had a tiff with our boss.

'I don't know him, sir,' I said.

'You know where he lives, don't you?'

'Somewhere near Vani Mahal, I believe.'

'Yes, yes, that's the place! As soon as you turn into Thirumalai Pillai Road, the first bungalow on the left, upstairs. You must go and see him immediately.'

'Sir, he won't even talk to someone like me.'

'Ah, no, no! Prakasam is not like that! He is . . . different. But meeting him just now would be embarrassing for me. That's why I want you to go.'

'But sir, he doesn't know me at all. Even here, in this studio, not many people are aware of my existence.'

Nadamuni didn't reply. He was reclining as usual, and I thought he was contemplating something. Suddenly, a snore emanated from him.

'I'll go and see him, sir!' I shouted.

Nadamuni Mama opened his eyes and asked, 'What was that?'

'I'll go and see Prakasam.'

'Oh, you will see him? What a great help that would be. I'll come with you right up to his doorstep. Then you go inside and ask him for it.'

'Sir, what should I ask him for?'

Nadamuni Mama paused for a moment. 'No, you don't have to ask him anything. I'll write him a note and give it to you.' While I worked, he made five or six drafts of the note, tearing each one up as soon it was finished. When the final version was ready, he put it in an envelope, which he even sealed. This annoyed me even more.

That evening both of us walked to Vani Mahal. 'There, can you see it? That's the house,' said Nadamuni Mama.

'Yes, I know.'

'Will you go in and ask him? I'll wait for you here.'

In those days, there were such large puddles of filthy water in the area around Vani Mahal that you couldn't always tell the pavement from the road. Moreover, it was always pitch-dark after sunset.

'Fine,' I said.

'I'll go home. After you are done with Prakasam, come over to my place and tell me.'

'Yes, sir,' I said.

Nadamuni Mama hesitated a little, and then began his slow walk home. He lived near the Mambalam Railway Station. My house was in West Mambalam, not far away.

I tucked my shirt neatly into my trousers, opened the gate to Prakasam's bungalow and entered the compound. There was a Muslim family staying downstairs, and a few people were about. I asked them if Prakasam lived there. 'This way to the staircase,' a small boy guided me.

In the veranda upstairs, Prakasam sat reclining in an easy chair in the semi-darkness. He was in his vest and pyjamas, smoking a cigarette. He didn't see me till I was almost upon him. Suddenly aware of my presence, he said, 'Who are you?'

'It's me,' I said.

'Who is "me"?'

I told him my name. It certainly couldn't have rung a bell. Perhaps he was satisfied with my answer: he rose, switched on the light and went back to the easy chair.

'What can I do for you?' he asked me.

'Nadamuni sent me,' I said.

'Who?'

I told him the name of our studio.

'Oh, Nadamuni Mama! How is he doing? It has been several months since we ran into each other,' said Prakasam.

I handed him the note. He tore open the envelope right in front of me and read it. Then, as though rendered inert all of a sudden, he gave it back to me without a word. I ran my eyes over the page and took in a few important lines. Nadamuni had, with great affection, asked that he be kindly repaid the sum of eight hundred rupees that Prakasam owed him.

'I am telling you the honest truth. Today, all that I have is just this.' Prakasam showed me his tin of cigarettes.

I didn't say a word.

'Sit down,' he said.

I did.

'What do you do?'

I told him.

'How long has it been since you joined them?'

'About a year.'

Prakasam told me, 'Join some other place before the year ends.'

I offered no response to his advice.

'Don't feel discouraged by what I have to say. They will just feed you well at mealtimes, keep you idle, and eventually make you permanently unfit for a proper day job. By then you will become what I am today: utterly useless.'

'Sir, you are all stars . . .'

'Yes, we are all big stars! Not worth a damn. When you have some kind of market, they feed you that rich pongal and rice with lots of ghee and put you to sleep. By the time you wake up, your face has vanished. As has your market. Others have arrived on the scene while you were asleep and got ahead of you. And you are left sitting there with a large belly, like a jackass!'

I couldn't understand much of what he said. I only knew that I couldn't possibly argue with him.

'Okay. Of what use is all this to a boy like you? Find yourself a job in a decent place and settle down in life while you are still young.'

Both of us were silent for some time. I asked him, 'So, what do I tell Nadamuni Mama?'

Prakasam shifted in his easy chair. 'What can I say? Not just eight hundred, I could give him even eight thousand. But I don't have a paisa to give.'

I sat still, staring at him in silence.

'All right, tell him to come and see me tomorrow. No, not tomorrow, on Saturday. I'll try to manage something.'

'Shall I tell him to come by on Saturday evening?'

'No, tell him to come in the morning. These days, I am never at home in the evening.'

Just then a woman came to the veranda, calling out to him, 'Prakash!' I recognized her immediately. She was a Telugu actress, widely recognized as a genuine talent. Even as recently as three or four years ago, her come-hither look and sexual charisma had bowled over the entire male population of south India. Her husband lived somewhere near Machilipatnam on the Andhra coast. Hard drinking and advanced epilepsy had ruined her, and now she barely had a foothold in the industry. It was said that she kept Prakasam around for stud duties, which—rumour had it—acted like a primitive cure for those epileptic attacks. I wasn't sure if Prakasam's ruin was to be blamed on the rich studio pongal or this woman.

'I am leaving.' I stood up.

She called out 'Prakash!' once more; then she put her arms around his neck and kissed him with great tenderness on the forehead. Prakasam remained wooden.

'Who is this young man?' she asked him in Telugu.

Prakasam made no attempt to answer her question. He turned to me and said by way of parting, 'Tell him to come on Saturday morning. I'll see if there is something I can do for him.'

'You won't tell me?' she baby-talked in Telugu and kissed him again.

I went down the stairs.

When I went to the studio on Saturday, I saw many people standing around in small, intimate groups. I asked them what the matter was.

'Nadamuni Mama is dead,' they said.

'Aiyo, our Nadamuni Mama?'

'Yes.'

'How? How did it happen?'

'Accident.'

'What accident?'

'Cycle accident. He was run over by a bus, sometime between eight and nine this morning.'

'Where, where?'

'Right here in Mambalam. The body is now in Royapettah Hospital.'

Nadamuni's corpse was indeed in Royapettah Hospital. Five or six people of some importance in the studio soon left for the hospital in a car. I, who had shared a room with him in the studio, was also taken along. We stopped the car near the old block of the hospital complex and walked in. The morgue was closed. There was a police inspector somewhere, and we had to find him and seek his permission. The car in which we had arrived left for Nadamuni's residence, perhaps to bring his wife and anyone else who had to come to the hospital. We waited under a tree. The door to the morgue remained locked.

Just then our boss arrived, looking grief-stricken. I recalled Nadamuni Mama's babbling in his sleep and wondered if it had been a plea in advance for the honour of this visit.

Our boss exclaimed to the senior people in our group, 'What is this? How did it happen?'

It had been many years since Nadamuni last rode a bicycle and he was hopelessly out of touch. But this morning, for some reason, he had been cycling down G.N. Chetty Road in Mambalam. He had moved to the edge of the road so that the bus behind him could halt at the Raghavaiah bus stop. The Corporation had, in the course of its routine effort to widen a few roads, dug this one up on either side and spread blue metal stones over both strips. The bus had taken off from the stop and was on its way. Nadamuni, who was floundering with his bicycle on the uneven surface, was somehow caught between the left rear wheel and the mudguard of the bus. The driver didn't know this. Neither did the passengers. Nadamuni had been dragged along with the wheel. He was thrown off only when the bus reached Vani Mahal. Before he died, all he could manage to do was identify himself.

'Why did this man have to go about on a bicycle?' the boss wanted to know. Then he took the police inspector aside and had a few words with him.

After thirty minutes or so, we were able to have a look at Nadamuni's corpse. The body was being carried into the morgue just then. His head was swathed in bandages: only his eyes, nose and mouth were visible. But for those bandages, there would have been nothing there that resembled a human face.

Our boss left after making just one more arrangement. Even if the bus had already cut him up into little pieces before the police could, Nadamuni's body would have to be dissected again for the coroner's examination, which would take a whole day. This was to be avoided, our boss insisted. Even if they had to do it for statutory reasons, they should just go through the motions and deliver the body at Nadamuni's residence by afternoon at the latest. To get this done, they were free to use the boss's influence at every stage of the process, whenever it became necessary.

We managed to bring Nadamuni's body to his residence before two in the afternoon. Since the body was in several pieces, it had been bound from head to foot to give it some kind of shape. At Nadamuni's residence, along with Nadamuni's wife and children, Raja was also weeping noisily.

Now he would never get his money back. Maybe the poor man didn't even give it a thought and was actually mourning the ghastly death of his dear sister's husband. Only I knew why Nadamuni Mama had gone down G.N. Chetty Road that morning towards Vani Mahal. He died before he could collect on his loan. Poor Raja, would he tell his sister now about the money he had lent her husband? Even if he did, would she pay up?

Nadamuni Mama's face, or what little of it could be seen between the bandages, still retained a look of repose. In the midst of all that noisy grief, cries and theatrical bustle, he looked very much like he had when he reclined in the studio. If someone had supplied the sound of snoring, one could have sworn that he was just fast asleep.

I stayed on till they carried him away to be cremated. By then it was evening, and while they went with him in the direction of Kannammapettai, I set out towards Vani Mahal.

Going by the experience of our first meeting, I had expected Prakasam to be seated on the veranda. But I found only a small servant girl there. I told her I had come to see Prakasam.

'Oh, he is not at home,' she said.

'The lady?'

'Oh, the lady?' She hesitated a little and then went inside. The actress came out, saw me and went back in without a word. A little later, the servant girl came to me and said, 'They want you to come in.'

I removed my slippers and entered. It was a large bedroom. Prakasam was lying on the bed, smoking a cigarette. The actress was reclining beside him, gently stroking his head.

'Come in, come in. I am very sorry, young man. I couldn't raise any money,' Prakasam said.

'Nadamuni is dead,' I told him.

'What? Dead! When? How?' He was obviously shocked by the news and quickly got off the bed. When I told him that they were on their way to cremate Nadamuni, he even wept. 'I have never seen him ask anybody to repay the loans he gave out. Where did he die? Right here? Near Vani Mahal?'

When I left, he was already lying prone on the bed again. I came down the stairs and stepped on to the street. Something made me turn around and look back at the house. The actress and the servant girl were standing at the top of the staircase near the banister. The actress was still there, watching, as I walked away from the house.

From the original Kadan (1973)

Why Tell Father?

At quarter past eight, Bangalore Cantonment station was barely lit and wore a deserted look. When the old woman, accompanied by a girl who must have been twelve or thirteen, entered the platform carrying her bedroll and baggage, she saw nobody whom they could approach for information.

As the old woman looked around, the girl asked her, 'Paati, what have you kept in this trunk?'

'Does your arm ache? Give it to me, I'll carry it.'

'But you are carrying two bundles already!'

'Is there a bus that can take you home?'

'There is, Paati. I could even walk home,' she offered.

'You must not walk alone in the dark.'

'But we came here alone, didn't we?'

'You father was not home yet, was he? After asking me to leave, he didn't even come to help me board the train.'

The girl didn't speak.

The tea stall on the platform was in a recess in the wall. There was a magazine stall nearby that had been left unattended.

'Find out at that tea stall if the Kanyakumari Express will come here.'

The girl set the trunk on the ground and entered the tea stall. The old woman rested both hands on the trunk, her breathing raspy and loud enough to be audible two feet away.

'Yes, it will come here,' the girl told her when she returned.

'Why don't you ask them where we can find the ladies' compartment?'

A faint crease of complaint formed on the girl's face. A girl ought not be sent to a tea stall alone at this time of night.

'You stay here. I'll find out and come back.' The old woman hobbled away slowly. The terrible ache in her legs was evident in her gait.

'Come. They say we must go to the other end,' said the old woman. She picked up the trunk herself.

'Paati!' the girl protested.

But the old woman started walking, the trunk clasped in her arms. Suddenly, the air turned slightly cold. The platform had been extended way beyond the station building. Though there was an asbestos roof, the open space on both sides made this area very cold.

The old woman stopped only after she reached the end of the platform. A few people could be seen moving about in the station—in all, there must have been fewer than twenty.

'You carry on, girl. I'll manage,'

'I'll leave, Paati—let the train come.'

'It will get very late if you wait for the train. It is already very late. I didn't ask you to come with me, did I?'

'Paati, how would you have carried everything by yourself?'

'The same way I brought everything when I came here. I am used to it now, having to do it all the time.'

'But your trunk is really very heavy, Paati.'

'That's why I told you I'd carry it myself, but you were adamant.'

'*Madras se Bangalore aanewali Bangalore Express . . .*' The announcement came over the loudspeaker in a hoarse, unintelligible voice.

The girl said, 'Paati, your train is coming.'

'This is an incoming train, not departing.'

'How can you tell immediately, Paati?'

'I know all this, girl; the only thing I don't know is where to live.'

'You can stay with us, can't you, Paati?'

'Is your word enough?' The old woman sat down on the trunk. Suddenly, the girl started crying. 'Look here, look here . . . why are you crying? What happened? Don't cry. Don't cry.'

The girl continued to weep.

'Please stop crying! Aren't you my darling?'

After considerable effort, the girl let her weeping subside a little. 'I feel very sad, Paati,' she said.

The old woman was silent.

Just then a family came and stood near them: husband, wife and four children—two boys under ten, a little girl and an infant that kept staring at the old woman. The wife handed the infant to her husband. 'Ladies' compartment, right?' she asked the old woman.

'Yes.'

'Kanyakumari train, right?'

'Yes.'

'Will it be crowded?'

'Not many people take this train. Are they twins?'

'Yes,' replied the woman wearily. 'Is this your granddaughter?'

'Yes. My son lives in Munireddypalya—his daughter.'

'Where are you taking her?'

'I am not taking her with me. She has come to help me board the train.'

The lady's husband said, 'Won't it get very late?'

'I kept telling her not to come, but she was adamant.'

'Where in Munireddypalya?'

'There is a cremation ground in front of the market. Somewhere near there.'

'I'll drop her there on my way home.'

'No, no, I'll go home myself,' said the girl hurriedly.

The old woman stared at the man for a second.

His wife said, 'You will only have time to go directly from here to your workplace. He is on night duty today.' This last bit was addressed to the old woman.

A lot of people had arrived on the platform by then. The wife asked the old woman, 'But you said there won't be much of a crowd?'

'These people are here to take the train to Madras. Two or three trains pass through here at this time.'

'You seem to know everything.'

The old woman looked at her granddaughter's face. Again, sobs came heaving out of her. The old woman put an arm around her and led her to a corner.

'What's the use of you and me crying, my darling?' she said.

'Why are my parents like this, Paati?' the girl asked through her tears.

'What's happened now? They are just fine. They face so many hardships, running the family.'

'No, Paati. You could've stayed with us, couldn't you? Why did they ask you to leave?'

'No, no. I left on my own. I want to go home. Don't take any of this to heart. You had better leave now. I will board the train with these people. You will be able to go home alone, won't you?' The girl wiped her eyes. 'I am going, Paati,' she said. The old woman embraced her and gave her a kiss.

The man said, 'I'll take the little one home.'

'No, she will manage by herself. Walking on the main road in Munireddypalya, there is nothing to be afraid of,' replied the old woman. 'Run along, girl. Your father did tell your mother that he would come to the station, but he hasn't. Don't know what kept him.'

Wiping her eyes and cheeks, the girl moved away, looking at her grandmother all the while. A bell rang on the platform. An announcement came again over the loudspeakers about a train's imminent arrival. Beside the old woman, the husband handed the infant back to his wife before picking up their suitcase and bag. The old woman began gathering all her luggage in one spot. When she was done she was startled to see that her granddaughter had come back. 'What's the matter?' she asked.

'I'll leave after you board the train, Paati.'

For the first time, the old woman's eyes seemed watery.

Very slowly, a train pulled into the station. The family standing with the old woman got ready to climb aboard. But the old woman was sceptical: 'Ask them whether this is the Kanyakumari train or the one to Tirupati.'

It was indeed the train to Tirupati, half an hour behind schedule.

The husband said, 'Our train will also be late, then.' He asked his wife, 'Can you board by yourself when the train comes? This old lady is here too, she can help you out. I'll head for my duty.'

His wife replied half-heartedly, 'All right.'

He turned to the old woman and said, 'Is the little one going home? I'll drop her home on my way. Will you come with me, little one?'

In a manner visible only to her granddaughter, the old woman shook her head. 'Her father had said that he would be here. It looks like he is on his way . . . Over there!' she said. The girl looked in the direction indicated by the old woman. There was no sign on her face of having recognized anyone.

It was past nine-fifteen when the Kanyakumari Express finally arrived. The platform was packed; passengers waiting to board the train to Madras clustered in a few spots along its length. They must have known that the compartments they had to board would halt near those spots. There was not much of a crowd in the ladies' compartment on the Kanyakumari Express. As the old woman was climbing aboard with her bedding and baggage, the mother of the twins shoved and pushed her way in at the same time. Although the old woman didn't get a window seat, she brought her face near a window and stood gazing intently at her granddaughter. The girl looked elsewhere, as though she was afraid to look at her grandmother's face. As the train began to pull out, the old woman said, 'Here, keep this.' The girl involuntarily extended her hand. The old woman placed a folded ten-rupee note in her granddaughter's palm and closed her fist.

'But you don't have anything yourself, Paati!' cried the granddaughter.

'I have everything I need. Go home safely,' shouted the old woman.

The girl tried to keep up with the train, but she had barely taken three or four running steps before the train left the station.

Walking briskly, the girl exited the platform.

'Has Paati left already?'

She turned around on hearing the familiar voice—her father. 'Why didn't you come inside, Appa?' she asked him.

'I couldn't buy a platform ticket. The place was so crowded.' She, too, had not purchased a platform ticket. She didn't tell her father about it.

From the original Appavidam Enna Solvadhu (1993)

Inspector Shenbagaraman

I had never imagined that the name Kantimathi could belong to a man. But here stood this six-foot giant in front of me, answering to that very appellation. Is it right to call a mere schoolboy a man? He was only a boy after all; my classmate. Full name: Kantimathinathan.

In those days, exams—quarterly, half-yearly or annual—were a dreaded prospect for all of us. If we successfully 'cleared' the annual exams, we had nothing to worry about. But if we couldn't manage that, then our marks in the quarterly and half-yearly exams assumed great significance. If they were not good enough to be taken into account—to compensate for our poor performance in the annual exams—we were held back for one more year.

Detained students were called 'second-year' boys. A student was not automatically promoted to the next class merely because he had spent two years in a class. He had to sit for his quarterly, half-yearly and annual exams all over again.

·I had just entered the fifth form. Later, when the education system was changed to 10+2+3, this fifth form became equivalent to the ninth standard. Kantimathi became my classmate. He was a 'second-yearer'.

It took me a few days to discover that his house was located in the same neighbourhood as mine. He appeared much older than me. At that age, even if a boy is just a year older, he looks much bigger. It is also the age at which boys discover the secrets of human existence. Kantimathi was truly a much older boy, who knew all the secrets. It amazes me when I think of it now: how could a boy like him have been fast friends with someone like me? Harigopal, who was forever raising alarms and sounding sirens, had warned me that his company would lead me to sin and ruination, but I continued to be very friendly with Kantimathi.

Kantimathi felt terrible about being detained. He couldn't grasp the intricacies of maths, floundered in Tamil, and the English language got stuck in his throat. It wasn't that he was not a hard-working boy. He simply wasn't cut out to be a student. He told me that his father was dead and his family lived in a village near Tirunelveli. His uncle had brought him to Secunderabad so that he could attend school here. Kantimathi sat at the back of the class whereas I was a frontbencher. In fact, friendship between us in that class seemed highly improbable; the big boys lived in a world of their own.

Then, all of a sudden, a rabid Tamil lover was appointed as the new principal. The man wanted to produce a Tamil play. Out of perhaps a thousand students in our school, barely a hundred and fifty were Tamil. The administration roped in twenty luckless boys out of that number to take part in the production. Kantimathi and I were among the twenty.

Even in that group, the chances of us striking a close friendship were indeed quite slim. But, as destiny would have it, there were three female roles. I was chosen to play one, and Kantimathi another.

I don't know how he expressed his outrage at this proposition. As for me, I tried everything, including bawling my head off. But the principal threatened: 'Look here. Just shut up and play the role given to you, or I'll send you home with a TC.'

Those were the days when a boy who had been dismissed from one school could never get admission in any other. It wasn't even as if our principal was a determined browbeater. Of the twenty of us, I was the only one whose voice hadn't cracked yet. The other two female characters appeared in the comedy scene. Women with deep baritone voices would naturally make the scene even more hilarious. And if a six-foot-tall girl appeared on stage, there wouldn't be any need for her to speak her lines or act in any manner. We rehearsed that three-hour play for three months. Everyone floundered and flailed about during the first few days. But as time went by the structure of the play, its various dimensions and the significance of each character became clear to all of us. Kantimathi and I actually began to get involved in our respective characters. There were two role models for comediennes at that time: T.A. Mathuram and C.T. Rajakantham. The latter was Kantimathi's favourite. He had watched a really bad Tamil film on each of the seven days that it played in our town just because Rajakantham was part of the cast. My role was tragic. Luckily, I recalled a Telugu film called *Kanakadara*, with Kannamba in the lead, which had run for many months. The heroine Kannamba sees no end to her trials and tribulations: her husband gets thrown into prison; she is viciously slandered; her two small children are carried off and abandoned in a dark forest. Finally, when she is sentenced to death and about to be hanged, her husband, her abandoned son—brought up by a jungle warrior, now a strapping lad—and her daughter, all turn up miraculously and save Kannamba from certain death. In that final scene, Kannamba, overwhelmed by happiness at her good fortune, laughs and cries alternately, showing great intensity of feeling. It scared me out of my wits. I chose Kannamba as my role model for this play.

At last, the day of our performance arrived. Our school auditorium was packed with more people than just the families of a hundred and fifty students. The play began. Perhaps three months of rehearsal had not been adequate, or perhaps it had been a bit too much; at any rate, we forgot our lines and stood on the stage, gaping, in almost every scene. When we eventually managed to remember our lines, we blurted them out at the wrong time. But our audience had come prepared to enjoy whatever we had to offer them. Whenever Kantimathi walked on to the stage, it seemed as if the explosions of laughter would bring down the hall itself. He performed every kind of clowning act he could manage. If the same lines and gestures were used in a film today, the censors would cut them out without question. Standing in the wings, I vaguely understood that there was something obscene in those lines and those pendulous movements of the hips, but I didn't know exactly what they signified at the time. My portrayal of the heroine's heartbreaking destiny must have been extremely funny. I fell dramatically on my dead son's corpse, my hair loose in tragic abandon, and sang out a dirge in Bilahari raagam. The audience was rolling in the aisles. As the song ended, I also burst out laughing. How could I help it? At least my mother and sisters, who were in the audience that night, should have cried along with me.

By the time we started for home that night after removing our make-up, it was already past ten. As Kantimathi and I walked down Oxford Street, a small car came from behind and stopped near us. A stentorian voice, clearly used to expressing nothing but authority, boomed out: 'Dei, what are you up to, loafing around on the streets so late?'

At once, Kantimathi shrank to something like three feet and replied to the owner of the commanding voice, 'We had our school play tonight, Mama.'

'Who is that fellow, da?'

'He was also in the play, Mama.'

'Was Swarnam there?'

'Mami said she couldn't come out today, Mama.'

'Okay, get in the car.'

That small car had four tiny doors. Kantimathi contorted his long torso and squeezed himself in through the rear door. It was dark inside and there was no way I could've known what his expression was trying to convey, if anything.

'Why have you abandoned him in the middle of the street, you ass!' the voice reprimanded.

'You get in too,' Kantimathi told me in a conspiratorial whisper. I sat beside him in the back seat. The first thing I sensed in the darkness was the odour coming off that man. It was sweet, bitter, hot and sour at the same time. The car started.

'Who is he?' I asked Kantimathi, in the same hushed tone.

Kantimathi made no sound, opening his mouth wide instead to let me lip-read his answer in the dark. 'Mama, Mama.'

I too sat with my mouth safely shut. The car rolled on past the street where I lived. The sight of Kantimathi, the six-footer all shrunken and quiet, silenced my tongue as well. We turned on to a main road and, after passing seven or eight bungalows, stopped at a fork in the road near Keyes High School, the biggest girls' school in our town. The vast triangular area in between was fenced in with a short compound wall, and in the middle of the ground stood a bungalow. I knew that the house and the compound wall were painted blue. We took that road whenever we went to the temple, vegetable market, flour mill or railway station. Since the bungalow was at quite a distance from the road, passers-by couldn't see inside the house clearly. As far as I was concerned, it was home to people who were beyond my imagination. But now, in the dark of night, Kantimathi's mama drove right up to the gate. Was this where he lived?

The car came to a halt in the portico. A man there gave us a stiff salute. He ran to switch on the veranda and portico lights. Kantimathi's mama got out first and the two of us followed. He was an inch taller than his nephew. There was a crescent-shaped patch of very dark hair at the back of his head, but the rest of his scalp was sparkling golden in the light. I had never set eyes on such pristine baldness.

'Kanti, bring this fellow in,' he ordered, and strode into the house with a rhythmic clacking of boots.

Kantimathi told me sotto voce, 'You come in too.'

Infected by his conspiratorial mood, I whispered back, 'Who was that?'

'I told you already. Mama. Mama.'

'Yes, Mama, but what's his name?'

'S. Shenbagaraman,' Kantimathi replied in a serious voice.

'Is he a military man?' There was considerable army presence in our town in those days.

'No, police inspector. Inspector of police.'

'Inspector Shenbagaraman, Inspector Shenbagaraman, Shenbagaraman in plain clothes,' I whispered dramatically to myself as I entered the bungalow.

It was an old-fashioned mansion. There was an enormous hall beyond the veranda. Two chandeliers were suspended from the ceiling, and helped me see the strange objects in the hall more clearly. Four pairs of antlers were mounted on the wall. There was a massive oil portrait of a large moustachioed man wearing a big zari turban, zari angavastram, long coat, pant and boots, and leaning lightly on a drawn sword. Complementing this was a portrait of a woman of indeterminate age in a silk sari with a rich zari border, assorted gold necklaces and chains around her throat, rings on all her fingers, a stone-studded tiara, a nose-drop, earrings and a gold waistband; she stood leaning her right elbow on a high stool.

There were separate rooms leading off from the hall on either side. At the sound of Shenbagaraman's boots, a woman rushed in from one of the rooms. She must have been under five feet, plump going to fat, but with a very fine face that spoke of superior qualities. Her jet-black hair curled in waves down to her ears. She wore gold-framed spectacles.

Shenbagaraman placed a booted foot on a stool. She removed the boot, lifted his foot slightly and pulled his sock off too. Then she did the same with the other foot. Then she fetched him a pair of rubber slippers from one corner of the hall. Shenbagaraman put them on and disappeared into another room.

The tension eased a little. The lady smiled at me and asked Kantimathi, 'Who is this boy?'

'He also acted in the play along with me.'

'Hasn't he washed his face yet? He's still got make-up on!'

I wiped my face with my hand.

'Wait here for some time. Let me attend to him first,' she said and went to the room into which Shenbagaraman had disappeared earlier.

'Who is this lady?' I asked Kantimathi.

He opened his mouth and answered soundlessly: 'Mami.'

'I'm going home,' I said. I had a half-mile walk in the dark still ahead of me.

'Don't, don't,' he shook his head vigorously. 'Take your leave of Mama before you go.'

At this rate, I concluded, I might never reach home that night. How had I got trapped in this place where everyone was practically dying of terror? So what if he was an inspector? Why was everyone acting so scared? Was this how Kantimathi spent all his days? Would he have performed his vulgar clowning act if his mama had been among those three hundred people just a few hours ago? There was no way he would have dared. He had been sure his mama would not turn up.

Shenbagaraman and his wife emerged from their room. He had changed into a veshti with a wide red border. His chest was covered with thick curly hair. He asked Kantimathi, 'Had your dinner?'

'No, Mama,' was Kantimathi's fawning reply.

'What are you doing?' he asked me.

I couldn't understand his question. I gaped.

'Have you had your dinner?'

'No. Not yet.'

'Come. Let's eat.'

'No. I must be going home.'

In fact, the thought of seeing my mother and sisters at home was terribly embarrassing. They had sat in the front row at the play, and although my mother had sternly warned my sisters not to look at me, they had had the time of their lives, concentrating solely on me and falling over with laughter. The make-up man, in his overzealous efforts to turn me into a girl, had wrought changes in my body above the waist that would have shocked even Mother Nature herself. My sisters had laughed only a bit less than everybody else. They would be waiting for me now.

Shenbagaraman asked me, 'Where do you live?'

'Lancer Barracks.'

'But we passed it on our way!'

'Yes.'

'You could've told me to stop! I would have dropped you off there!'

I looked at Kantimathi, but his eyes seemed to be focused on something ten or more miles away.

'What was your part in the drama?'

'I played the queen.'

'What?'

'I was the queen.'

'Then you must have worn those fabulous dresses and danced on the stage?'

'The king dies right when the play begins. The queen goes mad at one point. There's some swaying then.'

Shenbagaraman broke into a loud guffaw. The sight of his mirth encouraged his wife, Kantimathi and the policeman who had first turned on the portico light, to relax and smile faintly.

'He even sings a dirge in the last scene, Mama,' said Kantimathi, who had mustered a little courage by now.

'What song is it? Let's hear you sing it for us.'

It must have been eleven o'clock. At home, not only my mother and sisters, but also a lot of tongue-lashing and perhaps even a spanking awaited me. How could they know that I was being held captive in a policeman's house?

'Sing, da. Come on, *sing!*'

Doing away with the tear-jerking vibrato altogether, I sang the song set in Bilahari raagam for this inspector of police. The divine angel who personified that raagam must have been floating around in distress somewhere in the cosmic void. I went through the song in quick time, eliminating all refrains, never singing the same line twice. It was a few moments before everyone realized that I had actually finished. Shenbagaraman clapped enthusiastically. He turned to Kantimathi and asked, 'Dei, you fellows are going to put this on again?'

'No, Mama. It was only for today.'

Shenbagaraman came up to me and patted my back appreciatively. 'Where did you say your house was?' he asked.

'Lancer Barracks.'

'What is your name?'

'Chandrasekharan S.'

'Kanti. Take this boy and drop him home. Listen, boy, I'll come to your house sometime. Kanti, take the cycle if you need to.'

I said in a frightful panic, 'No cycle, Mama, no need.' In our town, if you rode 'doubles' on a bicycle, or if you had no lamp at night, or rode without a proper working bell or brakes, a policeman would materialize out of nowhere and fine you at least two rupees.

Shenbagaraman laughed. 'Never mind, boy. Do you want me to ride the cycle myself?'

'No, Mama. No, Mama.'

He laughed even more loudly this time. 'Don't worry about anything. Kanti will drop you home safe and sound.'

Even Shenbagaraman's wife appeared to be in high spirits. That hall indeed overflowed with a lot of energy, enthusiasm and happiness that night.

The rear tyre of the cycle had no air. We both walked at that midnight hour. Kantimathi didn't utter a word. It was only when we reached my house that he said, 'I'll be off, da.' The usual warmth seemed to be missing from his voice.

'What took you so long? Where've you been loafing around? Everyone's been waiting for you to arrive for dinner and you went off somewhere? Didn't you head home straight from school?' There was slight anger and irritation in Amma's volley of questions. One of my elder sisters and the younger one were still awake. When they saw me, they were overtaken by fits of helpless giggling.

'Go. I don't want to eat your food!' I said peevishly.

My sisters giggled even more. Appa shouted, 'What is this, giggling like idiots in the middle of the night?' Although it seemed that their laughter had subsided, I could see that it would burst forth again any minute. They giggled right through the following week. Only my mother provided some consolation: 'You did act very well, but you should have had some dialogues as well.'

The day following the play was declared a holiday for those who had participated in it. I had an oil-bath and, despite my mother's strictures, flopped down immediately after on a pile of bedding. When I woke up, I was running a high fever.

In our house, anyone who was unfortunate enough to contract a fever had no option but to endure the additional agony of drinking milagu kashayam, a peppery concoction. I drank up my share of this medicinal potion and sat there, blowing furiously to ease the burning sensation in the insides of my mouth.

Suddenly a small car pulled up at our house. It didn't occur to me that it might have anything to do with me. I simply thought that someone had lost his way and stopped in front of our house by mistake. Amma went to the gate. A tall man got out of the car and asked her something. She nodded as if to say, 'Right here.' Then she turned in the direction of our house and called out, 'Chandru!'

I swaddled myself in the cloak of frailty that I had been unable to muster for the play, and asked feebly, 'What is it?'

'Come here. Someone's come looking for you.'

I went to the gate. The tall man saw me and broke into a smile. 'Chandrasekharan, you seem to have forgotten everything overnight.' I recognized him: Inspector Shenbagaraman. He was not in uniform today as well.

I didn't know what was expected of me: how I should welcome him to our house and be generally solicitous as the host. But he came in on his own and sat down on a stool. He told my mother, 'Your boy has quite the talent for singing.'

My mother accepted this without a word in reply. When a booted, moustachioed man enters your house and sits down without so much as introducing himself, what are you supposed to think?

Amma turned to me and asked, 'Who is this?'

'He is Kantimathi's uncle. Police inspector.'

'Shenbagaraman is my name. Tirunelveli district,' our visitor said. 'Poor thing! I asked him to sing at ten o'clock at night and he sang readily. Chandrasekharan, didn't I tell you that I would visit you?'

'Oh yes. Amma, he told me yesterday that he would visit us.'

'How come you haven't combed your hair? Is something the matter? Why are you looking dull? Didn't sleep well?'

'He's been running a fever since this afternoon. He went to sleep after an oil-bath,' said Amma.

'Let me see.' Shenbagaraman put the back of his hand to my neck. His hand gave off the pungent odour of cigarettes.

'Oh, this is really high fever! Did you take him to the doctor?'

'Not yet. His father will take him when he comes home.'

'Chandrasekharan, comb your hair.' He turned to my mother. 'I'll take him to the doctor and drop him back.'

My mother stood there puzzled by this man, not quite knowing what she should do.

'Don't worry. Two doses of carminative mixture, and he'll be all right. Let's go, Chandrasekharan.'

I wore a freshly ironed shirt, and made a half-hearted attempt to comb my hair before I set out with him. I wasn't sure where to sit in the car. I had sat in the back last night and so I was heading there, when Shenbagaraman said, 'Come here, Chandrasekharan. Sit next to me.'

I took the front seat. A steel rod with a knob on top stuck out from the floor of the car. As he drove, Shenbagaraman pushed it this way and that. It bumped against my shin every time he did that. I had never sat in the front seat of a car before and observed the mechanics of driving so closely. 'What is this?' I asked him.

'This is the gearstick. The car won't move without gears.'

'But you just keep pushing it?'

Shenbagaraman laughed. 'I'll teach you how to drive a car next year.' Then he lit a cigarette named after the Charminar, the most significant landmark in the city of Hyderabad. The car sped past the clock tower along Market Street and turned into Paranjothi Street, coming to a halt inside the Cantonment Hospital compound. 'Come, Chandrasekharan.' Shenbagaraman led me inside. Although my parents had told me that I was born here, we seldom visited this hospital. The Railway Hospital was a mile and a half from our house, but to get to this hospital, we had to walk something like a mile and three-quarters.

Shenbagaraman took me directly to the doctor's room without stopping anywhere on the way. The doctor stood up when we entered. 'But I thought your injection was due on Saturday!' he said.

'I've come for this boy here.'

'What's the matter with him?'

'Fever, he says. He went off to sleep after his oil-bath.'

'Come here, boy. Show me your tongue.' The doctor took my temperature too. 'Who is this boy?' he asked Shenbagaraman.

'Oh, you know him all right. He says he acted in a play last night.'

'Oh, that drama at the school here?'

'Yes. Isn't that right, Chandrasekharan?'

'Yes, sir.'

'I was there too! What was your role?'

'He tells me he played the queen!' Shenbagaraman guffawed. 'I believe he sang a song as he was dying. Am I right, Chandrasekharan?'

I was silent.

'So that's why he's got this fever!' Both Shenbagaraman and the doctor laughed.

The doctor took a measuring glass, dropped a pinch of white powder in it, and followed it with two tablespoons of a red-coloured liquid. Then he topped up the glass with water. 'Drink this, boy,' he said.

I took the glass and poured the mixture down my throat. The medicine tasted hot, sweet and bitter, all at the same time.

'You can sing again tomorrow and make sure everybody gets fever,' said the doctor.

Shenbagaraman stood up and we left the building.

'How does it feel now, Chandrasekharan?' he asked.

'I don't know, sir.' For some reason, I could no longer call him mama.

'That means you're all right now. Shall we visit a house here? Then I'll take you back to your place safe and sound.'

Without waiting for my reply, Shenbagaraman walked ahead with quick strides. We crossed over to the other side of Paranjothi Street. I knew two of the three houses on that side. One was the advocate's house. His son studied in our school, in the Telugu-medium section. The next house belonged to our principal. His son too was in our school, but in a different section. Of the riotous audience last night, he was the one who had laughed the loudest. The third house was maadiveedu. I had never seen any signs of life downstairs. Shenbagaraman went to the house and tapped on the closed door twice with his knuckle. After a brief while, a girl who appeared to be a servant opened the door. He entered the house with me in tow. Not two feet from the door was a steep, narrow stairway. At the end of our climb, we reached a balcony that faced the street.

'Come, Chandrasekharan. Come. Come in,' said Shenbagaraman.

I entered hesitantly, closely following the inspector into a hall. For a moment, I marvelled at how the narrow stairway and veranda had led to this grand setting.

On a mat spread out on the floor, a boy and an adolescent girl were playing carrom with much laughter and merriment. From their intense involvement in the game, I could tell that they had been at it for a long time. It was the girl who first saw Shenbagaraman. Within a second, her laughter and carefree air vanished.

'Akka!' she called out and ran away inside. The boy stood up.

'How's it going, Babu? Did you manage to beat Thilaka at least today?' asked Shenbagaraman. Babu stood stock-still.

'Sit down, Chandrasekharan. Babu, do you know who this boy is? A big actor!' Shenbagaraman chortled loudly and sat down on a sofa, as though he was on very familiar terms with the people who lived there.

A woman came into the hall from within. I couldn't tell how old she was. She was probably an older sister of the girl who had been playing carrom. Her lips, nose, eyes and brows showed in sharp relief, as though they had been etched, like in a painting. On seeing Shenbagaraman, she greeted him warmly: 'Welcome!'

Shenbagaraman nodded and smiled with the pleasure of someone thoroughly enjoying a rare spectacle. It seemed to me that she blushed a little. The world stood still for a moment.

'All of you came in yesterday?'

'No, just this morning.' She was trying to speak, trying to overcome her own sense of diffidence.

When Shenbagaraman gave her a big fond smile, she stopped talking.

'Where is your mother?'

The girl repeated his question to Babu in a language I couldn't understand. It must have been Marathi. Shivaji Rao's family, in the first house in Lancer Barracks, talked among themselves in a vaguely similar tongue.

Babu was not very responsive. The girl hesitated.

'What's the matter with Babu? Is he not well? What's wrong, Babu? How are you feeling?' Shenbagaraman asked him with a friendly smile.

Babu mumbled one or two words in reply and went away from there.

The girl said, 'He's only a young boy.'

Shenbagaraman, still smiling, asked her, 'Aren't you a young girl yourself?'

My presence made her blush deepen.

Shenbagaraman immediately said, 'Oh, he is no stranger: he is our boy. Aren't you, Chandrasekharan? Come, sit down here.'

I sat down next to him.

'Won't you give our Chandrasekharan a cup of tea or something?'

'Oh yes. Thilaka! Thilaka!'

'Why, won't you make it yourself?'

Her discomfiture showing on her face, she said, 'I can't enter the kitchen.'

Shenbagaraman laughed aloud and then lit a cigarette. Hurriedly, the girl put a small stool before us, and placed an ashtray on it.

It must have been well past nine o'clock when we left. Shenbagaraman spoke to the girl's mother and an old man at great length and with considerable eagerness. Babu and Thilaka were nowhere to be seen, but their sister stood in a corner the whole time, listening to everything that was being said.

At home, my mother was extremely worried. My father too was equally anxious. Shenbagaraman dropped me at the gate and drove off. I felt very confused: what would I tell my family? Appa didn't ask me anything, but Amma kept grilling me. I told her only about our visit to the hospital.

The next morning, Harigopal cornered me almost as soon as I entered the school. 'Someone told me he saw you at that maadiveedu next to our principal's house!' he said.

'Who told you?'

'Someone I know.'

'What did he say?'

'That you'd been to that maadiveedu.'

'Which maadiveedu?'

Visibly angry, Harigopal glowered at me. 'Dei, are you feeding me lies?'

I didn't understand what, of all that I had said, could have been construed as a lie.

'Look here, Chandrasekhar. If you keep hanging around with these loafers, you'll definitely fail this year.'

I left him and went on to my class. We had English in the first period. Our English teacher, Prakash Rao, rolled his r's like all Telugus normally do. Kantimathi was the first to point this out to me. Ever since, as soon as Prakash Rao entered the classroom, I would turn around and look at Kantimathi, and he would smirk and shake his head. Today too, when Prakash Rao entered the classroom, I turned around, but Kantimathi pretended not to notice me.

During the lunch recess, I went over to where he was standing. The boys were still laughing over his performance in the play. Even amidst all that light-hearted banter, Kantimathi looked quite upset with me.

'Did you come to school yesterday?' I asked him.

'Yes, I did.'

'I didn't. Wasn't it supposed to be a holiday for us?'

'Not for me. After all, I am only a second-year . . .'

The way he spoke made me feel sorry for him. But I covered up by saying, 'I had fever.'

'Oh . . .'

'Why are you angry with me?'

'No, I am not.'

I couldn't understand the change in his attitude. 'Then, why won't you talk to me?'

He couldn't understand it either. 'Oh, nothing,' he said in a mildly appeasing tone.

But something had happened between us. Before, although I never visited his house, he would come to mine every weekend. Every day after school, he would wait for me so we could walk back home together. But ever since the play, all this solicitousness seemed to have come to an end.

'Why are you hanging around me all the time these days?' Harigopal inquired.

'Whatever I do, you keep scolding me!'

'You are my friend, close friend.'

'Yes. I am your close friend.'

But very soon, I grew tired of Harigopal's endless diatribes. The reason why I hadn't got close to him till then although we had studied together for many years was his compulsive need to find fault with someone or other all the time. Now, in addition to Kantimathi, his mama also became the object of his fulminations.

'How could you go into maadiveedu and such places just because that man took you?'

'What is this? Why are you going on and on about maadiveedu? There are many maadiveedus all over town.'

He laughed derisively. 'In this whole town, there is only one maadiveedu and that's the one you've been to.'

'Okay, so what if I went there?'

'Go ahead. Keep going there, and you'll also end up taking two injections every week.'

'But I don't have fever or anything!'

'You won't catch a fever. You'll catch a disease.'

'Disease. What disease?'

'Get lost. Your kind will learn only the hard way.'

I was in a state of acute distress for a whole week. Twice or thrice, I noticed Kantimathi break into a grin when he saw me, and then hold it back and look the other way. He was a lot older than I was, so how could I possibly question his actions? I found it highly embarrassing to make repeated overtures to him at school. Harigopal had always hated him. But then, was there anybody at all that Harigopal liked? I seemed to be the only one who had won his affection. Even though I was completely deaf to all his bluster and words of gratuitous advice, he kept coming back to me again and again. Perhaps in some previous incarnation, he had been a mother elephant and I, her little baby elephant. We might even have been some other kind of beasts, but with a similar relationship. He must definitely have kept a relentless watch over me like he was doing now.

We had a class test that week. I managed to do quite well in maths and history-geography: there was no prospect of my marks in these subjects being underlined in red ink. But I scored less than twenty in all the other subjects. Kameshwara Rao, after making me stand on the bench, asked me: 'Hanging around with these second-year boys all the time, are you planning on becoming one yourself?' Any student who got less than twenty marks in three or more subjects had to stand to 'attention' inside the principal's chamber for half an hour. As though he was happy to see me among them, our principal remarked: 'What do you say, shall we stage another play next year also? I'll let you play Lord Krishna.'

We had five successive holidays. I managed to get through the first two days, but on the third, I couldn't bear it any longer: I went straight to Kantimathi's house. The constable at the gate asked me in a bullying tone, 'Who are you? Where do you think you are going?'

'I want to see V. Kantimathinathan,' I told him.

'There's nobody like that around here. This is the police inspector's house.'

'He must be here. I know Kantimathinathan lives here.'

'Get lost. I'm telling you he isn't here; you're bothering me, unnecessarily insisting that he is.'

I felt sad. It seemed as if the whole world was conspiring to prevent me from meeting Kanti.

Just then, Kantimathi's aunt came out of the house into the garden. She stood there and gazed at us inquiringly.

'She knows who I am,' I told the policeman.

'Get out of here! Or I'll break your skull!' said the policeman.

I raised my hand to wave at Kantimathi's aunt. The policeman immediately hit me with his baton. 'Aiyo!' I cried out.

Kantimathi's aunt rushed towards us as I stood there crying. She asked him what the trouble was. I told her in Tamil, 'I've come to see Kantimathinathan.'

'Oh, but he is out of town right now!' she said. I was surprised to hear her refer to Kantimathi in respectful third person. Then she asked me, 'Who are you?' in respectful second-person plural. I was truly amazed: this lady talked to me as though I was already a grown-up and distinguished man.

'I came here late one night, don't you remember? I sang a song, and you listened along with the others!' I said.

'Oh, you're that boy! I was wondering why your face looked so familiar. Come, boy, come in.' After extending this warm welcome, she turned to the policeman and scolded him, 'If you ever raise a hand against any of our visitors again, I'll send you packing. Mind it!'

As soon as we went inside the house, she said, 'Show me your hand.' My wrist was already swelling up. She brought Iodex and applied it. For the second time that day, my eyes brimmed with tears.

I stood there not knowing what to say. 'Sit down, thambi,' she said. 'There was a telegram saying Kantimathinathan's mother was ill. So he left immediately. You know, it takes three whole days just to get there. We have asked him to send a telegram if his mama needs to go there too. How are you, thambi? You sang very well that day.'

I found myself in great distress, scarcely knowing what to say. Her face had the serenity of a temple icon. It seemed to me that she was incapable of rancour or rage.

'Will you have something, thambi? Shall I make some tea?'

Because I didn't know how else to respond to her question, my reply came easily: 'All right.'

She went inside. A minute later, she called out from there, 'Why don't you come in here, thambi?'

I went in hesitantly. It was a very spacious kitchen. In those days, cooking was mostly done on wood-burning stoves. On that kitchen ledge, which had a large chimney above it, she lit a small Primus stove and heated some water. When it came to a boil, she put a spoonful of tea leaves into it, turned off the stove and covered the vessel with a lid. Then she turned to me. 'What had your mother cooked in your house today, thambi?'

This time I had something specific to give her by way of a reply. 'Who does the cooking at home, thambi? Do your sisters also cook sometimes?'

'My eldest sister is a good cook, but she is also very stubborn. She and my mother are always quarrelling.'

'Women who cook well are good at quarrelling too. I heard that my husband came to your house?'

'Yes. I had fever. Kantimathi's uncle was the one who took me to the doctor.'

'Where did you go after that, thambi?'

I didn't fully grasp the implications of that question. But out of an unconscious instinct for self-preservation, I held my tongue.

'Did you visit maadiveedu?'

I didn't say a word.

174

'Is that girl really beautiful?'

I lost all my defences in that moment.

'Which girl?' I asked her.

'How many girls did you see in that house, thambi?'

'There were two girls. I know only one girl's name: Thilaka.'

'She is the younger one. Her akka was also there, wasn't she?'

'I don't know her name.'

'Sakkubai.'

'Oh.'

'Is she very pretty?'

'Yes.' I added, 'You are very beautiful too.'

She turned her face away. A moment later, she was sobbing her heart out.

I tried to get away from there without making a sound but—

'Thambi, why are you leaving before you've had your tea?' Her shining eyes glowed like two burning coals in her dark, beautiful face.

She cooled the tea by pouring it in and out of two tumblers and gave it to me. Even then it was too hot for me. She watched as I drank it, one small sip at a time.

From outside came the sound of a car approaching the house, and we heard the gate being opened. While I sat in the hall drinking my tea, Kantimathi's aunt went out to the veranda.

The inspector saw me and exclaimed, 'Oh Chandrasekharan! When did you get here?' He was in uniform. The crease on his khaki trousers was as sharp as a knife.

'I came some time ago,' I said.

'Do you know, I was planning to come over to your place this evening?'

'I didn't know, sir.'

'How could you have known? I didn't tell you, did I? Swarnam, did you offer Chandrasekharan something to eat, or were you planning to send him off after giving him some warmed-up weak tea?'

'Will you eat here, thambi?' she asked me.

'I've already eaten.'

Shenbagaraman said: 'If we ask you to have dinner with us, you say your mother is waiting and you have to go home. When we ask you to lunch, you say you have eaten already. Tell me, when should we invite you?'

I stood there not knowing what to say.

Shenbagaraman's wife removed his boots and socks. He took off his shirt and handed it to her. Then he asked me, 'What brought you here? Is everything all right with you now? No fever?'

'I came to see Kantimathinathan.'

'He's gone home to his village. My akka has suddenly become paralysed in one leg. Kantimathi is my akka's son, I'm sure you know that.'

'I do, sir.'

'He's not doing well at all, Chandrasekharan. He doesn't get more than twenty marks in any subject. And this is his second year. I don't know what to do with him. What do you think?'

I gaped at him, speechless.

By now, his wife was ready to serve him food. She waited, leaning on the door frame.

'Come, Chandrasekharan. Come. Come in.'

His plate was laid on a small table. I stood a little away from it. 'Sit, Chandrasekharan. Swarnam, bring Chandrasekharan a stool,' said Shenbagaraman.

The food was more or less similar to what we ate at home. 'Don't you eat meat?' I asked him.

Shenbagaraman laughed, 'What do you think we are? Here, I can invite someone like you home to eat. In my village, my akka wouldn't even serve you water; they are that orthodox. Has Kantimathi never told you all this? What do you boys talk about, then?'

'We have never talked a lot to each other. He never speaks of his people back home. He only said it was a tiny village.'

'His father died very young. Unlike me, he sired seven children.'

I kept my mouth shut. His wife served him rasam.

'Now my akka is very ill. If something happens to her, Kantimathi will have to look after everybody. But look at him, he simply has no aptitude for learning.'

'He is a very good student, sir.'

'You can say that, but shouldn't your principal agree with you? What is your rank?'

'Eighteenth.'

'Oh, so you're also the same type!'

'I came sixth last month.'

'So it seems you've been promoted this month.' He laughed. 'Don't worry about Kanti, I tell my wife, I'll get him into the police department. She says no. He'll go astray, it seems! Do you think my ways are evil, Chandrasekharan?'

His wife served buttermilk.

'I am going to have a short nap. Why don't you too sleep for some time? We'll go to a film in the evening.'

'Film?'

'Don't you like films? *Ek Din Ka Sultan* is playing at Chitra Talkies. You follow Urdu films, don't you?'

'I'll go home first and then come back here.'

'Or stay at home. We'll pick you up. If others at your home want to come along, we can take them'

'Can they all—my mother and sisters—come along too?'

'We'll pack them all into my little Austin car. No problem.'

'But what about mami? Don't you have to take her?'

His wife was cleaning the table with her head bowed. Shenbagaraman looked at her. 'Won't you come along too, Swarnam?' he asked her. She stood there, without giving him a reply.

'You come along too,' I told her.

She looked at me, an impassive expression on her face.

'You come along too,' I repeated

'We should go, then, Swarnam, shouldn't we? If Chandrasekharan wants something, there can be no appeal, right? You go on home, Chandrasekharan, and wait for us. We'll be there on the dot at half past five.'

Amma was quite firm that she couldn't go without Appa's permission. My brother and sisters were simply thrilled that they were going for a ride in a motor car and would also be watching a film. As early as four o'clock that evening, they were all ready to go; having scrubbed their faces and combed and plaited their hair, they hung around near the gate in breathless anticipation. Appa usually returned home from office around half past five. If he came home early today, Amma would be able to see *Ek Din Ka Sultan* with us.

Appa came home exactly at half past five; but there was no sign of Shenbagaraman. From five in the evening, every minute had sat heavily on us like a huge burden. After five-thirty, time froze for every one of us except Amma. Then it was a quarter to six. Our faces went slack with disappointment, and Appa remarked with his usual sarcasm: 'Some obscure police fellow comes along and says "I'll take you to a film," and everyone here is so naive that they stand in the middle of the road waiting for him.' Amma fetched a bundle of greens to chop.

Suddenly, Shenbagaraman's car appeared on the horizon. Regardless of the many potholes, it raced at breakneck speed and stopped in front of our house. His wife sat next to him in the passenger seat. He got out and walked into the house. 'Chandrasekharan, are you ready?' he asked, just as Appa came in after having washed his face.

'This is my father,' I told Shenbagaraman.

'Why don't you also come along with us?' Shenbagaraman invited him.

'No. You people carry on. I've just come home from work. After all, cinema will always be around,' said Appa.

'Chandrasekharan, take everyone and go sit in the car,' Shenbagaraman told me.

I went to my mother in the kitchen and informed her, 'Inspector mama's wife has come.' She got up and followed me.

The inspector's wife looked radiant that day. Her jet-black hair cascaded from the crown of her head. Set in her dusky face, her eyes and rows of even teeth appeared very beautiful. She was wearing the gold-framed spectacles. She gave my mother a lovely smile. My mother said, 'Won't you please come in?'

She hesitated: 'He is upset because we are already late for the film.'

My three sisters, my brother and I squeezed into the back seat. There is a law of physics which says that matter is compressible. All five of us—granted, we were physically small—were able to clamber into the back seat of a Baby Austin and even close the door. Thus, we were able to prove that this particular law of physics held good even under such extreme conditions. Shenbagaraman's wife suggested: 'Why don't one of you come to the front if you wish?' She sat my youngest sister in her lap. The car rolled away slowly.

As he drove, Shenbagaraman asked me, 'So you thought I wouldn't come, didn't you, Chandrasekharan?'

'No, sir. Nothing of that sort.'

'The car wouldn't start. Neither did Swarnam. I asked her to come only because you wanted her to.'

'I don't understand these Urdu films, thambi,' she told me.

'Your mother could have come along too,' said Shenbagaraman.

'Where would she have sat in this car if she had?' asked his wife. The car turned into Kingsway, and then into General Bazaar Street where it entered the compound of Chitra Talkies. Two or three attendants at the theatre came running to us as soon as they saw the car. We streamed out. 'Where is Karam Singh?' asked Shenbagaraman.

'He'll be here at seven. Go ahead and be seated, saar,' said the one who looked like he was the manager of the theatre.

I asked Shenbagaraman, 'Isn't Karam Singh the owner of this place?'

'How do you know that?'

'My father knows him very well. We also get to see films here without buying tickets.'

'Then you're a policeman already,' said Shenbagaraman.

We sat in a separate enclosure called the special box. Even though the theatre was brightly lit, this box was partially dark. Generally, people in the lower stalls twist their necks to see the people in the upper stalls. But they really cannot see anyone in the special box. The sofas were padded with thick cushions that gave off a musty smell from lack of frequent use. Someone brought us orange-flavoured soda. In those days, any cold drink that you could pour down your throat was called a soda. 'Tell them to bring us some good tea during the interval. Do you have Rimjim? Biscuits and cakes? If you do, bring them,' Shenbagaraman ordered. Then he added, 'Tell Karam Singh to come and see me as soon as he comes in.'

The film began. In all Hindi movies, you feel completely lost in the beginning, like someone who's been blindfolded and let loose in the jungle. But within half an hour, it becomes clear who the good man is and who bad, which woman is smitten with which man, and which one is betraying her husband. Then you can reconstruct the conversations in the film according to your own imagination. It took me some time before I grasped that *Ek Din Ka Sultan* was about Emperor Humayun.

Shenbagaraman sat in the two-seater sofa nearest to the exit. He made me sit with him. His wife, my sisters and my brother sat in the adjacent sofas. Shenbagaraman lit a cigarette. In those days, there was no ban on smoking inside cinema houses. In fact, some people went to cinema houses only to smoke in peace.

As the film went on, Shenbagaraman kept up a steady stream of chatter, though none of it concerned the film's plot or screenplay. The actress Mehtab appeared on the screen for the first time. She had a small mouth, thick lips and eyes that weren't exactly large. Sometimes, I thought, she resembled a small monkey. But she was a wonderful actress. As the film continued, you forgot to notice her thick lips and small eyes. Even before I turned thirteen, I had already seen several of her films, weeping my heart out at their tragic climaxes. Shenbagaraman wouldn't have wept like me, though. As soon as she appeared, he gripped my hand and whispered urgently, 'Look at her, look at her.' I was looking at her all right. 'Look at her elbow, her elbow!' he hissed. Her elbow was nothing more than an elbow. 'See how all the three humps are visible on her elbow,' he said. It took me a while to make out what he meant, for they kept showing only her face in close-up shots. When she reappeared after a lengthy scene in which she hadn't figured, it took some time for her elbow to become visible on screen.

'Yes, I've seen it,' I said.

'Only that sort of female is the genuine goods. You know, these blowsy fat types, they are just cows. Whenever you meet a girl, you should ask her to bend her elbow first and see for yourself.'

After that, I hardly paid attention to anyone in the film. I only watched their elbows. Shenbagaraman shifted restlessly on the sofa. Then he told me, 'You sit here and watch the film and keep an eye on everyone,' and went out.

During the interval my brother and sisters asked me, 'Where is Inspector mama?' But Shenbagaraman's wife didn't ask me where he was. She chatted with my sisters about home, school and teachers. Karam Singh came but on seeing that Shenbagaraman was not there, he left immediately. Cakes and biscuits arrived on separate plates for each one of us, followed by some piping-hot tea. The film resumed. Sher Shah defeats Humayun who flees from the battlefield and jumps into a river. A water carrier inflates his buffalo-skin water bag and throws it into the river for Humayun to clutch and drift ashore. The emperor is astounded by the reward sought by the water carrier. The man wants to be king for a day, one day only, and that day, all his orders should be carried out. Humayun agrees.

It was ten when the film ended. My younger brother and sister had fallen asleep. I too was drowsy. But Shenbagaraman's wife was wide awake. The senior employees of the theatre had gone home. Only the men at the ticket counters and the gatekeepers were still around. A man entered the box and said, 'Clear out, all of you!'

We stood around in the theatre's veranda. The crowd began to pour in for the next show. In those days, people who went to the night show were not considered respectable. Only rowdies, loafers, gamblers, thieves and bad characters braved this stigma for the pleasure of watching the night show. Many such men walked past us. They stared at us; some whistled. They must have thought we were their own kind.

Shenbagaraman's wife took great pains to try and keep things normal; she talked with each one of us, asking us about this and that and forcing us to reply. But it was past ten o'clock at night; how much longer could we wait there, menaced by that army of delinquents? I remembered a serial I had read in the Tamil magazine *Ananda Vikatan*. It was a Tamil translation of R.K. Narayan's English novel *The Dark Room*. A woman who is angry with her husband leaves home in the middle of the night when all her children are asleep. The next day, as if to prove that everything is still normal, the husband takes the children to watch a film. As soon as the show begins, he tells his children he will be back soon, and leaves; the children have no one to turn to after being abandoned. He has gone to visit his mistress.

I knew that very instant where Shenbagaraman had gone that night.

Paranjothi Street was less than half a mile away from Chitra Talkies. If I ran all the way, I could get there in less than ten minutes.

I asked Shenbagaraman's wife, 'Should I go and get him?'

She asked me in turn, 'Did he say where he was going, thambi?'

'No. But . . .'

'No, thambi. He might have gone to some other places also. I don't want you to go to such places.'

They had put out all the lights in the theatre. We were not afraid because we had Shenbagaraman's wife with us. We were only afraid of the tongue-lashing we were sure to get from our parents when we finally made it home.

At long last, Shenbagaraman arrived. He exuded a strange combination of odours. Wordlessly, we all got into the car. The next day, Shenbagaraman's wife visited my house when I was away at school. She spent a long time talking to my mother.

Kantimathi didn't return from his village. His mother could no longer move about, so he couldn't go to school in a distant city. Shenbagaraman continued to visit our house once or twice a week. My father stopped referring to him as 'policeman' after the day he took us all for the film.

We never went together to the cinema again. I did watch a few films with him, but after *Ek Din Ka Sultan* his wife never came along with us.

Shenbagaraman, who everyone thought was beyond destruction or decay, fell ill one day with fever. He had returned home late one night in the pouring rain. After changing into a veshti, when he sat down to eat, he toppled forward along with his chair. His face met the plate with great force; he hurt his earlobe and bled profusely from the wound.

A policeman came by our house a week later to inform us. Appa and I went to see him that evening. Shenbagaraman was very glad to see Appa. Both of them talked and joked for a long time. If he hadn't been reclining in bed, and if a tabletop cluttered with numerous bottles and pills hadn't stood beside him, any observer would have thought it was a meeting between two old and fond friends.

I sat in a corner, listening to their conversation. At some point, Dr Perumal came in and attended to Shenbagaraman. I wondered why the doctor, after seeing this man who bubbled with lively banter, had pulled such a grim face. We left around eight. As we were exiting the gate, a policeman came up to us and said that the inspector had asked for me. While I went back inside, Appa went away to the vegetable market.

Shenbagaraman brightened visibly when he saw me. He asked warmly, 'You didn't even say a word to me, Chandrasekharan?' I went and stood near his bed. He stroked my cheek. As soon as I saw that his eyes were wet, I too started crying.

'Don't cry right now, Chandrasekharan. There's another ten or fifteen days to go,' he said.

I stopped crying.

'Do you remember, we visited a house the other day?'

'Maadiveedu, sir?'

'Good boy, you're absolutely right! You must go there without anyone knowing about it. No one!'

'Yes, sir.'

'Whom did we meet there that time, do you remember?'

'There was the boy Babu, his sister Thilaka, their mother . . .'

'You didn't see anyone else?'

'Thilaka's akka.'

'Sakku. What's her name again?'

'Sakku.'

'You must go and see Sakku.'

'Will she talk to me?'

'She will. She knows you.'

'Yes, sir.'

'Go and find out what Swarnam is doing.'

I went to the room between the hall and kitchen. I found Shenbagaraman's wife there, seated in front of a large framed picture of Ambal, the Great Mother, and reading aloud from a book of slokas.

I went back to his room. 'She is sitting in front of God's picture,' I told him. He took out a fat paper envelope from under his mattress. It was crumpled and worn from having been stashed away for many days.

'There's a little money here. Give it to Sakku, or even her mother. Do you remember the old man who was also there? He must not know anything about this. That boy is also a bad sort. Did you notice how he didn't bother to respond when I called him?'

'Yes.'

'Be careful with the money.'

I rolled the envelope and stuffed it into the pocket of my half pant.

'Tell Sakku . . .' As he started to say this, Shenbagaraman broke down.

His wife rushed into the room almost immediately. 'What's the matter, what's happened to you?' she asked in panic.

'Oh, nothing. You see, I was talking to Chandrasekharan, and suddenly I remembered my appa and amma.'

His wife was visibly moved. She stood there for a minute with a look of commiseration on her face. 'Would you like some arrowroot gruel?'

'Okay.'

She left.

'Say that I will come and see them. Tell them not to worry about anything,' he told me.

'Okay.'

Shenbagaraman was silent for a little while. 'I want to see her, Chandrasekharan,' he said and started weeping again.

Again, his wife came rushing in.

'Nothing, really. I just told Chandrasekharan to come and visit me every day.'

She looked at me. Unable to meet that look, I averted my eyes.

I didn't sleep a wink that night. I had stashed the envelope under my pillow, but it peeped out whenever I moved. I hid it inside my maths notebook, but the notebook gaped open, like a crocodile waiting for its prey. I tried to conceal it, piling other books on top and stacking a few more on the sides. Alerted by my staying awake till as late as ten, my mother felt compelled to ask, 'What's the matter? What's happened to you?'

'I believe Inspector is very ill. Is that true?' I asked her.

'Appa also told me. What can we do? I am very worried, particularly when I think of her!'

'Think of whom?'

'His wife, naturally. She was also married off when she was nine, just like me. How bright and clear she looks, like an idol made of gold! I don't know whose sin or curse it is that they don't have any children. There's not a single temple they haven't been to. I believe everyone from that man's house is pestering him to get married again. But he has stubbornly refused to do that. Your friend, Kantimathi, and his mother—I believe they simply can't stand Swarnam. And still, fifty to hundred rupees are sent from here every month to keep that family going.'

Amma turned out the light.

When I left for school the next day, I tucked Shenbagaraman's envelope safely into the pocket of my half pant. Although I had given my word, I was daunted by the prospect of delivering the envelope secretly at maadiveedu.

Our principal's son was in the habit of hanging about on the street all day long. There was no hour of the day or night when people didn't move about on Paranjothi Street. Thanks to Harigopal, I had earned all kinds of notoriety at school. Now I had to go and knock on maadiveedu's door and wait in full view of the whole street while someone came down to let me in. I suffered acute fits of anxiety. I had walked along Paranjothi Street five or six times that day, during the lunch recess and while going home in the evening after school. Each time, the street was swarming with people, as if their only mission in life was to keep me from approaching that door. Some of them even knew me. I was hoping that I would spot someone from that house on the first-floor veranda, but it was empty. Just once during my reconnaissance trips along the street, I sighted the old man.

I had to keep vigil over the envelope for another night at home. This time, I fell asleep. I didn't know how much money he had stuffed into the envelope. I assumed that he hadn't enclosed a note along with the money. If there was one, who would it be for? It could only be addressed to Sakku or her mother. What would he have written? Why send it in such secrecy? After all, so many people worked for him; and so many others came to see him. Couldn't he have entrusted one of them with this task? Adults didn't have to worry about seeing, or being seen by, anyone: they had no one to be afraid of. I had my principal, and his son, and Harigopal. God knew who else was watching me from secret vantage points: what tales would they carry to my family?

I decided that I would definitely get it done on Sunday. The envelope had become pathetically deformed from being hidden away in my half pant pocket and many other unlikely places. Even if the envelope contained a lot of money, its exterior had become tattered like a beggar's rags.

At noon on Sunday, when it was so hot that even flies and crows had stayed away from the street, I knocked on the door of maadiveedu. Who should see me then but our principal's son who sauntered on to the street. I gave him a half-smile and knocked on the door again.

'It doesn't look like there's anybody home, does it?' he commented.

'Nobody's home?'

'If there were, wouldn't they have opened the door?'

'But how could they go out and still latch the door from inside?'

'There is a back entrance to this house. In fact, all of them use only the back door.'

'How do I get there?'

'You see this alley next to the advocate's house? Go in there and turn right. Second door on the right. The first one is ours.'

'Don't you use that entrance?'

'Why would we need to use the back door?'

I followed his directions: I went down the alley beside the advocate's house and reached the rear entrance of maadiveedu. There was a big lock on the back door.

Shenbagaraman's money weighed on me like an immense boulder. I should have cast aside my diffidence and embarrassment, and gone there on the first day itself. Ought one stop oneself from doing what has to be done just because some people might make fun? Could one put it off indefinitely?

I had an idea. I went to the hospital on the other side of Paranjothi Street. Since it was mealtime then, I would be taken for someone bringing food to a patient. It was not a big hospital. Two big halls and seven or eight smallish rooms, that was all. It was adequate for the population of our town. If Shenbagaraman had been admitted here, he would have had no problems sending messages to the people in maadiveedu. If he could walk a little, he could even have made a short visit. It was that close to the hospital.

Upon reaching the hospital, I noticed a small new block behind the main building. I could see nurses moving about there. There must be some patients in that block as well, I concluded. It was possible that the doctor who met me the other day was also there. I could ask him about the people in maadiveedu. Several people stood outside the first room in that block. Although they were in plain clothes, you could tell they were policemen from the square set of their shoulders. One of them signalled to me. 'Aren't you the boy who lives in Lancer Barracks?' he asked me in a hushed whisper. 'Yes,' I nodded. 'Go in. Inspector has asked for you.'

I was startled. Was Shenbagaraman really in this hospital?

To keep the room cool, they had hung wet vettiver blinds outside the windows in that room. Shenbagaraman seemed to be having difficulty breathing. His wife sat quietly on a chair at his bedside. She stood up when she saw me and said, 'Where have you been, thambi? He's been asking for you since morning.'

'When did you come to the hospital?'

'This morning.'

I went near Shenbagaraman. He could not speak, but his eyes seemed to ask me anxiously: 'What happened?'

I shook my head to indicate that I hadn't yet done what he had wanted me to. His face fell. I whispered in his ear, 'They've all gone somewhere. There's nobody home.'

He relaxed a little. His lips trembled, as though he was trying to say something. I knew what it was. Sakku.

His eyes were pleading with me to bring her there.

I ran out. I went again to maadiveedu and knocked hard on its street door.

This time the principal himself came out. 'Chandrasekharan? Isn't your name Chandrasekharan?' he asked me.

'Is Sundar at home, sir?' I asked him. His son's name was Sundar.

'Dei, Sundar! Come here. Chandrasekharan has come to see you,' he called out and went inside the house. His son came out.

'Do me a favour, please,' I begged him.

'What is it?'

'Will you send word to me when the people at this maadiveedu come back from wherever they've gone? I'll be in the hospital over there. You know the special ward at the back? I'll be there.'

He stared at me. If he had continued for one more moment, I would have broken down and wept. 'Okay,' he said.

I rushed into the hospital again, but this time they didn't let me into the ward. The doctors had inserted a tube in his lower abdomen to pump out water. Even his wife had been told to stay outside.

Shenbagaraman breathed his last that evening, five minutes after rahukaalam set in. I was the one whom his wife first embraced when she broke down in her grief. Before the sun set that evening, his uncle, Kantimathi and one or two others arrived from the village. We loaded his body on to a police van and sat in the back. Kantimathi didn't speak to me even then. I went to maadiveedu again the next day. It was still locked. Nobody knew where they had gone. They must have gone out of town, surely; perhaps to their village. For all anyone knew, someone in their family might have been on his deathbed.

Many times during the following week I had the urge to hand over the envelope to Shenbagaraman's wife. But I felt it would only hurt her more if I did that. Whenever she saw me, she wept, 'Where has your inspector gone, thambi?' Kantimathi turned his face away at the very sight of me. Shenbagaraman's Baby Austin stood in the garage, unused.

One day after they had all left for the village, the principal's son told me, 'They've come back.'

I ran there right away. This time, I went straight down the alley leading to maadiveedu's back door and finding it open, I ventured in. There was a staircase there too. It took me directly into the kitchen. Thilaka stood there fanning a wood-burning stove. 'Who are you?' she asked me.

'Is Sakku here?'

Before she could reply, Sakku and her mother came in. In a loud and intimidating tone, the woman growled at me, 'Who are you?'

'I had come here once with Inspector,' I said.

'So? You think you can just walk in here whenever you feel like it? Get out of here!' she screamed shrilly.

I shook with trepidation. She picked up a broom.

'I came to hand over something from Inspector.'

'But that fellow is dead and gone, isn't he?'

'He died here, in the hospital down the road. I came here many times that day. None of you were here.'

'It was a good thing we weren't here.'

'He wanted to see Sakku.'

'When he was dying?'

Sakkubai, who was standing behind her mother, started crying; at her mother's admonitory 'Keep quiet!' her weeping subsided immediately.

'What did that man ask you to give us? How could we have known that he was going to come here and die in this hospital? I sent word to him even on the day before he died. The bastard told us not to come. We left for our village immediately. He seems to have caught it the very next day. What did that crook ask you to give?'

Sakku said, 'Amma.'

'You shut your mouth, you hear! What did he give, da?'

I handed over the worn, crumpled envelope. There must have been thirty or forty ten-rupee notes in there.

'If the fellow had to give us money, why couldn't he have given it in BG?' she said.

Hyderabad currency at that time was called Halli Sicca and Indian currency was known as BG, or British Guarantee. Both were rupees, but BG had higher value—a hundred BG rupees were equivalent to a hundred and seventeen Halli Sicca rupees.

'Don't come through the back door again,' she said. I walked through the front veranda; it was Sakku who came down the stairs and unlatched the street door to let me out. When she was sure that we were out of her mother's earshot, she asked me, 'Did he ask to see me, really?'

'Yes. He could not breathe at all. Even then, he was thinking of you.'

'I would've come running, but my mother dragged me off to the village.'

I had already reached the street. She still did not let me go and kept asking me: 'He asked for me? Are you sure?'

'He couldn't speak. But I know he did.'

While she stood there staring at the street, I moved on. Sundar came down the street, looking curiously at me. It must have been lunch recess at school.

From the original Inspector Shenbagaraman (1990)

Children

The patriarch himself had come to the railway station. Although having to cover her head with the end of her sari was a bit awkward, Vandana felt pleased. Carrying her suitcase, her husband boarded the train first, located her seat and kept the suitcase safely underneath. Dhanraj got in with his father and sat near the window. Vandana picked up her bag and the food hamper. Her husband took them from her and stowed them conveniently inside. By this time, Vandana's brothers-in-law had arrived on the platform. One was in a shirt with a floral print. The younger was in striking red. Both carried helmets and stood by deferentially in their father's presence.

'Um, get in,' said Vandana's husband. Gripping the handle on the compartment's door, Vandana placed her left foot carefully on the steps. Leaning firmly on it for a moment, she climbed into the compartment. At home she was comfortable using her foot in this fashion. While boarding a train, however, she could neither forget nor hide it.

Her husband got down and stood with his younger brothers. 'Dhanraj, let your mother sit near the window,' he said.

'Appa,' pleaded Dhanraj. Vandana got up and stood beside her son, pulling the end of her sari over her face. 'Sit, sit,' said her husband. Vandana remained standing. Now her father-in-law told her, 'Um, sit down.' Vandana sat down on the edge of her seat. By this time, her red-shirted brother-in-law had brought four bottles of Thums Up, one of which he extended towards Vandana. 'Take it, Amma,' said Dhanraj.

The brothers were talking among themselves. Of the three, only Vandana's husband was in ordinary clothes. Like the others, his face too had not seen a razor in two days. However, of the three, he was the one who spoke in a measured way. His younger brothers were unable to say anything without gesticulating freely with their hands.

'Come on, drink it up fast. The bottle has to be returned,' he urged Vandana now. She felt awkward, having to draw hard on a straw in front of her father-in-law. She managed to finish her drink somehow and held out the bottle. Her red-shirted brother-in-law went to return the bottles.

The patriarch said, 'Look after your health. Don't be careless like you were here.' Vandana kept her head bowed.

Her older brother-in-law inquired, 'Do you need anything, bhabhi?'

'No,' she replied, 'I have brought plenty to eat.'

'Chittappa, Chittappa! Wafer biscuit, Chittappa!' cried Dhanraj. He was enormously proud of his uncles. Vandana placed a hand on his shoulder. Even so, a big packet of wafer biscuits arrived soon. Vandana collected it and kept it in the food hamper.

Signs indicating the train's imminent departure could be seen. Not only had the crowd thickened on the platform, but a lot of people were rushing forward. At the same time, many who had come to see someone off stood waiting, looking visibly tired. How many times could they repeat, 'Write a letter when you reach home, look after your health, give everyone my love, keep an eye on the luggage, count all the pieces, make sure nothing is missing.'

It was hard on Vandana to see the patriarch standing. He was the only one in that house, apart from her husband, who didn't refer to her as a cripple. Their family was not all that affluent. As they had been tenants for a long time, the rent for their house was raised to one hundred rupees only after her wedding. Her husband had joined a small bank right after his school-leaving certificate examination. Both his mother and father had been unhappy over their eldest son going to work elsewhere instead of minding the family business. They couldn't demand much money and gifts as dowry based on the strength of his job alone. It was only by pointing out how difficult it was to get a lame girl married that they were able to specify and get precisely what they wanted in terms of gold, silver and diamonds. Everything was invested in the family business. As though it had been pending only the eldest son's marriage, a telephone arrived in their house. A petrol pump, too, was acquired. It was Vandana's husband who looked after that business, going in regularly every morning and evening. When an employee embezzled money, her husband didn't hand him over to the police; instead, the fellow was given an increment and the money recovered through monthly deductions from his salary. On a festive occasion, that man offered her obeisance by prostrating at her feet. He might not have noticed that one foot was shrivelled.

The train started moving. Without uttering a word, Vandana's husband gently waved goodbye. Vandana looked out of the window. Her brothers-in-law were waving vigorously. If their father had not come to the station, Vandana would have responded. Now, Dhanraj had to do it on her behalf as well.

As the train gathered speed, she could get a second's glimpse, even amidst the crowd, of the father and his sons going back. They would walk together till they reached the exit gate of the station. Then her husband would go on foot in one direction and one of her brothers-in-law would take his father home on his motorcycle in another.

Vandana leaned back comfortably in her seat and loosened the covering over her head. She felt flattered that the patriarch had come to the station. Her father and mother would ask her in disbelief: 'Really? Really?' After she and her husband had moved out to set up their own household, he hadn't visited them even once. Last year, both her brothers-in-law got married in consecutive months and now there were two more daughters-in-law in the house. Gossip had it that neither woman stayed home in the evening. It was even said that one of them visited a five-star hotel now and then with her husband, returning home drunk.

'I am hungry, Amma,' said Dhanraj.

'Look, the ticket collector is coming this way. We will eat after he is gone.'

'No, Amma. Now, *now*, Amma.'

Vandana opened the packet of biscuits and gave him two. Before she could close it and return it to the hamper, Dhanraj took two more. Vandana walked to one end of the compartment to wash her hands.

There were many passengers in that compartment who were travelling standing. Vandana particularly noticed a number of girls. Fair-skinned, dark-skinned, wheatish-complexioned; short and tall; with combed and plaited hair or with bobs and coiffures shaped like film actresses; sari- and jeans-clad; with or without a bindi on their forehead. No matter how bold these girls were, everyone still needed their parents' help to arrange their marriage.

If you need favours from someone, you end up having to accept their decisions as well. Her second brother-in-law's wife had grown up in America; she had also been educated there. Concerned that she might be lured into following some white man, her parents had come to India to find her a groom—or so people said. Once, during her visit to Vandana's house, she had asked Vandana when the two of them were alone, 'Bhabhi, may I see your foot?' It appeared to Vandana as though her sister-in-law had even felt sad on seeing her deformed foot. Vandana had expected her to come to the station today. If the train had not been scheduled to depart at seven, she might have.

Vendors serving coffee and breakfast had passed them four times. 'I am hungry, Amma,' Dhanraj had whined once more. Vandana cast a swift glance at the people sitting next to her and those on the opposite side. Barring one lone person who was asleep, everyone was eating something.

Vandana dragged the food hamper out before her. The puris and vegetables she had prepared at four that morning were still warm. Fruit and a bottle of pickle were at the bottom of the hamper, along with a water bottle. Besides these, there were some snacks that had been bought from a shop the previous evening. 'Let this first morsel of the day help us perform only good deeds,' she prayed.

Of late, she had begun to have doubts about what was good or bad. She had no worries about herself. It seemed as though everything she needed in life had been arranged for her in some fashion: a husband who, even if he didn't earn a lot, respected her and others; a son; in a few weeks, another child to follow; a father-in-law who came to the station when she went to her maternal home for her delivery; and two sisters-in-law, who were still innocent of the world. While they were still living at her mother-in-law's place, her husband had taken a bank loan and bought a flat. It was all fine, all fine *today*, but it felt like a big time bomb was ticking under everything, waiting to explode.

For example, the autorickshaw which brought them to the railway station that morning had been driven so rashly as to churn her stomach. Even at that early hour of the morning, ten to fifteen people on the road had narrowly escaped with their lives. The same could be said of the vehicle's occupants. This was, however, routine business for the driver. He must have been, at the most, as old as her brothers-in-law. They, too, drove their motorcycles in a similar fashion. With their open hair flying in the wind, the wives held their husbands tight as they kept chatting about something or other. Even on this train, a lot of people stood near the open doors of the compartment. At least a few among them must have had reserved seats. Even so, they were clinging to the steps precariously enough to agitate any onlooker. Who, indeed, was feeling upset? Vandana looked around. No one appeared to be suffering from an upset stomach.

'What's the matter, Amma? Why do you keep sitting all the time?' said Dhanraj.

'See that boy standing over there, at the far end? Give this to him and come back.'

'Come on, Amma. I don't know who he is—some beggar, he must be.'

'That's why I am telling you. Go give that boy a puri and come back.'

'I won't.'

Vandana waited for a few moments. When the boy looked in their direction, she beckoned to him. She was surprised to see the boy limping as he walked towards her.

When she gave him a puri with a small portion of vegetables inside, the boy begged for one more, extending his little finger. After receiving that as well, he stood at a spot where she could see him.

Picking up a stainless steel plate, Vandana wiped it with the end of her sari and placed a few puris on it along with some vegetable and sweets. 'Do you want pickle?' she asked. Shaking his head, Dhanraj started eating the sweets. Then he gestured with his hand for water. She poured water into a tall tumbler and gave it to him.

'Biscuit . . .'

'Eat them later, no?'

'No, I want them now.'

After he had finished eating and washed his hands, she wiped his hands thoroughly dry. Serving herself a piece of pickle, she began to eat. Back home, her husband too would have finished eating and be ready to set out for the day. The bank he had joined initially had been merged with another large bank. Although there was not much improvement in the pay scale, there were other perquisites. Even his father himself had opened an account there in Dhanraj's name. The petrol pump account had been there from the start. Now her husband went to his father's house as well as to the petrol pump to collect cheques for depositing in the bank. He was probably in conversation with his father right now.

The passengers in that compartment were restive; they couldn't sit in one place. On top of their bustle, vendors selling coffee, omelette, vada, biscuit and cigarettes passed by every five minutes. Two people had come from elsewhere on the train to chat with the family seated opposite Vandana. Since they were huddling in a cramped space, Vandana moved closer to the window and made room for them next to her. An old woman in that family didn't stop talking. After a short while, all of them left to go somewhere else. Dhanraj moved to the opposite side, then came back to her immediately, saying, 'Let's play chess, Amma.'

Chess had arrived in their home only five or six months ago. Vandana's husband had bought a chess set and started to play by himself, using Sunday supplements for reference. One day, while he was engrossed in trying to solve a puzzle, Vandana had pointed to a piece and said, 'This one.'

He was surprised. 'You know this game?'

'A little,' she had replied.

'But you never told me!'

Since then, they had played at least one game a week. Whenever her husband began to lose, she would say, 'Here,' and teach him the right move. He had no qualms about losing to her. Feeling extremely happy, he even said once, 'You are so wicked!' Then he taught Dhanraj. 'But if you want to play an advanced game,' he had told his son, 'you must challenge Amma!'

Vandana felt like she needed a short nap. 'Let us play after some time,' she said.

'Whenever I ask you for something, you say, "Later, later,"' complained Dhanraj. Vandana was taken aback. Dhanraj was such a clever boy!

When the box was opened out and placed face downwards, it became a chess board. Vandana picked up the pieces and arranged them on the right squares.

'I'll play white,' said Dhanraj.

Within fifteen moves, Dhanraj's position had become hopeless. 'Try this,' Vandana said. After making her move, she pointed to one of his pieces and said, 'Move this here.' Without her being aware of it, her knight was in a position to take both his king and queen. 'Dhanraj, let's start a new game,' she suggested.

'No, only after we complete this one.'

'See this?' At first he couldn't understand. Then she showed him by moving her knight to his king's square. Pulling a grim face, he moved his king. Vandana took his queen.

'You never told me about this earlier,' said Dhanraj. Then he moved his rook without any defence to the king's row.

'No, no. Your rook will be taken,' Vandana said.

'You teach me all the wrong moves.'

'Such situations do arise in this game.'

Dhanraj kept staring hard at his pieces. Suddenly, he pushed all the pieces off the board and then punched her hard on her thigh.

'Amma!' Vandana screamed. Dhanraj was ready to hit her again. The other people in the compartment were watching them now.

'What happened?' Vandana asked him, ignoring her own pain. Dhanraj glowered at her with hatred in his eyes.

Vandana collected the chess pieces and closed the box. The hatred in her son's eyes frightened her more than his sudden attack. She thought for a moment about the child she was going to deliver shortly. She then thought about all the children yet to be born to womankind.

From the original Kuzhanthaigal (1994)

The Cart Track

The jeep inched its way through the forest, crushing dried leaves and twigs under its wheels. Subba Reddy sensed that it was about to come to a halt. He couldn't see much more than the jeep's floor and the policemen's boots from where he lay. When the jeep stopped, the two policemen jumped down. One of the policemen told Subba Reddy in Telugu, 'Get out, young man.' Subba Reddy could not get up on his own. With the help of the policeman who had called him 'young man', Subba Reddy first pulled himself into a sitting position and then got down slowly from the jeep.

It was a familiar spot. There, in the middle of the jungle, was a small house. Built many years ago for an employee of the Forest Department, it lay abandoned, stripped of all its doors and windows. The police had a temporary outpost there.

Subba Reddy caught the eye of a policeman and said, 'Sir . . .' The policeman nodded and made a move to free Subba Reddy's hands. Suddenly he stopped himself and loosened Subba Reddy's pyjama instead.

Another jeep arrived just then. A police sub-inspector and two more policemen alighted from it. The sub-inspector's eyes fell on Subba Reddy. The look in his eyes caused Subba Reddy to hold his breath for a moment.

'You got just this one?' asked the sub-inspector.

'Yes,' replied a police constable.

'What have you got to say for yourself?' asked the sub-inspector as he approached Subba Reddy. Subba Reddy stood still.

'I'm asking you something! Yet you don't answer?' The sub-inspector swung his cane. Though the blow was aimed at Subba Reddy's shoulder, it actually fell on the bamboo staff which had been inserted behind his back to bind his elbows together.

Subba Reddy still remained silent.

'What've you got in your mouth, a guava?' The sub-inspector swung his cane harder. This time, it connected with Subba Reddy's neck and tore at his flesh.

'Amma!' cried Subba Reddy.

'Did that hurt? What about when you set fire to the police station, did it hurt then?' The sub-inspector swung his cane wildly at the prisoner. Subba Reddy turned this way and that, trying to expose only his back to the shower of blows from the cane.

'Where are the other three fellows?' asked the sub-inspector, continuing to hit Subba Reddy. One blow landed directly on his ear and another on his head. Subba Reddy slumped to the ground with a thud. Since the staff inserted behind his back kept his frame rigid, even his fall was awkward.

Another police van arrived then. Everyone straightened up on seeing the officer in the van. The sub-inspector saluted, and went up to him immediately.

The officer asked him, 'Have you rounded everyone up?'

'No, sir. There was only this one fellow there.'

'Naansense! Four of them were together in this!'

'No, sir. When we surrounded the place, there was just this one fellow.'

'Shut up! How long must we keep chasing after these young rascals?' The officer cursed the sub-inspector in unprintable language. 'Catch the other three fellows before the night is over. Dead or alive.'

The officer came to Subba Reddy, who lay in a crumpled heap on the ground, and nudged his face with his boot and glowered at him. 'Where are the other three?' he bellowed. When Subba Reddy didn't answer, the officer kicked him in the face.

'Badmash! Have you heard of Golconda Goli?' asked the officer.

Subba Reddy had: they applied chilli powder to the wet end of a ruler and shoved it up one's rectum.

'You'd better tell us where the other three are hiding before the sun sets. If you don't, you won't leave this jungle alive.'

The atmosphere lightened up considerably after the officer left. Though it was very hot, the place was densely shaded and cool. The sub-inspector crumpled his empty cigarette packet and threw it away, and then held out his hand to a constable. The constable gave him a bundle of bidis. The sub-inspector lit one bidi and put the rest in his pocket.

The policeman said, 'Saar?' The sub-inspector threw the bidis back to him, and walked into the building.

The four policemen went off in different directions with their lit bidis. They returned after a while. Subba Reddy signalled to one of them, saying, 'Saar . . .' Understanding what he wanted, the policeman helped Subba Reddy to his feet and took him aside. Subba Reddy felt acute pain in his ear and chin; they hurt much more than the rest of his body. His shoulder ached terribly too. If they untied his hands for ten minutes, it would ease the pain considerably.

The sub-inspector appeared at the entrance to the building and asked, 'What's the arrangement for food?'

The constable who had accompanied Subba Reddy replied, 'Have to bring it from Alir, sir.'

'Go there quick and get it. My stomach is burning. Also buy four packets of cigarettes.'

Two policemen left in a jeep. The sub-inspector told the other two, 'Bring that fellow inside.' They took Subba Reddy into the building.

It was a small house with two tiny rooms and a veranda. Not a single window frame in the house had been spared; they had been torn from the walls and carried away. Only two folding cots and a water pot had been left behind. The sub-inspector lay down on one of the cots. They brought Subba Reddy before him.

The sub-inspector looked at him from where he lay. 'Look here, young man. Don't get beaten to death. Tell us where your comrades are.'

Subba Reddy didn't say anything. The sub-inspector was disappointed. 'Take him away from here,' he ordered the policemen. They dumped Subba Reddy in the other small room where he sat in semi-darkness.

Subba Reddy squatted on the floor in the half-light. If he pressed the staff trapping his elbows against the wall he could get rid of it. Then his bound hands could be freed with some effort. He had taken a severe blow to the ankle bone. With a foot like that, he wouldn't be able to run fast. He knew this place well. He had holed out for two nights with Mallikarjun and Rama Reddy in this very house. Alir Railway Station was about three miles from here. If he could get there somehow, the police would never be able to catch him. He could hide in Pointsman Rajaiah's house. He had taken shelter in Rajaiah's house on many occasions in the past and given the slip to the police.

The police didn't even know his name. But they knew that there had been four of them. It had all happened because of that fool, Rama Reddy. Their plan had been to burn down Jangaon Police Station in a surprise operation, giving the police no grounds for suspecting any of them. Subba Reddy had climbed on to the terrace of the police station with a bottle of kerosene and a small bundle of rags. He had tied the rags along the beam of the tiled roof which sloped down from the terrace. All that was left to do was pour the kerosene and light a match, and then jump down and escape. At that moment, Rama Reddy had panicked and begun to fire at the police station from his position behind the bushes. Seeing this, Krishna Rao had also started shooting from another corner. The police had immediately been alerted. They had closed the doors and returned fire through the windows. In all this chaos, the flame from the match had not caught. Below, guns were going off on all sides. Subba Reddy had jumped down and run towards the bushes. The police didn't even know that he had jumped down and got away. But they had somehow caught on that it was an attempt to set fire to the police station. A large police force had immediately been deployed in the region.

The police only knew of this attempt at arson. They didn't know that Subba Reddy and his comrades had also murdered the kotwal of Ghanapur. The man was a Muslim, but that was not why he was killed. Rather because he was a symbol of the oppressive and exploitative power structure. No one suspected their group of having murdered the kotwal. The man had taken a cobbler's daughter for his mistress. She had acquired other patrons as well. The police thought that somebody had killed the kotwal to settle scores. Their primary suspect had immediately gone into hiding.

The policemen didn't know a great deal. They didn't even know for sure who they were after. And so their methods to extract information from Subba Reddy would be extreme. Third-degree methods. Golconda Goli was one such. There were others far more horrible. There had been six men in Subba Reddy's gang once, but two were taken by the police. No one had seen them since. It was rumoured that one of them was wandering in Warangal town, insane.

The police were waiting for something. They couldn't interrogate him in that house. They had to shift Subba Reddy somewhere else before they could begin: Who are the other three? What are their names? Where are they? Talk. Talk. Talk.

Subba Reddy shuddered. He had barely withstood the cane blows. What else would they do to him, he wondered. They would hang him upside down from the ceiling and start a fire below. They would bring his elbows down below his knees, insert a stick through them and tie him up; then they would hit him on the buttocks with a cane. They would pluck out his pubic hair in bunches. They would push a needle into the soft flesh beneath his fingernails. They would use a pair of small pliers to pull out his nails.

The more Subba Reddy thought of such things, his stomach started to burn like a fireball. He knew one thing about himself. He would never talk, no matter what the police did to him. So they would only step up the torture.

Should he run to the sub-inspector right now and tell him everything? But what was there to tell? He could reveal the names of his comrades. But would it be so easy to apprehend them? They would be even more alert, now that they knew that Subba Reddy was in custody. So, all he could give the police were mere names. Would they release him just for these names? Would they believe that those names were the only information they could get out of him?

Then there was something else, too. The people who vomited out confessions to the police were a type by themselves. They begged and fell at everybody's feet right from the moment they got caught. They cried loudly, rolled on the ground and behaved in such a way that they had to be dragged along bodily. They humiliated themselves to a point where the enemy became exhausted with boundless disgust and contempt for them, and thus managed to save their skins. But Subba Reddy had done nothing like that. He had kept his mouth shut from the beginning. He had not betrayed any sense of fear or terror. The policemen must have concluded that he was a deep one. If he said that he was ready to confess now, they would consider it suspect. And if they didn't find his comrades where he said they would be, their rage and blind fury would know no limits. He wouldn't get out of that jungle alive.

When the time came, he decided, he wouldn't fight death too hard. Life would be worth living only when all the policemen in the world had been eliminated. Even if one policeman were left alive, it would be better to die than to live. But the police never hand out death so easily or generously. They would kill him slowly, little by little.

His stomach turned when he thought of this. His head spun, and he felt like retching. But in all this, one thing was certain. He would not open his mouth. It was not something he was capable of doing. The intensity of their torture would increase. They would tear up his rectum. They would singe his flesh with a red-hot iron rod and sprinkle salt water on his wounds. They would make him eat the excrement that he would release involuntarily during torture.

Subba Reddy moved a little and peeped into the next room. The sub-inspector was asleep. He couldn't have slept a wink last night. He must have stayed up through the night till Subba Reddy was captured in the early hours, and then hurried away on the trail of the other three. But they had gotten away.

What would have happened if one of the others had also been caught? Disaster. One of them might have confessed on seeing the other fellow being tortured. It would have meant the end of everything. Apart from the four of them, all their comrades who lived in the Railway Colony would also have been nabbed. All the firearms and ammunition they had gathered at great risk would have been seized.

Subba Reddy pressed his elbows against his back and relaxed the staff to which they were bound. It came loose. He bent his arms at the elbows and slowly brought them over his head to the front. It was a good thing that they had tied his wrists with ordinary rope: they hadn't had handcuffs when they caught him. Getting out of them would have been much more difficult.

Subba Reddy peered out carefully through the window opening in his room. He could not hear or see anyone. The jeep was there, but the two policemen were out of sight. They couldn't have gone very far. Perhaps they were standing guard around the corner of the building. Could he afford to attempt an escape and risk being caught? What would happen then?

A man who burns down police stations, who does not flinch from killing policemen, who thinks nothing of killing people in cold blood—if such a man is captured again? Subba Reddy's guts twisted and tightened.

But not to try to escape was sheer insanity. He would never get another opportunity like this again. After their meal, they would definitely take him somewhere else. And this time the handcuffs wouldn't be forgotten. The interrogation would begin tonight.

Golconda Goli.

Subba Reddy stood near the window and made a hissing sound four or five times. Nothing happened. He raised his bound hands to the top edge of the window and tried to pull himself up. That didn't work; so he pressed down on the lower edge with his hands and drew a leg up on to the edge. He strained a little and managed to sit precariously on the windowsill. It was a good seven or eight feet to the ground. If he jumped from that height, the sound of twigs and dried leaves being crushed underfoot would give him away.

Subba Reddy looked out from his perch on the windowsill. The jeep stood there, innocent and blameless. He clutched the windowsill with his bound hands and gently lowered himself outside. When he hung by his fingers from the windowsill, it was hardly a foot or two to the ground. He let go of the windowsill and landed softly. Stretching himself on the ground close to the wall, he slowly crawled to the corner of the building. He found himself at the back of the house. There was only a wall here, not even a door or a window. Less than five metres from the wall, the bushes began. Then for a mile or so, the jungle was densely wooded.

Subba Reddy crept to the edge of the bushes. But a man couldn't crawl through them. He tried to go forward on all fours, but his bound hands made it difficult and slow. Still, to think of freeing his hands before reaching the cover of the jungle would be rank stupidity. He could scarcely believe it! Just when he had thought the show was over and had abandoned all hope, how easily he had broken out! He had escaped, when there should have been double the normal security and vigilance because they were 'terrorists'. But policemen are always more paranoid about robbers and thieves. They never expect political prisoners, idealists and principled revolutionaries to attempt escape like common thieves; perhaps that explained their slackness in guarding Subba Reddy.

From that point, Subba Reddy stood up and began walking. He could find his way through the area even if he was blindfolded. This route through the jungle would take a little longer. If it normally took one hour to reach Alir Police Station, this detour would stretch it to two. Still, this was the safest route for the moment.

He was impatient to free his hands. But the knot was very tight. Even if he rubbed it on the sharpest stone he could find, he would probably scrape his hands without doing the slightest damage to the knot. It could only be cut with a knife. Rajaiah's house would be the best place for that. No one had ever suspected Rajaiah. No one thought that Rajaiah was even capable of thinking of anything. They all thought he was a real imbecile. But no one knew of the rifles and ammunition he had pilfered from the Railway Protection Force. Subba Reddy and his three comrades had stayed in Rajaiah's house many times for days on end.

Hunger and thirst began to gnaw at Subba Reddy as he walked. He had had a couple of biscuits and tea the previous night; that's all. Now it was well past noon. When even the policemen had gone hungry themselves, how could they have given him anything to eat? After a sleepless night in pursuit of Subba Reddy's gang, and with nothing to eat, it was only natural that the sub-inspector and those two policemen had fallen asleep from fatigue and hunger. What a stroke of good fortune that had turned out to be!

His ears, his shoulders, his ankles—they all ached terribly, but the hunger was far the worst. The area was very quiet. News of his escape hadn't spread yet. If he didn't have to take this detour, he would have reached the railway quarters in Alir by now. It wasn't so bad though. If he cut across, he could reach the cart track in ten minutes.

Subba Reddy walked fast, unmindful of the terrible ache in his foot. He didn't really have to walk on the cart track; keeping a little to the side would take him just as fast to Alir. It was a useless, barren stretch. The trees here were felled only for firewood, that too, perhaps once in six months. So, there was no chance of being seen by anyone now. There would be no danger of that even if he took the cart track. It was now thirty years since the country had become free. This place had been fallow like this for three hundred years. The few hundred tribals in this area had lived here for generations, for centuries, like cattle, eating berries and half-cooked maize which grew wild on this land.

He reached the cart track. The railway station was less than half a mile away.

Hearing a familiar sound, Subba Reddy jumped aside to hide among the trees. He had overlooked that blind turning in the track. It could only be the police jeep which had gone to bring food from Alir. But before he could take cover, Subba Reddy knew that the policeman who was driving the jeep had spotted him.

From the original Vandippaathai (1978)

A Longing for Truth

One day, all of a sudden, Manickaraj came up to me in the office when no one else was around and said, 'I have handed in my resignation letter, saar.'

I had been expecting the unexpected from him for some days now, but I'd never imagined he would give up his job.

'Have you given it in writing?' I asked.

'Yesterday, saar.'

I moved the account ledgers and papers in front of me to one side. 'What's the problem?' I asked him.

Manickaraj rolled his eyeballs up and brought his eyelids over them. 'I don't want to go through this birth lying again and again in this false, illusory life, saar,' he said.

I am prone to laughing even if a person sneezes in a slightly different way than normal. But I didn't want to hurt Manickaraj's feelings, so I held my breath and pretended that I had hiccups. My eyes became red and a couple of teardrops collected in them. 'What do you mean by lying?' I asked him.

As much as he could, Manickaraj kept his face looking calm and peaceful, like a Jain idol. But he must have found it painful. 'I have borrowed money from so many people. They want their money back. Am I not lying to every one of them?' he said.

'You won't need to lie if you leave your job, is it?'

'I'll get my provident fund and gratuity amounts. Then I can repay all my debts and lead a peaceful life, can't I?'

It had been ten years since I had started working here. Manickaraj had joined the company many years before me. But even after fifteen years of service, not much money could have accrued in his provident fund account from his paltry salary.

'How much do you owe people?'

Manickaraj ran through a fairly long list and finished with a total of nineteen hundred rupees and change. I noticed that he had left out the thirty rupees that he owed me. Perhaps I didn't look like much of a creditor to him.

Just then Bhagavathar entered my room. He wasn't a singer, which is what a real Bhagavathar ought to be. He worked in our company for a daily wage of three rupees, for only two or three days a week at that. Even so, you never saw him without an angavastram on his shoulder. We called him Bhagavathar only for this reason. He answered to that nickname as though he was born to it, without feeling particularly honoured or ashamed. Although Bhagavathar paid his respects to me, he was really waiting to meet Manickaraj. Manickaraj took his leave and went out into the garden with him. After a quarter of an hour, Bhagavathar came to me and said respectfully, 'I'll be going, saar.'

'Aren't you on duty today?'

'Tonight, saar. I am on the night shift at nine.'

'What's wrong with this Manickaraj? All of a sudden he says he wants to resign.'

'I don't know, saar. Maybe he doesn't like his job.'

'Can you suddenly start hating your job after working for so many years? Is it possible?'

'I don't know, saar. Isn't that a matter for his conscience?'

'Conscience? What conscience? What *is* conscience, I say? You tell me!'

'It's the heart, saar. If the heart doesn't like it, it weighs heavily on the conscience. Isn't that right?'

I could see a black cat trying to cross the road in the distance. After it had safely reached the other side, I asked Bhagavathar, 'How much does he owe you?'

His reply was prompt: 'Five hundred, saar.'

'Five hundred? You mean, *five* times *one hundred*?'

'Yes, saar. Five hundred is right.'

'Then what are you doing here, working for a daily wage? How much more money have you put away? Can you spare me three hundred?'

Bhagavathar laughed. 'You are pulling my leg, saar.'

'I mean it,' I said. 'Just last month, I borrowed eighty rupees from that cross-eyed Pathan. On that loan alone the interest comes to ten rupees a month.'

It was obvious that Bhagavathar was paying no attention to what I was saying. As soon as I finished, he took out a sheet of paper from his shirt pocket and gave it to me. It was an application for a job—Manickaraj's job.

'Get out of here!' I snapped. 'Be off!'

Bhagavathar stubbornly held his ground. His grin and fawning manner never failed to protect him.

'Go, go,' I said. 'Don't keep standing here, where I can see you!'

'They'll have to employ *someone*, so why not me, saar?'

The logic of his statement made me even more furious. 'Get out of my sight! Come to me again, and I'll crack your skull!' Bhagavathar knew that my words were no real threat. With a disarmingly cordial smile, he took his leave. I intended to submit his job application personally at the administrative section at four o'clock when I visited the cafeteria for coffee.

I presented myself in our accountant's room at a quarter past four. He too had just had coffee. 'Have you received Manickaraj's letter?' I asked him.

'Yes. It came in this afternoon with the secretary's signature.'

'What reason has he given?'

'Well, I can't make any sense of what he has put down. He says he wants to leave; and we seem to be telling him— ah, very good, we are glad you want to leave.'

'He is quite old. Will he have the money to survive at least for some time?'

'How much will he get from us? I'll send for his papers.' He hit the call bell a couple of times. 'Go to Kuppuswamy and get the Manickaraj file,' he told the man who came in through the swing-door.

'Which Manickaraj?'

'As if there are nine fellows here called Manickaraj, and I need to be specific! Go! Just get the file. Wants to know which Manickaraj!' The papers arrived in two minutes flat.

'Here they are. With PF and gratuity and everything, it amounts to three thousand and thirty,' said the accountant.

I mentally subtracted eighteen hundred from that number.

The accountant added, 'There is eight-hundred-odd outstanding from the loan he took for his daughter's marriage. He has also taken an advance on his salary. Then there's his mess bill, and payment for this and that from our stores. The total should touch a little over one thousand.'

'So he will have two hundred left.'

'Two hundred? No, two thousand I think.'

'No, just two hundred,' I said and left. Bhagavathar's job application remained in my shirt pocket.

Manickaraj had left by the time I got back to my desk. He ought to have gone home by one, but he had been hanging around the office, reluctant to leave. He had finally left just a while ago.

The office closed only at half past five. I went directly to Saidapet. There, in Mettupalayam, I looked for Manickaraj's house. I don't know how Mettupalayam—the high district—had earned its name; it looked as if all the rainwater and sewage from everywhere had flowed into that ditch of a place, turning it into a vast slushy tract. The old tile-roofed houses and huts in the district had no electricity. I wanted to find Manickaraj's house quickly, before it grew dark.

I couldn't find anyone who could recognize him from my description. Short guy. Small-headed. Bald. Been working in our office twenty years. Wears a kurta all the time. Has a brother in the Territorial Army. Got a daughter married off last year. Has taken to attending a great many pujas and bhajans these days. His name is Manickaraj. Maybe he is called Manickam around here. Manickaraj. Manickaraju. Manickaraja. Manickam. All this was no help.

Finally, a man in a small provisions store asked me, 'Is he a Mudaliar?'

I ought to have begun my search by mentioning his caste. I found his place easily after that. I needn't have wandered around in that maze of slushy lanes for so long.

Even though it was a tiled house, the roof sloped down steeply as in a hut. When I called out for Manickaraj, seven or eight adults and children emerged, all bending quite low. They straightened their backs only when they were out in the open. From what I could see, at least ten families were living in that house. Of those who came out in response to my call, none belonged to Manickaraj's family. A little later, his wife appeared, with a ten-year-old girl in tow. I remembered then that his wife was mute. Manickaraj had not returned home yet.

'I'll ask him to come and see you at home,' said the girl.

'Yes. Tell him to make sure he does,' I said and started out. In the swiftly falling darkness, I could see a kurta-clad form approaching, with a carry bag in his hand. Yes, it was Manickaraj.

'Hello, saar. When did you come? Please come in,' he said.

'Just walk with me for a minute,' I told him and took him to the end of the alley. It led to a passably good road; there was even a street light there. Manickaraj had smeared a lot of sacred ash and vermilion on his forehead: he looked frightfully religious.

'How many children do you have?' I asked him.

'Five, saar. I married off one daughter just last year. You attended the wedding.'

'Is there anyone in your family, apart from you, who earns a living?'

'They are all women, saar.'

'Then how do you plan to live after you quit your job?'

Manickaraj seemed overwhelmed by confusion and uncertainty. He fended them off as best as he could by indulging in his new habit: he rolled his eyeballs up and brought his lids down on them. 'I don't want to spend this life speaking nothing but lies,' he said.

I felt faint for a moment. A life without falsehoods! If only there were no such thing as a lie, how wonderful life would be!

Manickaraj must have sensed my state of mind. He said in an even louder voice, 'I have survived so far by lying to every man who has ever lent me money. I no longer want to spend my days telling lies.'

I continued to stare intently at his face. When his eyes met mine, he seemed acutely embarrassed.

We stood there for some time without speaking. Manickaraj's embarrassment increased steadily. At one point, he couldn't bear it any more; 'I'll be off,' he said abruptly, and turned to go. I grasped him by the shoulder and stopped him.

'What you tell your creditors, only *that* is a lie?' I asked him.

'Do you mean to say it is not?' he said stiffly.

'That may be, but is that the only lie?'

'I don't know. I don't like it, that's all.'

'Okay, so you repay your debts to ensure that you don't have to lie any more. But all your money will be gone in no time. And you won't have a job. Then, how much of the truth will you be able to tell the people who are going to lend you money?'

'Why worry about something that is going to happen sometime in the future?'

'Sometime in the future?' I ask incredulously. 'What does that mean? After a hundred years? Right now, in less than two or three months, you will find yourself penniless. What are you going to do then? Now, when you still have a job, it is hard to get people to lend you money. Who will give you a loan when you are unemployed? Then, you will have to lie even to borrow!'

'I have vowed never to borrow money again.'

'Very good. When it comes to borrowing, it's all lies before *and* after, right? And how do you intend to run your house without borrowing?'

'Did I arrange to come into existence? Will I have to arrange to die?'

'Right, let's say that's true. Similarly, you didn't arrange to become an adult either, or to marry, or to father five children, or to be in debt. Then, why do you bother with arrangements for paying off your debts?'

'That's my duty.'

'There's also a mute wife dependent on you. And those little girls. Isn't it also your duty to protect them from destitution?'

Manickaraj looked at me with irritation. 'Go away, saar,' he said. 'Who are you to interfere in my personal affairs?'

I was prepared for this. 'God knows how it's come about, but I am neck deep in your affairs. After all that's happened, what's the point in just giving up without having something to show for it? If you had thought about all this before you resigned, no one would be able to point a finger at you. Leaving your job is no simple matter. There must be proper thought and reasoning behind it.'

'I have taken this step after a lot of consideration. You don't have to come and give me counsel, like a guru.'

The sarcasm in the term 'guru' made me want to hit him.

'Oi, you think you have found a guru like no one has ever seen before? What advice did he give you? What did he tell you?'

'Don't show disrespect for my guruji.'

'I'm not showing disrespect, I am only *asking* you. Did he summon you and tell you to resign?'

'No, but he did tell me to give up falsehood.'

'You mean you know for certain the difference between truth and falsehood? You think you are a very wise man, don't you? *I* think you are a big fool. Of the two, which is the truth?' Manickaraj stood silent. I continued, 'I am not someone who claims to know the past, present and future. I cannot cut open your breast and find out what lies inside. But this I certainly know. And I know it better than anybody else. Your wife and children have no one but you. There's no way they'll survive on their own. So far they have at least half filled their stomachs, even if you've had to borrow the money to feed them. Now you attend one or two bhajans, make up your own meaning of what you hear, then you throw off the only means of sustenance all of you have. If you want to renounce the world and go into the jungle, that's fine. But whoever said you have to clear your debts before you do? If a man really wants to disappear into the jungle, he won't bother announcing it.'

I surprised myself. I had not planned to speak in this manner.

'You can do what you like to yourself. Who am I to stop you? The trouble with you is that you say one thing and do something else altogether. That won't solve your problem. You talk grandly about not lying to creditors any more. In the past fifteen minutes, you have told me about fifty lies. I too would like to learn all about lies; right now, I don't know very much. But I do know that distinguishing between truth and falsehood isn't as easy as marking right or wrong in a second standard child's arithmetic sums. If you are sure that what you are doing now will eliminate falsehood from your life forever, go ahead and do it.'

I felt deflated. Before I began my speech, I had thought of a number of arguments that would have certainly undermined his decision. It was only when I began to talk to him face to face did I realize that I too had acted on instinct. Manickaraj must have come to his decision in the same manner. I needed to be alone to savour my defeat in full. I moved away from him and started down the road. But before I had taken ten steps, he ran after me and caught hold of my hands. He was crying.

'Manickaraj, what happened?' I asked him, greatly upset.

'I don't understand a thing, saar. Not a thing. They say one must not take big decisions in such confusing times. But I have done it, saar. Where will I go now? What will my children do? Will they starve to death? Saar, I even gave it in writing! If I refuse to leave now, they still have the right to throw me out!'

Next morning, I went to the secretary's room as soon as he entered the office. 'What is it?' he asked.

'We must reject Manickaraj's resignation.'

'Who is Manickaraj?'

'He is the attendant who works for me. He wasn't in his right mind when he resigned. There is absolutely no reason for it.'

'Ask him to put this down in writing.'

'I have already brought his signed statement.'

It is now ten years since that incident. Manickaraj is still employed there. The same kurta, the same bald head. Has he grown slightly shorter? I saw him four days ago. He looked through me, but deep down, he must have felt grateful. I am sure that his wife and children still remember me. All this is necessarily guesswork because, within a month of forcing Manickaraj to withdraw his resignation, I did exactly what I hadn't wanted him to do—resign on a sudden whim.

From the original Unmai Vetkai (1974)

Revelation

Unlike the other tourists around her, she had not chosen the Chinese airline for the delicious Chinese meals they served on the flight. In fact, she found it tiresome when foreigners extolled the virtues of Chinese cuisine, and when the Chinese themselves bragged about their food.

As the plane taxied out of Taipei airport, a male voice sounded over the public address system, and the stewardesses began what seemed to her like a strange dance in accompaniment to it. But it was no dance; they were miming the safety procedures which passengers had to follow in the event of certain emergencies. There is a life jacket under every passenger's seat; if the plane falls into the sea, the jacket will help you stay afloat. There is a trapdoor to the overhead compartment above every seat. In case of a sudden decrease in cabin pressure, the trapdoor will open automatically and release the oxygen mask. Passengers should pull the mask on to their faces and breathe normally. In the event of an accident, you can use the emergency exits which are located here, there and over there. Please extinguish your cigarettes now and fasten your seat belts. After these announcements were made in Chinese, an English version followed. She didn't know a word of English.

A young stewardess, with a fresh pimple on the tip of her nose, came to her. 'Would you like to watch the film?'

'Which one is it?' she asked, and the stewardess mentioned a title. 'Hm, yes.'

The stewardess gave her something which looked like a stethoscope to clamp on to her ears.

'What is this?'

'You can hear the dialogue and the music only if you have the earphones on. Those who don't wear this can only *see* the film on the screen.'

'Then why didn't you give it to everyone?'

'Because we charge for this.'

'How much?'

'Two American dollars and fifty cents.'

'Oh, that much!'

'Yes. That's the standard charge on all international flights.'

'Then I don't want it.'

She returned the stethoscope-like gadget. Ten American dollars was all she had. She had had to pay four hundred Taiwan dollars for them. In the black market, the rate was even higher.

She woke up with a start and sat upright in her seat. She had dozed off, watching the silent figures on the screen, and had no idea when the film had ended. There was an announcement in Chinese over the loudspeakers. 'In a few minutes from now, we shall be landing in Tokyo. Please fasten your seat belts and extinguish your cigarettes when the "No Smoking" sign is switched on. We hope you had a pleasant flight. On behalf of the captain and the crew, I bid deplaning passengers goodbye.'

She peeped out of the window. It was as though the starlit sky had descended to the earth. There were millions of stars out there in the dark, of different shapes, colours and lustre. As the plane approached the jumble of stars, she could make out the skyscrapers of Tokyo and, somewhat indistinctly, its streets down below. Suddenly, the plane climbed and reached the outskirts of the city, and then began to lose altitude.

Her stomach churned. She turned away from the window and trained her eyes on the plane's interior. The 'No Smoking' and 'Fasten Your Seat Belts' signs were blinking rapidly. The stewardesses did another pantomime in time to the voice that boomed from the loudspeakers. Amidst the rows of blue lights, the dark spots between them appeared like a swarm of moths. The plane rushed forward at great speed. Suddenly its wheels touched down on the runway; it shook and rattled, then began to slow down. Finally, it came to a halt in front of a huge building.

Many passengers disembarked at Tokyo. Even those who had to travel further visited the transit lounge to look around and make purchases at the duty-free shops. But she didn't leave the plane. The mere idea of setting foot on that soil was abhorrent to her. Once, not long ago, the Japanese had killed the Chinese as though they were no better than pigs. She was not even born then. But her grandmother was forever bemoaning the horrors of those days.

These days her ceaseless laments included present-day troubles as well.

'Ask Dominic not to come back. Let him stay safe and well somewhere in America. He should never come back to this wretched country. My darling, you and Dominic should never come back here.'

Her aunt too had given the same advice. In fact, the entire family was of the opinion that Dominic should never return. All three generations of the family loved him more than life itself. He was their only hope, their only salvation. If he came back, the government of Taiwan was sure to throw him behind bars. He might be sentenced for five years, seven maybe, or even ten. He had publicly criticized the Taiwanese government in America and had read 'undesirable' books and pamphlets. He had even participated in a factory strike once. In America, no one arrested him for these offences, but if he ever came back to Taiwan, they would certainly put him in jail.

After an hour or so of peace and quiet, the plane was bustling again. Many new passengers came aboard. A fat lady sat down in the vacant seat next to her, cradling an enormous carry bag on her lap. She had a hairy upper lip, and even her chin looked as if it had been shaved with a razor. As soon as she sat down, the lady asked her something. She couldn't understand the language the lady spoke; it was certainly not English. Perhaps the fat lady did not know English either.

The loudspeakers began their familiar babble. A stewardess walked down the aisle, checking to see if the passengers had followed the instructions. When she came to the fat lady, she took the carry bag from her lap and crammed it under her seat. The plane began to move.

Rows of blue lamps stretched to the very ends of the world. The plane passed them at a dizzying speed, and suddenly took off, nose in the air. Again, the streets, buildings and lights of Tokyo. Mere moments later, this vast, borderless megapolis gradually began to float below them, receding further and further until you could only faintly see it in the distance, and then, nothing at all. Let Tokyo be damned!

Why should I despise Tokyo so intensely, she wondered. Just as she had not been born when the Japanese had massacred the Chinese, there would now be many in Tokyo who too hadn't been born then. If she told them, 'You people slaughtered us like pigs,' they might exclaim in genuine surprise, 'Oh, really?' She felt a moment's regret that she had not got out at Tokyo.

After they had eaten, the fat lady leaned back and went to sleep. A stewardess came down the aisle asking the passengers something. She anticipated the question even before the woman reached her, and told her promptly, 'I don't want to watch the film.' The stewardess seemed to wonder whether she ought to wake up the fat lady. After a moment's hesitation, she moved on to the next row.

The film started. It was a different one this time. As far as she was concerned, it was a silent movie. Four cowboys surround a farmhouse, kill an old man and his wife, set fire to the house. The young son of the slain couple fights them. They bind his hands and feet and thrash him. Once the job is done, they go on their way. In the young man's handsome face, there is rage and a passionate resolve to seek revenge. He will mete out hard and cruel punishment to those four evil men.

She no longer saw the young man's face; it was Dominic's face which loomed large in her mind's eye. What strength and resolve glowed in his handsome face! When their family had sought refuge in Taiwan, Dominic had been a mere stripling, not yet ten years old. Many among the refugees became wealthy. Even her father found a steady job in a factory that manufactured woollen vests and managed to provide for his family. But Dominic's father had never been able to hold down a job for even one year. To fulfil the secret dreams of his grey-haired mother whose eyes had been widened by unresolved anxieties—it was with this unspoken vow that Dominic had migrated to America.

Was she going over there to marry Dominic? Or was she travelling all that way just to make sure that this pool of memories, stagnant now for over three years, had not dried up altogether?

'Dominic!'

'Yes?'

She gave no answer.

Dominic grasped her by the shoulders and looked directly into her eyes. Suddenly a deep sadness welled up in her, and a stream of tears flowed from her eyes. He stood still, just looking at her. And then he spoke to her: 'You know, you are still a child. So it's natural that you feel like crying whenever someone goes away. But two years from now, even three maybe, if you still weep when you think of me, then we must live together. Even if it has to be in the Arctic. All right?'

She nodded her assent. He continued to gaze at her intently. Then he pulled her towards him and kissed her on the lips.

She wiped her lips. The lady in the adjacent seat drooled in her sleep. She bemoaned her bad luck at being seated next to such a repulsive person, and scowled in distaste. Then it also occurred to her that a Chinese-speaking person would have jabbered till she got off at San Francisco. If it had been a man, he would have pawed her, certainly, in an attempt to make the most of these few hours of sexual opportunity. He would have rubbed his thigh against hers; on the pretext of whispering gallantly to her, he would have brought his face close to her ear and furtively kissed her cheek. Then she wouldn't have been able to think of Dominic. When she had learned that Dominic was leaving, she was ready to give her life, and herself, to him. But he had gone no further than that one tender kiss. He was a man. Only those unsure of their manhood sought petty pleasures whenever they got the smallest opportunity. Her Dominic was a real man.

The film had finished, but many passengers slept unaware, earphones still on. She had missed the ending this time too. Did that young man avenge his parents' death or did he also end up being defencelessly slaughtered, like his parents? She had never ever pondered over the endings of stories. Whether it was a mythological yarn, or a modern detective story, it was her nature to accept without question. Then why did she now worry about how this film had turned out, that too a film she hadn't even watched? What made her think that the young man would have died without taking revenge?

With every passing moment, she grew more weary and exhausted. It was her first ever flight. People at home still tended to call her 'my child'; her toys were still intact, put away neatly in boxes. But she scarcely felt a childlike wonder and delight in this journey. She was a grown-up now, an old, worn-out hag even. If she put on a little more weight, one wouldn't be able to tell her apart from the sleeping mass of obesity in the next seat.

She gingerly moved the fat lady's legs out of the way and went looking for the toilet. Her lower abdomen and ankles ached from the strain of having sat in the same place for hours, ever since she boarded the plane at Taipei.

But her walk down the aisle led her not to the toilet but to the pantry. Two stewardesses sat there, holding hands. When they saw her, they hurriedly let their hands drop.

She stood there, hesitating. One of them called out, 'Hi!' She too said, 'Hi!', and then asked her the way to the toilet.

Before she opened the door and came out, she smoothed her skirt one more time and looked at herself in the mirror. She *was* a pretty girl. Her dress had been made especially for this journey. The hem of her skirt was half an inch lower than necessary. That was on her mother's insistence. 'In America, you will need this extra half-inch.' America, America. Ask Dominic never to return. You and Dominic, the two of you just stay put there and be happy. Don't come back to this wretched country.

There was sudden excitement among the passengers. The city of San Francisco, there it floats, down there, below us. Fasten your seat belts. Do not smoke. We hope you had a pleasant journey. We look forward to having you fly with us again.

Suddenly, the fat woman gripped her hand. From the many folds of slack flesh surrounding her eyes, she appeared to be pleading desperately for something. 'I don't know English, either,' she told the fat lady, but the lady did not release her hand.

The plane came to a halt near a huge building at the airport. Everyone moved towards the exit.

She and the fat lady took their hand luggage and walked along with the others. It was like crawling down an endless man-made cave. They came to an abrupt halt. In front of them, the floor of the cave sloped down steeply and the steps kept moving. All a person had to do was step on the moving staircase and it would take her down on its own.

She understood how the escalator worked and put a foot forward. For a moment, she felt she was floundering, and then it was all right.

Her hand was still in the fat lady's grip. She turned and signalled to the fat lady to come along. But the fat lady pointed to the moving escalator, her eyes stupid with terror.

Again, she invited the fat lady to get on to the escalator. Her hand was extended now and grew rigid.

She abruptly jerked her hand away, but the fat lady had understood the situation by now and let go of her grip. The gap between the two women kept widening.

She felt sorry and ashamed. When she reached the bottom, she turned around and looked up at her. Still standing in the same place at the top of escalator, the fat lady fondly waved goodbye.

To fill out the necessary details in her application form to enter the United States, she had to seek help from one of the ground staff of the Chinese airline. He asked her harshly, 'Why didn't you get this done on the flight? You were supposed to.'

'I didn't know.'

'If you didn't know, why didn't you ask someone? They gave you these forms on the plane, didn't they?'

'I didn't know.'

'But you do know how to lie down on your back, right?'

She remained silent.

When he asked her where she was going to stay in the US, she took Dominic's letter from her handbag and gave it to him. He entered the address carefully in the form.

After her luggage had been examined thoroughly, they let her go. She had the feeling of having been released suddenly into open space.

Beyond the barrier, a large crowd milled about. Everyone was eagerly looking for someone, and when they saw the person they had been waiting for, they waved. But the passengers could not recognize them that easily. She too looked for Dominic among the hundred-odd faces beyond the barrier; she even thought she heard someone call out her name. But she could not see him.

She stood there paralysed. But it was not really possible for her to stop and collect herself. The passengers behind her pushed against her back and shoved her forward. All alone in this strange place, and without knowing a word of the language, what can I do at this midnight hour? God! Didn't Dominic get my telegram? Why, it was he who arranged for my ticket! Dominic! She walked past the barrier. Suddenly, someone reached for her suitcase. Frightened, she looked up at the man's face. He gave her a half-smile. She hesitated for a moment, then dropped her suitcase and handbag to the floor and threw her arms out, crying, 'Dominic!' She hugged him fiercely. 'Come, let's go,' said Dominic. She followed him, her eyes brimming with tears.

He turned to her abruptly and asked, 'Would you like to eat something? You had dinner on the flight?'

She said she didn't want anything.

'We don't have much time, either. Our bus leaves in half an hour,' he said.

The way he spoke to the taxi driver made her uneasy. They reached the bus station in fifteen minutes.

'Stay here,' Dominic told her and went off to buy tickets for their journey. She looked around. They were in an enormous waiting hall. There were rows of chairs, some of which were fitted with a small television set on one armrest. A few people sat glued to those sets while they waited.

There was a cafeteria at one end of the hall. She could see the staircase and a portion of the first floor from where she stood. The door to the restroom, which she had learnt to recognize instantly by now, caught her eye.

Dominic was standing in the queue. He accidentally bumped into the man in front of him, and when the man turned to glare at him, he mumbled something. Must have been an apology.

His very posture seemed to suggest he was constantly apologizing to the world around him. Even when he walked ahead carrying her suitcase, his posture was not erect; he slouched along, shoulders hunched. In Taiwan, where he had often lived on just one meal a day, even there he had never appeared so crushed.

Soon it was Dominic's turn at the ticket window. He put the money on the counter and said something to the lady. There was an exchange between them before she took out a bunch of tickets, passed it under a punch and handed it to him. Then she took her time handing out his change.

Dominic walked towards her, tickets in hand. He seemed an old man now. He smiled weakly. 'How was your flight?'

She didn't think there was much to say about it. 'It was all right.'

'This is the only flight where you are served proper meals.'

'Yes,' she muttered, and stood staring at him.

'What are you staring at?' Then, giving her another weak smile, he embraced her again. This time, for some reason, she didn't want to close her eyes.

When an announcement sounded over the loudspeaker, he said, 'Come, it's time for us to board our bus.' He walked ahead of her, carrying her suitcase. Three years ago, his hips had stayed firm and strong when he walked. Now, even that part of Dominic had grown weak.

Passengers were already waiting in a queue to board the bus. Noticing the suitcase in Dominic's hand, the bus driver came to him first. Dominic went with him and kept it along with the suitcases heaped in the low bay on one side of the bus. The driver entered the bus again and got a baggage identification tag which he tied to the suitcase. Then he tore off the check from the tag and gave it to Dominic. Again, Dominic displayed the same grovelling attitude.

He came and stood beside her, complaining that they should have handed over the suitcase earlier. She muttered, 'Oh, really?'

She remembered her father, mother, uncle and aunt; she also recalled the image of Dominic that they had cherished in their memory. But her own memory could not be retrieved in that splendid moment of revelation; it lay hidden somewhere.

They boarded the bus and took their seats. The bus was very comfortable, warm enough to help them withstand the cold.

'When will we reach home?'

'Home?' asked Dominic and laughed lightly. Then he said, 'We'll get there tomorrow morning.'

'Are we going to spend the whole night on the bus?'

'Yes. We could have stayed overnight in San Francisco. But it would've cost us at least twenty dollars.'

The bus sped along steadily, droning like a swarm of insects. She looked at Dominic. He was fast asleep. Somewhere in the bus, a black girl was singing in a small voice. She must be putting her baby to sleep.

From the original Prathyatcham (1974)

King under Threat

Two recent news items—unrelated to each other—reminded me of Vijaya Rao and Raghuram. The first was that the American surgeons who were treating the actress Sridevi's mother had operated on the wrong part of her head. The other was about the chess match between Kasparov and a computer. Both items made me feel as though forty years had vanished in an instant.

Before talking about humans, I must talk about a building called Kohinoor. The film company that I worked for functioned out of several separate buildings dispersed over eleven acres. If one drew a map of the campus, its perimeter would look like a camel sitting on the ground. Kohinoor was located on the camel's head.

Not all of our company buildings had a name. In fact, Kohinoor had not been built with a company office in mind. It was a two-storeyed building with thick compound walls and somewhat small windows, suitable perhaps for housing a secluded zenana in a modern Indian city. After our boss bought Kohinoor, its rooms were crammed with bundles of old papers and books which had accumulated in various departments across the company. It is my belief that those bundles of paper had never been untied by anyone.

I was allotted the upstairs hall in the Kohinoor building. Had they put my table in any of the other rooms, no human would have been able to enter that room. The architect who designed Kohinoor could not have cared a whit for people who needed to stretch their legs to lie down.

Since Kohinoor was located in a corner, without much human traffic, it had become a place to relax for many people in our company. One such person who came in for a daytime snooze beside those bundles of paper was Vijaya Rao. After studying law in college, he now worked as an actor in our company on a monthly salary. As far as I knew, he had been given a speaking part only once in his entire career. In that film, the hero, having lost all his wealth and money, stands forlorn in front of a paan shop and begs the shopkeeper, 'Aiya, could you give me some water to drink?' The shopkeeper says, 'Go, go away.' Vijaya Rao was the shopkeeper. It was he who looked pathetic in that scene.

Vijaya Rao made great efforts to ingratiate himself with me. He had to pass me on his way to the room where he usually napped. No matter how friendly his smile appeared to be, when I saw him I could only think of all the mendicant's roles he had played. One day, after he had gone in to snooze, I peeped into that room. Vijaya Rao was not napping that afternoon; he was playing chess with himself.

'Why are you playing all by yourself? We can play in the hall, under the fan,' I told him.

From that day forth, his daytime naps became a thing of the past.

My prowess at chess surprised even me. After I had arbitrarily moved a piece, without any kind of plan or forethought, Vijaya Rao would say, as if broken-hearted, 'What's left for me in this game?' and sigh deeply. Having witnessed his agony for several days, I told him, 'You go ahead with your nap, Vijaya Rao. I am fed up of playing chess.'

'No, sir. I won't sleep a wink till I beat you.'

The next time I played with him, I deliberately lost my queen and then played aimlessly for a while. After about fifteen moves, Vijaya Rao sighed. Worried, I asked him, 'You're winning this time, aren't you?'

'Look here,' he pointed. My bishop was in position to take his king. Neither of us had noticed this situation in time.

'Vijaya Rao, it's obvious that I can't play chess to save my life. That's why mistakes like this happen whenever we play. Let's not play any more.'

'No, sir. I *must* beat you in at least one game. I'll bring Raghuram sir along tomorrow.'

'Who, Raghuram from Editing?'

'Raghuram from Stores. He knows how to play chess. All three of us can play.'

'Listen, you have to work only when you put make-up on. But if I keep playing chess during working hours, our boss is likely to say, "You can go home and play, boy," and send me packing.'

'Not at all. How will anyone find out about our chess game here in Kohinoor?'

'It's talk like this which lost us the Koh-i-noor, that queen of diamonds.'

Vijaya Rao laughed. 'Don't worry, sir. This Kohinoor won't get lost. And you won't go anywhere either.'

'Who is this Stores Raghuram? Is he the boss's secretary's younger brother?'

'Yes, yes. They assigned him to Stores after the secretary put in a word. Over there, nobody is allowed to do any work.'

'Bindu Madhavan . . .'

'He is the only one there who can work. If the others were to take up anything, it would only lead to some major confusion. Once, because of an error in the order sent by Raghuram, we received four tons of common pins, instead of four tins.'

'A magician I know eats common pins.'

'To eat four tons of common pins, he would need to live for four hundred years.'

Vijaya Rao even slept for an hour that afternoon; so confident was he of beating me the next day with Raghuram's help.

The next day, I had a sty in my eye. It took four days for the sty to ripen with pus and burst, and for my life to be restored to normal. I returned to the office, only to find Vijaya Rao and another person playing chess at my desk. Angrily, I asked him, 'What's this, Vijaya Rao? Isn't there a time and a place for playing chess?'

He said with a laugh, 'Let's see if you can beat Raghuram now.'

'I have to attend to my work first. We can play later. Come by this afternoon.'

Vijaya Rao and the other person arrived punctually at two o'clock. The boss's secretary resembled a string bean. As secretary, he had adopted a silk kurta and a zari veshti as his uniform. Raghuram, his brother, wore a two-yard veshti and shirt, both washed and dried at home but never ironed. He also wore a wrinkled coat over his shirt. Anyone might have asked why the coat was necessary. Raghuram was very thin. The coat was a close fit and made him look even spindlier. Only a deathbed vow could have compelled a man to wear a coat like that in the peak of summer.

I was surprised to learn that Raghuram, too, was a law graduate. How did these people, so educated and learned, end up loitering inside a cinema company, not knowing what to do with their time? I played the same game with Raghuram as I had with Vijaya Rao. When it was my turn to make the eighteenth move, I faced a double check: my king was under threat from two directions.

'Did you see that?' crowed Vijaya Rao, as if he was the one who had defeated me.

We started our game rather early the next day, at one o'clock. This time, Vijaya Rao started advising me, ostensibly to help me out. Although this annoyed me, I couldn't stop him. Game after game, Raghuram showed me up as a ludicrously inept chess player. My brute determination that I must somehow beat this Raghuram took me by surprise when I finally became aware of it. I had never seen even the lowliest employee in our company treating Raghuram with any respect. But what extraordinary genius resided in that man!

When I closed my eyes, only chessboard squares and pieces swam inside my head. In one position, two pieces were poised to attack the queen and block the king with a knight; in another, my bishop and queen were simultaneously trapped and floundering. The chessboard itself—at various levels and from various angles— stretched, shrank, bent and folded upon itself. Pieces moved of their own volition. Suddenly they stood up to attention. While a lone piece rose towards the sky, others sprouted legs like ants and crawled away. The sky itself turned into a gigantic chessboard, and various planets and stars became chess pieces. Now and again, jet planes streaked across the sky with a deafening roar.

The black king and white king guffawed loudly, snarled, even cried piteously from their injuries. The numberless permutations of a chess game came and went whenever I was half asleep or just drowsy. I found it impossible to forget and fall asleep. Wooden pieces, plastic pieces, ivory pieces and china pieces—all pursued me relentlessly. Openings that were impossible to win against kept appearing in my dreams and reveries. Yet, when I played a real game, I struggled, unable to recall any of them properly.

All the opening gambits I thought up after considerable effort, forgetting rest and forgoing sleep, were easily countered by Raghuram, who reliably defeated me every time. Vijaya Rao was now completely outside my awareness. In a way, even Raghuram, his stick-like limbs, and the coat that tightly gripped his thin, cadaverous body, had slid away from my consciousness. Chess games and pieces had become my whole life and world.

The strange thing was: no sty erupted in my eyes again. In fact my health was better than usual; although I went without sleep for weeks on end, I attended office regularly, experiencing no fatigue or exhaustion at any time. I would finish my professional duties for the day in just half an hour and wait for Raghuram to arrive. As soon as he came in, without even exchanging pleasantries, I would arrange the chess pieces on the board. At a shop selling second-hand books, I had picked up a chess book that had details of a game Napoleon had played with an officer when he was under custody in Elba and of several games he had played later in Helena with the governor of that island. I memorized all the games in that book. I tried out moves from every one of them against Raghuram. He, however, drove Napoleon to retreat right at the outset, acting like some latter-day incarnation of Wellington. For all his triumphs, Raghuram played his game in a laid-back manner, chewing paan, talking about old times, and getting up every now and then to spit betel juice from the upstairs veranda.

Holding my head in both hands, I would sit with my attention completely focused on the chessboard, not permitting anything to distract me. I would then proceed to lose in extremely humiliating ways. Having decided that the rest of my life would be spent solely in losing to Raghuram at chess, I lived with no thoughts of tomorrow. I could honour and accept my near and dear ones, family chores and professional duties, only in so far as they supported my chess playing. If someone had told me that my sole purpose in being born was to play chess with Raghuram, I wouldn't have argued.

That this was not true became clear during the next round of retrenchment in our company. Our boss sent even his secretary home. The savings from his departure would have been six or seven hundred rupees at the most. If the secretary himself was axed, how could his younger brother survive? Unsurprisingly, Raghuram too was given the pink slip. Later, all junior artistes on a monthly salary, including Vijaya Rao, had to go home.

I couldn't even think of my working life without Vijaya Rao and Raghuram. What would I do from eleven in the morning till six in the evening? What *could* I do? Raghuram didn't even drop by for a farewell visit. Why bother with bidding farewell to a man who kept losing horribly in chess, he might have thought. However, Vijaya Rao did come in to say goodbye.

Kohinoor became the place where I wandered like a ghost during the day. The bundles of old papers and books surrounding me seemed like fellow ghosts. There were no humans around to play chess with. For a day or two, I set up the pieces on the board and tried to play the game from both sides. Playing with Vijaya Rao seemed far better in comparison. After the downsizing, additional responsibilities came my way. In the alchemy that time wrought, I extricated myself gradually from the invasive hold of chess.

A few more changes occurred in the next two months. Having developed a distaste for cinema, I gave up my job. I lived in another city for a year. On Pongal that year, Tamils in that distant city celebrated 'Tamils Day' in a marriage hall. The screening of a recent Tamil film was a highlight of the celebrations. Vijaya Rao was in the film. He had not risen higher in life, it appeared. He was one of five or six patients who waited in a clinic for the doctor.

Within a month of my return to Madras, I saw a familiar face in a shop. Rather, a familiar *coat*: Raghuram.

'Raghuram, Raghuram! How are you? You went away without even saying goodbye! Where are you now?'

Raghuram showed scant regard for my excitement at seeing him. It seemed like he hardly recognized me.

I was unfazed, however. I asked him, 'Do you play chess these days? Whom do you play with?'

'Chess?'

'Yes. Chess. Even with your eyes closed, you could make champions and gladiators bite the dust.'

'Yes, I used to play a little. I haven't been keeping well. Even my hearing is somewhat dull.'

Only then did I realize that he was standing in a medical shop. No major changes were apparent in his body: still the same old string-bean physique. But there was an unhealthy intensity in his face.

'What happened?' I asked him.

'I am being treated for TB. I've had it for the last six months.'

'You?'

'Yes. I was coughing every night, so the doctor told me to bring an X-ray of my chest. When I did, he said it was a wonder that I was still alive. It seems that one lung had totally collapsed.'

'I am really sorry to hear this, Raghuram.'

'A whole lot of pills every day for the past six months. There's very little room in my stomach for food.'

I didn't laugh. I wrote his address down, telling him that I would meet him the following week.

When I went to his house, his elder brother told me that he had gone out to get a second X-ray done. Raghuram returned after seeing his doctor with the X-ray. There was doubt writ large on his face.

'Is it getting better?' I asked him.

'Better? The doctor says there's absolutely nothing wrong with me. He has asked for another X-ray.'

The riddle was solved when the third X-ray was taken. The first X-ray was not Raghuram's. It belonged to someone else who had come to that X-ray clinic on the same day.

His worries over, Raghuram became cheerful. Putting a handful of supari into his mouth, he said enthusiastically, 'Come, let's play a game.'

I went later to the X-ray clinic to inquire about the other person. Records going back six months were no longer available. I wondered which doctor that person might have gone to. Whichever doctor it was, he would have looked at the X-ray and told him that there was absolutely nothing wrong with him. With no further treatment, that person with a collapsed lung might have died within a week.

From the original Rajavukku Abatthu (1996)

Husband, Daughter, Son

When she spotted Shanmugam at the end of the street, Mangalam knew instantly that he had come with a message.

'Ramu Saar will be coming home late tonight. He sent me to inform you.'

'Why? Does he have to work late in the office?'

'In the office? They lock up the place at five o'clock sharp, 'ma. It seems he is going somewhere else.'

Mangalam glanced at the wall clock. It was half past four. 'You are going back to the office, aren't you?'

'Yes.'

'In that case, ask Ramu to come straight home today. If he has to visit someone, he can do it over the weekend.'

'He will have left by the time I reach.'

'Tell him if he is still there.'

'I will, if I see him. I'll tell him that you asked him to come home right away,' Shanmugam said and left.

One night last week, when Ramu had not come home even after eleven, Mangalam set out alone to inquire at a few places where she thought he might have gone. In the first two establishments, the lights were turned off and everyone had gone to sleep. The third was a 'recreation club' meant for card sessions. There too, the tables and chairs had been moved to a corner and stacked neatly, and the attendants were about to latch the front door. One of them said that Ramu had left at around eight that evening. Mangalam walked down the streets at that midnight hour, to see whether Ramu was standing somewhere near the bidi shops or idli-and-egg food carts which were still open for business. Only after she had returned home did she wonder if roaming the streets alone like that had been wise. She even felt afraid. She hadn't had a spot of gold on her person, but her assailant in the dark would have found out only later, and when he did, it would have only enraged him further.

Ramu did not come home that night. Despite herself, Mangalam had dozed off at dawn. The old woman who delivered milk to her house wore herself out knocking repeatedly on the door; eventually, she kept the packet on the doorway and left. The packet had leaked from a corner, and a small pool of milk had collected on the floor.

When Ramu finally returned home, children in the neighbouring houses were preparing to go to school, and the adults were about to leave for office. But Mangalam did not even ask him why he had stayed out all night. He had simply spread his mattress on the floor and flopped down on it.

There was a time when everything in their house was done at the right time and in the proper manner. Most outsiders would still remember Ramu's father as a fine person. He had organized the wedding of their first daughter, Lalitha, with such modest grace! Even the watchman at the wedding hall, who found a seat only in the fifth round of the wedding feast, was given the same attention as all other guests. A couple of relatives who had misplaced their umbrellas during the wedding were provided with two brand-new ones when they were returning home. The groom's parents had bought Ramu a gold ring as a ceremonial gift for the young brother-in-law. Ramu's father took the ring from him. He was fifteen then; he couldn't have known about the possibilities of gold ornaments.

But there were many other things people did not know. How Mangalam was forced to part with one piece of jewellery after another. Or how, after they had settled on a groom for their second daughter, Uma, Ramu's father had gone around asking all kinds of people for a loan of five thousand rupees on the eve of her engagement ceremony. It was even rumoured that someone had loaned him the money. But he had gone missing the next morning. When the groom's party arrived in the evening, he was nowhere to be found. The family looked for him first in the houses of relatives and friends, then at his office, and later in police stations and hospitals. He had vanished without a trace.

But over time they kept receiving random pieces of information: He had another family in the same town with a daughter of marriageable age. He had borrowed money from a lot of people—not small amounts, but one, two and five thousand. What did he do with all that money? He had not done much for his second wife either. In fact, he had taken some of her ornaments too and sold them.

Mangalam found it all puzzling. Who was this person she had lived with for so many years? Even after living together for twenty-five years, how could he keep so many secrets from her? Had he deliberately concealed his other life, or had she blinded herself to it? Could such a blind and ignorant woman ever retain her husband? Was that why he had run away?

Mangalam felt each moment of her married life rise to the surface from the abyss where it was buried a long time ago. He had coddled her too, scolded her, caressed her, and sought her advice. He had done things to please her on many occasions, tossed their children in the air and played with them, and stayed awake at night to give them medication. Why, when Uma was hospitalized, he had stayed up on the hospital veranda all night long. He had asked her to make his favourite ridge-gourd chutney every other day, sew buttons on his shirts, forbidden the 'dot kolam' in front of the house for some reason, blabbered all kinds of things in his sleep, lain ill for days, wept inconsolably at his mother's death, and cleaned up the cobwebs from the high corners of the house. But he had also, without her knowledge, lived with another woman and raised a daughter. He would have coddled that woman too, scolded her, sought her advice, tossed her little baby in the air, and cleaned up the cobwebs in that house. How had he found the time for all this? The energy? Above all, what had motivated him to engage in so many activities? Was he such a deep person, an incredible achiever? Where was he? What was his life like? Would she ever see him again?

Uma's wedding was called off. Ramu's education came to a halt. In those days, there was no correspondence course or evening college. You couldn't clear each paper separately. There were three parts, each with a set of papers. A student had to complete each part in its entirety in one go, and all three of them to graduate. If he could not attend college for some reason, it was the end of his education. Ramu started going to work.

For survival, the household had to depend on the salary from Ramu's job. His father's office had no option but to recognize that he was still alive. Without his signature of approval, they could not give Mangalam any monies that were due. Years later, even on the day of his superannuation from the job, they could not give the money accrued in his account to anyone without an official certificate that he was no longer alive. Uma found a job writing receipts in a chit fund company. Within two months of her daughter's new job, Mangalam learned through someone else that Uma had got married. She could not believe it. Uma had eaten that morning as if nothing out of the way had happened and carried some curd-rice for lunch. Mangalam had meant to ask her when she came home that evening, but she could not bring herself to do so. It was the same the next day, and the following day as well.

A fortnight later, when Uma told Mangalam on her own that she was going to set up home with her husband, the question still stuck in her throat. Mangalam didn't even ask whether her son-in law was young or old, vegetarian or a meat-eater. It seemed that Uma, too, never thought of telling her mother. She took away a few pots and pans from the house. Of the silver items collected over the years for Uma's wedding, only the small vermilion box was left. Of the stainless steel utensils, there were four or five. Uma didn't ask her mother for anything more by way of dowry. She also didn't volunteer any details about her husband or her marriage.

Mangalam complained to Lalitha once about Uma's conduct. 'What kind of a heartless girl is she? Am I a stranger? An enemy? Not one word to me, after all this! She said that she was leaving, but she didn't even tell me where she was going!'

Lalitha had come after a very long time. Her first child was born at her mother's place as per convention, but she hadn't visited Mangalam since the delivery. Now, it was her second child's third birthday.

'Even if she didn't breathe a word to me, she could have at least told you about it!' Mangalam sobbed.

Lalitha was silent for a while. Then she stood up. 'Uma did tell me before she got married,' she said.

'What?'

'Her plans to get married and move to a new house, she had told me about all that in advance.'

'What?'

'She'd told me. Ramu too.'

'The two of you knew everything; yet, no one told me?'

Lalitha stuck out her lip. Then she left.

Mangalam sat there for a long time, staring vacantly after her.

Ramu's health had deteriorated badly. His liver had never been strong; even as a child he had suffered from an inability to digest his food, and now his liver had been damaged further. When he lay in hospital for a month with an enlarged liver, Mangalam went for days without eating. But she stayed awake during the nights and cooked a convalescent's diet for him three times a day, waited endlessly for various specialists to ask them about Ramu's condition. None of the senior doctors spoke directly to her; they would tell other junior doctors, who would then abbreviate or alter the information before telling Mangalam. But one day, a senior doctor told her directly in Tamil: 'If your son continues to drink all kinds of rubbish and falls ill again, he won't survive.'

That time, Ramu had survived. But here he was, back on the path to becoming a chronic patient. But she still couldn't say to him: 'Ramu, stop drinking!' She didn't want a situation where she admitted knowledge of his drinking. In his presence, she couldn't even think of him as a drunkard. He too would want to believe that she didn't know, even though it was unlikely, given the extent of his addiction. He must act as if she didn't know; as if she didn't know and he didn't want her to know.

When the sun had risen, Mangalam stood gazing at her son who was lying unconscious on the floor. Whatever his other faults, his father had never come home drunk. She did not know how her husband had behaved with his mother. But in many ways, Ramu behaved just like his father. He never got irritated with her, nor shouted at her; but on many matters, he remained reticent and tight-lipped. He didn't breathe a word to her about Uma. She was not her daughter's enemy, was she? Wasn't she concerned about her daughter's welfare? But this had never occurred to either of them.

Even after the doctor had told them firmly that if Ramu started drinking again his life would be at great risk, he went off to drink. He must have arranged for the money from somewhere. At home, they were penniless, with poverty gnawing at them relentlessly. But somehow he found the money to spend on alcohol. Whereas she, on her part, had to regretfully throw away the food she had prepared for him.

'Ramu! Ramu!' she wanted to scream. 'Why do you torment me like this? No one in our family has ever died of drinking, da! Don't drink, da! For God's sake, stop drinking, da!' But because of the habit built over a lifetime, she could not enunciate a single word. For a long time, she could never look her son in the face. Only now, when he was asleep, was she able to look fully and directly at him.

This was how it had been with her husband. Now with her son, too? She felt a deep surge of sadness rise within, but she could not bring herself to weep.

From the original Kanavan, Magal, Magan (1989)

The Colours of Evil

A request from a small-town friend that I buy and mail him four law books opened up a whole new world for me. I discovered that the tomes which line the bookshelves that serve as a backdrop in the portraits of eminent judges and barristers aren't the only law books. Many publications did not have more than twenty or thirty pages. While some fat volumes were available for fifteen rupees, a few others, slim as a booklet of film songs, cost at least five rupees if not more. But above all, I learned that law books are not sold in all bookshops.

At first I looked all over, trying to find out where these special law books were available. This was not common knowledge even among those in the book trade. Finally someone told me to try Varadachary & Company on Linghi Chetty Street, a thoroughfare right opposite Madras High Court. The Government Law College was right next to the high court. With colleges, textbooks are a natural combination. Why didn't it strike me that there were probably shops selling law books in the vicinity of the high court? I even felt a little ashamed of myself. I went looking for Varadachary & Company.

Here, too, I must confess that I went *looking* for it. If a person with normal vision merely kept his eyes open, he would notice Linghi Chetty Street first and discover Varadachary & Co. almost immediately. But I stood in front of a shop and *asked* where Varadachary & Co. was. As it turned out, that very shop was Varadachary & Co. With my brain dulled from looking at glittering and showy signboards all the time, the signage of this shop hadn't caught my attention.

I felt diffident on entering the shop. Though I had stepped inside as if I was discovering the life source of the wicked magician in a Vikramaditya story, I could sense in every inch of that shop that thousands—nay, hundreds of thousands—of feet had walked inside it over the years. I've been living in this city for more than thirty-five years, but everything was still new to me!

The shop must have been very, very old. It wouldn't have surprised me if it had been established a hundred years ago. You cannot hide the age of an establishment no matter how hard you try. The doorstep might betray it, or a piece of furniture inside—a table, chair or cupboard—or the shade of the electric lamp that hangs from the ceiling. All that I chanced to see were clues to the shop's great age. When I walked in, only a couple of women were in the shop, looking after sales. They could have been

Varadachary's granddaughters, great-granddaughters, or even great-great-granddaughters. They probably worked there only because it was a family enterprise, and because they could never be seen working in any other office or commercial establishment. Since they had been brought up to be disciplined, they comported themselves with dignity and restraint. At the same time, their faces displayed an assurance that came from standing on their own ground, under a roof which was their own. Though they looked like a couple of children to me, I addressed them in respectful second-person plural and inquired about the law books I was searching for.

They had only three of the four books I needed. They told me that getting the fourth would be very difficult. I hadn't known until that day that those statutes, and books containing those statutes, even existed. But those children, who seemed to know everything, must have felt that telling me that the book would be *impossible* to get would be harsh, so they told me that procuring it would be *difficult*. One girl wrote a bill for the three books. The other took the hundred-rupee note I gave and returned the change. As I stepped out into the street with the bundle of books under my arm, I felt that my world had expanded greatly. I had barely walked ten steps along Linghi Chetty Street when I saw Anthony.

To say that I saw Anthony would be wrong. Dozens of people appear in front of a person walking on Linghi

Chetty Street at that hour. Just because these people are right in front of us, it doesn't mean that we see them. I didn't see Anthony; rather, it was he who spotted me first, and materialized in front of me, asking, 'How are you, saar?' Even at that point, I couldn't say that I saw him. Then he tilted his head very slightly to one side, and I recognized him immediately as Anthony. I too cried out, 'Anthony!' With my free hand, I grasped his shoulder. Passers-by on the street turned around and looked at both of us. In that moment, our meeting would have greatly expanded their worlds too.

Twenty years ago, when Anthony and I were twenty years younger, we worked in the same company. Anthony, Manickaraj, Manickavasagam, Munuswamy—all of them worked in my section. At a slight remove was one Nair. Although I was nominally their officer, we all did the same kind of work, the same amount.

Apart from them, our section comprised a small army of ten drivers, two cleaners, five members of a family who worked as sweepers, four members of another family who were employed as scavengers, nine watchmen and a dozen gardeners. We were accountable for the work done by this army. I must have written countless explanations for the jobs they had failed to do, and the ones they had fouled up! On top of those, applications for loans and for advances on salary, a moving letter of contrition for having been absent without permission for fifteen days, requisitions seeking leave for another fifteen days which were even more moving. I didn't write these applications with regular ink; rather, I wrote them with tears, salty as brine. No, that's not quite accurate. The letters were intended to bring tears to the reader's eyes, so it would be more precise to say that I wrote them with a pen dipped in onion juice.

Our sweepers, scavengers, drivers and gardeners faced the same hardships and sorrows that befell every human being. They were prey to ailments and diseases. Infants and old people in their homes passed away. They met with accidents and got injured. Sometimes, they had large, unforeseen expenditures to cope with. Though they appeared greatly troubled during those trying times, they recovered soon enough: they smiled, ate, slept soundly, had babies. Their supervisors—Manickaraj, Manickavasagam, Anthony and Munuswamy—and I, who supervised all of them, must have lived similarly.

On the surface, our economic conditions were much the same. All of us were perennially short of money. The signs of being half-starved showed on all our faces. Rising prices prevented our shortfalls from decreasing even slightly, and our salaries remained criminally low. So we applied for loans from the office, took advances on our salaries and, finding ourselves indigent even after all this borrowing, borrowed some more from outside sources. The five of us were somehow trapped in a situation where the risk of descending into insanity was ever-present. All the others had a direct relationship with the tools of their trade. We, who oversaw their work, were a flesh-and-blood presence among them, speaking and breathing in their midst. At the same time, the five of us were also connected to an invisible, phantom-like management through a telephone and via notes brought in by strangers, and we were accountable to this phantom at all hours.

This pressure of being accountable didn't torment the others the way it did the supervisors. Manickavasagam lost his mental balance once, and had to be tied down like a lunatic for months. Manickaraj handed in his resignation whenever he felt like it. Munuswamy kept up a constant chatter; it was his way of protecting himself.

Anthony was the only one among the supervisors who behaved normally. At the same time, he also managed to extract work from his subordinates through a combination of shouting and intimidation. From the beginning, my democratic instinct ensured that I never learned this method of yelling and threatening. Although I knew that for someone in my position this democratic instinct was sheer lunacy, I stubbornly refrained from intimidating anyone. This one factor kept the number of explanations I had to give to the management on a steadily rising curve, but I managed to go through my entire career without threatening anyone.

Anthony raised his voice quite often. But threats and shouts were useless. No threat could be carried to its logical end. And if you couldn't act upon it, you lost the little coercive power you had. Anthony knew this; in fact, everyone did. Yet he kept yelling at his subordinates. And he was far more successful in extracting work from everyone than I was.

We were more or less the same age. At the most, Anthony might have been older by a year or two. But he had been working there for many years before I joined. He had probably started when he was fifteen or sixteen. What kind of job could a fifteen-year-old from the slums of Narayanaswamy Thottam get? He couldn't have had much education. How much would they have paid him then? I felt very depressed whenever I thought of his life. But Anthony himself didn't seem to be weary.

Though it paid us less than a pittance, the company we worked for and its owner were highly reputed in the world outside. That was our boss's good fortune. Anthony got married before he turned twenty. When I joined work, he was a newly-wed groom. Within a few months after the birth of his first child, another was on the way. During her second delivery, that woman—how do I refer to his wife, as a woman or a girl?—developed fever and died within a day. The infant, too, died the next day.

Anthony and I did not begin to work together right away. After working for seven or eight years in all the sections, I was eventually forced to accept this assignment as super-maistry. By then Anthony, who was a deputy or assistant maistry, had already encountered the harsh tragedies of married life.

Now, I had run into Anthony while I was looking for the fourth law book, having already procured the other three. Though the figure who stood in front of me was a middle-aged man, I saw only the young Anthony who was compelled to bring his motherless three-year-old son along to work because the child couldn't be left in the care of anyone else. I couldn't imagine how I must have appeared to Anthony right then. It was possible he was thinking of my mother along with me. Once, inviting himself to my home, he came and removed all the cobwebs, dusted and cleaned the house. Then, during one Navaratri season, he brought coloured paper to decorate my house. I knew how to decorate a house by hanging colourful streamers but I had never done it because I felt that these decorations wouldn't be appropriate for the dolls we had. But when Anthony volunteered to do it, I couldn't turn him down. When I saw the colours on the sheets he had brought with him, I was taken aback. I couldn't have thought of a more bizarre colour combination even in my wildest fantasies.

But I reimbursed the entire amount for the decorations Anthony put up that year. Through the ten days of that Navaratri, I nursed a severe and relentless headache. The moment I stepped into my house, Anthony's colours robbed me of my appetite. I felt ravenously hungry, but my mind was repulsed by the very idea of food. But all this didn't blind me to Anthony's concern for me.

Even at work, the liberties he took with me led to embarrassment and, on a few occasions, to big, nasty rows. In those days, workers were still considered servants. Like all owners of large enterprises, my boss was terribly suspicious of trade unions and the labour legislation proposed by the then government. 'Union' and 'communist' were dangerous words to utter if we wished to hold on to our jobs. At any rate, after prolonged and bitter disputes, our company was forced to comply with a few sections of the labour statutes enacted by the government. These covered drivers. One by one, regulations concerning their working hours, pay scales, dearness allowance and overtime pay came into effect. Until then the management had not given the slightest thought to the worker, his mealtimes and his weekly holiday; and they continued to remain thoughtless in such matters out of sheer habit. Since our senior officers had no grasp at all of these regulations, people like us, who supervised these workers directly, had a hard time. Compared to what drivers earned elsewhere, our men were poorly paid. Nevertheless, their earnings were higher than ours. When the eight-hour day was first implemented, they would abandon their cars wherever they happened to be and go away for lunch. Similarly, they would walk off promptly at the stroke of three in the afternoon. All the resulting confusion landed on my head, and I had to deal with it all the time. The management started to get concerned over this issue. Our boss was forced to invite the leader of the All-Madras Trade Union, of which our drivers were members, for negotiations. They agreed on the following arrangement: drivers on the morning shift would be relieved for lunch at 11 a.m.; if they were out on duty at that time, then they would be relieved next at noon; if they couldn't be freed even then, the office would give them a lunch allowance. How much? Ten annas. Or sixty-two paise, according to the new decimal system.

This sixty-two paise deal might have appeased the drivers. But it created terrible bitterness among the four supervisors: Manickaraj, Manickavasagam, Anthony and Munuswamy. They earned very low salaries to begin with; and they too could not, on most days, get away for lunch at eleven or even twelve. But they were not entitled to the sixty-two paise. Yet these same deprived supervisors had to rush to the accounts section exactly at five past twelve, draw the money and disburse it to the drivers!

This issue led to many other complications. Whenever an officer of the company was provided transport, he was told to keep to the eleven-to-twelve lunch schedule (and it fell to us to remind him). The drivers felt as if we had punched them in the stomach. As a result the rift between the workers and us widened. Officers who went out on official duty snapped at us when they were informed of the time restriction. Even when their job was over and they were ready to return by eleven, their vehicles began having starting trouble; or being held up on the way by a procession. We, the supervisors, were given clear instructions: avoid paying the lunch allowance at all costs. Our drivers had just one goal: get the allowance by any means.

I drafted many applications for Anthony. Big loans, small loans, salary advance, advance payment, moving explanations for not reporting to work for a week or ten days, complaint to the inspector-general of police about the drunken and disorderly behaviour of some rowdy in Narayanaswamy Thottam, a letter seeking financial assistance from a Christian institution in San Thome to meet medical and educational expenses for his son, a letter of apology for failure to pay an instalment on the plot of land allotted to him by the Housing Board under its scheme for weaker sections. During that time, when our rancour and mutual hostility was growing over this sixty-two paise problem, Anthony asked me one day to write out a fresh application, more like a petition, for him. Though he was responsible for supervising the work of over forty people, his designation was still 'office boy'. Let them do away with this 'boy' business. Let them call me 'worker', or 'cleaner', or 'street sweeper'. Let them call me a clerk and increase my salary. But not this lowly 'boy', not any more.

Maybe the designation 'boy' was no longer appropriate or desirable. But I could not put down the alternatives suggested by Anthony with any apparent justification. I told him that we should let the management decide. But Anthony didn't agree and wanted somehow to get into one of the cadres which were governed by labour laws and protected by the trade union. 'But why do you want to be called a "clerk"?' Clerks were not covered by trade unions in those days.

Our petitions, and even protests in person, didn't yield any result. The management had a reply ready for every kind of grievance. If we asked them how they expected us to get along on such low salaries and with so few amenities, they cited other companies where workers were paid even less. And then they had their trump card: the threat of a lockout.

Now, even Anthony and I fell into bitter arguments. Both of us knew that there was no personal animosity, but his sudden disappearances and absences landed me in difficulties beyond the limits of endurance. Since I had no intention of betraying Anthony or any of the other 'boys' to the management, I was stuck in the office for ten or twelve hours every day. Manickavasagam, though he regularly came to work, would find ghosts in one corner and demons in another. Hiding under a bench or chair, he would loudly appeal to all the gods. One day, the racket he made brought a passing policeman to our office; he wanted to investigate. We sent word to Manickavasagam's people, but no one turned up. We heard that his behaviour was no different at home. Manickaraj handed in his resignation almost every other day. Munuswamy's relentless monologues were no longer a source of amusement to us; they caused terrible headaches. Often, when I found myself alone, I would bury my head in both hands and wish fervently for my life to cease right then.

Money, money which was always short, the self-imposed decree that I should never renege on my word to anyone, acting on behalf of the boss and in his interest regardless of whether he was right or wrong, the effort to appear cheerful without letting anyone know the hardships and sorrows that racked me. One awful day, I heard myself scream: 'Aiyo!' Two drivers who were nearby helped me up and sat me down. But I collapsed again and fell down limp as a heap of rags. One minute. Just one minute, that was all. The list of people who were to be allotted vehicles that day appeared in front of my eyes. And the overtime statement for drivers which I had to compile and dispatch that day. And the sheet of paper on which drivers put down their signatures after collecting their sixty-two paise. And the wedding invitation of scavenger Rajaiah's daughter and the contributors' list we had circulated to collect money for a wedding gift. I stood up. All the people who were around me moved away as if nothing extraordinary had happened.

Reflecting with some sense of awe on the power that work and habit exercised over man's behaviour, I sat down in my chair and resumed my regular duties.

Anthony was not in the office the day this happened: it was his weekly day off. Manickaraj, who was supposed to be my assistant in Anthony's absence, had gone off to have darsanam of a holy man who was in town for a few days. Anthony came in to work the next day and at the very first opportunity asked, 'Saar, I heard you fainted yesterday?'

I replied, 'Why, no!' It was true that I had felt giddy, but I was conscious throughout. In fact, one could even say that my self-awareness had been somewhat intense.

Anthony stood there looking at me. Just a couple of days earlier, we had had a nasty row. It was that same sixty-two paise issue again. One of the drivers had taken a rupee and given Anthony change. It was a paisa short because the poor man just didn't have the exact amount. Anthony had yelled at him, and as if to get even, the driver had taken the next three days off. We had a hard time because replacements were not easy to find. 'Will your home be drowned in a deluge if he gives you a paisa less?' I had asked Anthony. He accused me of supporting the drivers all the time and not doing a damn thing for the 'boys'. We went on repeating this acrimoniously over and over again, louder and louder each time, till our vocal chords felt as though they were close to being torn apart.

Now Anthony looked at me intently. 'Saar. Just go away from this place, saar,' he told me.

'Why?'

'Don't stay here, saar. This place is not good for you.'

'I'll suddenly be in luck if I leave this place, will I?'

'It can't be worse, saar.'

'Why do you say that?'

'There are lots of spirits in this place, saar.'

I felt a sudden jolt. Manickavasagam was the one who kept screaming of demons and ghosts. Had something happened to our normally sober Anthony too?

'What are you saying, Anthony? What ghosts? What spirits? There's nothing of that kind.'

'You are Hindu, saar, and you talk like this? There are five or six right here. Manickavasagam hasn't gone crazy, saar. It's these spirits who are chasing him around.'

'Why don't they chase everybody?'

'They do, saar, they do. They give each one a different kind of trouble. You know these rows I have with you? I abuse you freely? Do you think I do all this on my own? No, saar. It's all out and out the devil's work.'

'Then surely it's just as easy to say that everything is the devil's work?'

'The devil doesn't do everything, saar. It does only whatever is required to change a man into a devil. So far, no devil has even come close to you. But now it will. The day you fall into a faint, you are possessed from that very day. Or you will be.'

'You talk as if you know a lot about this. Have you ever seen a ghost?'

Anthony looked at me with contempt. 'I'm telling you for your own good, saar. I can't stand by and watch you go to ruin. That's why I'm telling you. From now on, you are going to faint again and again. Every single day. You don't faint for no reason, saar.'

Some work came up in the meantime and he had to leave. By then I was really angry. I wanted to grab him by the collar and deliver a couple of blows or punches. Until then, I had known him as a young man who had had the courage to stand up for his rights, an intelligent, hard-working man who was forced to accept his station as a humble office 'boy' because he had not been able to afford a decent education. Now that he revealed himself as someone who knew about demons and ghosts, it seemed to add a whole new dimension to him. Even though it had been a rough day for me as usual, Anthony's warning drifted back into my consciousness again and again.

When he was getting ready to go home after his shift, I sent for him. 'Anthony, tell me again what you were saying this morning.'

In those five or six hours, his speech had lost its keen edge. But a certain sobriety and resoluteness of manner had taken its place. 'Exactly what I told you earlier, saar. A spirit is going to possess you.'

Earlier, because I had been taken unawares by the sudden turn in conversation, I had been a little perplexed. But now I was more lucid. 'What is the name of that spirit, Anthony?'

'Spirits don't have names, saar. But they all share certain traits. They can't stand human beings. They can't bear to see people laughing, they can't bear to see people happy.'

'We are not exactly laughing and enjoying ourselves here.'

'How can we be happy after a spirit has come here, saar?'

'Have you ever seen a spirit?'

Anthony tried to leave without answering this question, just as he had done earlier.

'Anthony,' I called him. He stopped.

'Do you want to know which the real devil is? This arrangement which decides who will be rich and who will be poor; who the boss and who the servant; who the paymaster and who the labourer—that is the real devil. But for this devil, you and I and everybody, even if we are half-starved, can manage to be happy. But this devil has been around for many thousands of years. And it is growing more monstrous by the minute. If we can liquidate this devil, all the others you talk about will die on their own. And if they can't die, they will vanish into thin air. People keep talking of methods with which to kill this big devil. They say that they have already killed it in a few places. Some day we'll succeed in killing it here too. That's what I believe.'

To Anthony I must have sounded like I was already possessed. He went away.

Although I had bravely held forth on the subject, I often felt giddy and even blacked out for one or two seconds every now and then. I kept telling myself: this is not the devil's doing, not his doing at all. Anthony began treating me like a sworn enemy. If one does not heed another's genuine concern perhaps this kind of rancour is inevitable. Even when things weren't going his way, Anthony could be firm and authoritative; I had admired him for this quality. Now with all his talk about ghosts and spirits, I began to feel a mixture of awe and respect for him. It was Navaratri season again. If Anthony had not harboured enmity against me, I might have given him ten rupees and asked him to decorate my house. But he kept harassing me so relentlessly that I couldn't expect to be comfortable with him ever again.

Gradually, belief in the existence of evil spirits began to take root in me.

It was a time when prohibition was still in force; when policemen conducted themselves like they were supposed to. People who quietly drank at home and went to bed ran little risk of getting caught. But those who ventured out in a drunken state, rarely, if ever, escaped the attention of the police. That day when Anthony came in, he was quite sober. But within five minutes of his arrival, he snuck away somewhere for a drink and came back tipsy. Maybe he had brought a bottle with him and was swigging from it on the sly. There was a fairly heavy inflow of visitors to our office. Somebody in his line of work could not possibly be drunk on duty. He had hoped to keep it a secret.

I took Anthony by the hand and dragged him away to a corner. 'You don't have to totter around trying to prove something. Just go and lie down in the tools room, if it is all right with you,' I told him.

He tried to resist, flung his arms wildly, but after that one gesture of defiance, he calmed down. He lay down in the tools room like I told him to for the better part of that day. At the end of his shift, he came to my table just before leaving and stood staring at me. I was immersed in work: to me, at that moment, Anthony simply didn't exist. He lost his temper and blurted out, 'I went home today.'

'Oh, and where have you been living all these days? On the pavement?'

'I meant your home, saar.'

'Why did you go to my house? I don't even want to talk to you any more.'

He went away. I seethed in anger. Why should this fellow visit my house?

I found out only after I reached home. That year too, he had decorated my house for the Navaratri kolu. My mother had insisted on paying him in spite of his protests. I don't know what had possessed him because, right after that exertion, he had bought himself some illicit liquor. When I saw his handiwork, I felt anger and pity in turns. His decorations never had any special aesthetic quality. Given his meagre resources and experience, it was unlikely that he could have grasped things such as unity, harmony and contrast between colours. Still, his imagination and a kind of craft were evident. Many people of a similar station in life might not have had even the faintest idea of decoration. But his mind seemed to have a few recesses where some primitive aesthetic discrimination still functioned.

Though I had slaved like a dog and worked like an ox that day, sleep didn't come to me easily. All the lights in our house were turned off, but a street lamp lent a faint illumination to the front room. That was where we had set up the kolu. The arrangement of dolls at our home never followed a plan or organized structure. The lion often nestled close to the Taj Mahal, and Naradar, the puranic sage, stood right beside this mausoleum. Anthony's paper buntings that hung over the rows of dolls appeared eerie in that half-light. What a bizarre combination of colours!

Suddenly I felt that Anthony's choice of colours was trying to tell me something. Though professionals would have dismissed his handiwork as a product of ignorance,

I had a hunch that something imperceptible was hidden there. In the semi-darkness, his coloured streamers seemed to be mysteriously animated. I recalled his warning. Spirits! Anthony was warning me: Watch out, there's a ghost here! But then, could he really be acquainted with ghosts? Why had he not replied when I asked him if he had ever seen one? Why did he get angry? Had he brought those ghosts here, into my house?

I felt angry at the direction of my thoughts. I also felt ashamed of myself. There has never been a logical explanation to validate the possible existence of ghosts. One advances two or three steps along the way as you try to explain it, saying, 'That's right, that's right' at each step, and when the explanation reaches the fourth step, the whole edifice collapses. Perhaps it is for this reason alone that people who believe in ghosts withdraw from any argument on the subject.

Although I tried to reason with myself, Anthony's decoration seemed to have brought an unusual significance to the kolu which had, until then, never meant a thing to me. The old terracotta dolls became a source of terror. Anthony's paper buntings wafted from the ceiling as if bestowing strange powers of devastation on the dolls.

One by one, all the old ghost stories which I had heard years ago came back to me. I was surprised that someone like me, always an indifferent listener to such tales, had registered so much. Each story took shape and expanded in my mind without skipping even the most trivial detail. After a point, I stopped straining and resisting; I let my mind go where it would. I must have fallen asleep, because later I couldn't remember anything beyond that stage.

But on the following day, I felt quite sure that there was no connection between Anthony's buntings and the world of spirits. Somehow I felt that way when I heard about the fortunate turn of events in his life. He was getting married again. Uncertain whether this was going to be a happy event or a tragedy, Anthony had got very drunk.

It had been so many years since Narayanaswamy Thottam had turned into a slum area that nobody could visualize its earlier incarnation as a garden. Dozens of Anthony's relatives, both paternal and maternal, lived there. It is possible for a man who has lost his wife early in life to pass his days peacefully, bringing up his child. But surrounded by relatives as he was, Anthony could not avoid getting married again. All his relatives had one or more daughters. Anthony must have cited some fairly good reasons to have put off the inevitable for so long. But even he could not do it forever. Anthony must have decided on some girl or the other just to put an end to being nagged every day by four middle-aged women with marriageable daughters,

It was from the day he decided to marry again that Anthony started drinking regularly. I wondered where he found the money for it. For as long as I had known him, he always came walking to work, his pockets invariably empty. Even when he had fought for and won his right to an hour of lunch recess, he spent the entire duration sitting under a tree; I never saw him eat anything.

On the salary each of us earned, we led lives more or less similar to Anthony's. Had his wife been alive, she might have sent him off to work with a lunch packet. He should marry again at least for that reason. But if he started drinking like this, the next meal might become harder to come by.

He did not invite any of us to his wedding. But I wrote out something like an invitation on a sheet of paper and used it to collect gift money. The collection did not quite reach the sum of fifty rupees. At the time, we could buy a couple of vessels with that amount. Though none of us attended the wedding, I had arranged for the vessels to be delivered to his house two days later; but finally, I had to deliver them myself. I walked all the way to Narayanaswamy Thottam, but when I reached his house, Anthony was not there. Hearing someone ask for him, a woman emerged from another hut nearby. She turned out to be Anthony's new bride. I handed over the vessels to her and returned home. The reason for Anthony's taking to drink seemed vaguely apparent to me.

The bride was a mature woman, perhaps even older than Anthony. She looked educated. She must have had expectations from her husband and their life together. I might have been awed by Anthony, but all those qualities which I considered special, would they seem special to her as well?

He had made no effort at all to clinch this alliance. If a man lived in an area crowded with hordes of relatives, many decisions regarding his life were inevitably taken by these people. Perhaps they had reasoned that the girl's father would be rid of at least one burden. Perhaps it had been a case of genuine compassion for a man who was struggling to bring up a motherless child by himself. But what difference did all these reasons make to a mature young lady, a self-assured woman with expectations from life? Anthony must have sensed all this. Yet all his relatives had ganged up and got him married to this girl.

What a stickler for rules he had been! His entitlements and rights were so few. But he would never compromise on any of them. He would not remain in the office for even a moment after the stroke of eleven. If he was given a task even a second before the clock showed twelve, he would walk off as if he hadn't heard anything. A pity that all this didn't count for much with his aunt, uncle, grandmother and grand-uncle.

Anthony didn't turn up for work in new clothes the day he rejoined duty. Sometimes we tend to distress ourselves with imaginings. In truth, reality does contain possibilities of pleasure; I had hoped that this would be the case with Anthony. Instead, he became even more difficult to deal with, and started drinking heavily. Against all odds, his bride delivered a baby: a daughter. Another baby followed the next year: a son. It was around this time that I took permanent leave of that haunted office.

Twenty years later, here was Anthony again, walking down Linghi Chetty Street. I had sighted him maybe a couple of times during those two decades. He too might have seen me around. But on those previous occasions, we probably hadn't had the opportunity to stop and chat. He might have been standing inside a bus while I pedalled away on my bicycle; he might have been dawdling near Mount Road Post Office just as I emerged from the offices of Sudesamitran on the other side of the road. Dozens of buses, cars and scooters must have sped by noisily between us, in both directions. Above all, neither of us might have had the time for reminiscences. Or, there might have been strong reasons to avoid them. It does take some time for memories to cease gnawing at the heart. But now, I was just as glad at meeting Anthony as he was at running into me. Our appearance seemed to convey everything without either of us needing to ask the other how the past twenty years had been. Most of my colleagues from those days invariably said after the first round of inquiries were over: 'Buy me a cup of coffee, will you? Do you have three rupees to spare, I owe the eye doctor nine rupees.'

I asked Anthony, 'How are you, Anthony? Anything I can do for you?'

He was wearing an old, faded shirt, worn trousers and a tattered pair of chappals. His face was craggy and knotted like a dried-up yam. The way he spoke, squinting his eyes hard, suggested that he was postponing the purchase of a new pair of spectacles. He said, 'I don't need anything, saar. How are you?'

The dense traffic congestion on Linghi Chetty Street was entirely undeserving of bearing witness to the reunion of two long-lost friends. We climbed on to the front steps of a shop.

After a brief exchange of pleasantries I asked him, 'What are you doing these days, Anthony?'

'Now I am not doing anything much, saar. I got rid of that cursed job the year after you left. For fifteen years I slogged for them, losing my wife and child in the process; but when I left, they didn't even give me a thousand rupees, saar.'

'But then, they paid very low salaries, didn't they?'

'How they skimped on paying us ten annas for a mid-day meal!'

'You still remember all that?'

'Those scoundrels. The owner and his sons kept spending the whole loot on all the whores in town, built mansion after mansion for them, bought them cars. And the petty buggers were so stingy about giving us ten annas; made enemies out of good people like us. That's why they're going to be ruined, with nothing left for the next generation.'

'What is your son doing?'

'Those rascals, they have the heartburn and agony of so many workers on their heads! Their whole line will become useless and lie stinking in the gutters, you'll see!'

'Is your son employed?'

'Yes, saar. He is a fitter in a factory in Guindy Industrial Estate. He is married, even has a child now.'

'Why did you get him married off so young?'

'How will he manage for food, saar? I got him married to my elder brother-in-law's daughter.'

'Why? Is he not staying with you?'

'No, saar. You know that fine woman I got married to the second time? She chased him out of the house when he was barely ten.'

'Has he been working since then? From the age of ten?'

'No, saar. You know I have an aunt who lived near Chinnamalai? I took him to her and gave her fifty rupees a month to take care of him.'

'Then?'

'I was employed, see? Right here, on this street. I finished sixteen years' service and retired. When I retired, do you know how much that Marwari gave me?'

'How would I know?'

'Twenty-five thousand, saar. And where I worked with you for fifteen years? That owner fellow gave me eight hundred when I left. This man gave me twenty-five thousand rupees. I have kept five thousand aside for my elder daughter's wedding. The rest, I've lent here and there on interest.'

'On interest?'

'It's all safe, saar. Don't worry. I've lent it on pledges: house, plot of land, property, things like that. What are your sons doing, saar?'

I was proud of him. Even when hardships and tragedies pile up on you and recovery seems impossible, if you don't collapse entirely and hold on for a bit, isn't it true that the factors you hadn't taken into account until then find a way to bring you relief?

We left that shopfront and moved to another.

'That second marriage, that's what gave me no end of trouble, saar. She ran away three times. My people went and dragged her back. Now she lives by herself in Narayanaswamy Thottam. I live in Periyamedu.'

'She must have been possessed.'

Anthony screwed up his face. 'How can there be devils there, in that house, saar? If you come up to Greenways Road, yes, sure. Or on the other side, near the Adyar bridge. There are no spirits in Narayanaswamy Thottam, saar.'

As I kept looking at Anthony, I felt a surge of happiness. The Anthony I had known had been a victim of scarcity without reprieve; half-starved or worse most of the time, he had looked at the world with hate-filled eyes and been ready to destroy himself and take the world along with him to ruin. But now, all this was informed by a certain beauty and passion. It is not essential for a man to be affluent to love this world. Perhaps affluence in itself would make such love impossible. But if a man wants to hold on to his pride while he goes hungry, then everyone he comes across becomes his enemy. He must destroy them, at least in his mind.

'You told me that there were ghosts where we used to work. Do you remember that, Anthony?'

'Yes, saar. That place was full of ghosts. Not just there, but all around. Near Sun Theatre. Many inside that park. And on this side, that gramophone company's compound.'

'All those are not the real devils, Anthony. The condition where you find yourself without money, when you can't feed yourself or your children properly, that is the genuine devil. Poverty is the real spirit of evil.'

Anthony stood there, listening to my words out of respect for me. We were forced to abandon the front steps of this shop too. Along with the noonday sun, the traffic on Linghi Chetty Street had also reached a peak. Rainwater from a recent downpour, together with water from a blocked underground sewer somewhere, flowed down the street. People held down their natural sense of revulsion and continued walking. Some who didn't wish to step into the dirty water, climbed up and down the front steps of the shops along the pavement and found us in their way. Then I remembered the fourth law book I had to find. If I could get hold of that soon, I could send all four books in the day's mail.

'You worked right on this street, you said?'

'Yes, saar. Pratap Company.'

'Where can you buy law books around here?'

'Varadachary & Company, saar. Right over there.'

'I've just been there. I got three of the four books I wanted. Couldn't find the fourth one.'

'Try Seetharaman Store, saar.'

'Where is it? Around here?'

'No, saar, not here. It is in Royapettah.'

'On Pycroft's Road?'

'It is near Ajantha, saar, Ajantha. You know Ajantha Hotel?'

'Yes.'

'It's near the hotel. Go there, and anyone will show you the way.'

This was yet another aspect to the new Anthony. His world had grown big enough to include knowledge of shops where you could buy law books in the city of Madras.

'You told me about the Thousand Lights area. Are there ghosts here too?'

'Where, saar?'

'Here, in China Bazaar, in George Town.'

'Plenty, saar. You know that tree and the public lavatory near Flower Bazaar Police Station? You will find dozens there. Here also, near the Law College gate. The high court compound gate in front of Raja Annamalai Hall. There were many right here, saar, on this street. They brought those buildings down, and all the ghosts went away.'

'Then, do you mean to tell me that all the people here are dancing to the tune of ghosts?'

'Not quite like that, saar. Ghosts don't go to everyone. Have a cup of tea, saar?'

We went to a small tea stall and ordered two cups. Once again, I noticed the stream of sewage on the street. Before I could cancel the order, the boy from the stall had given Anthony two cups.

But the tea tasted nice. When I offered to pay for it, Anthony stopped me with a firm hand. I couldn't wait to get out of the street. Perhaps Anthony had some work here. Or he might have wanted to meet someone else. He occupied the front steps of yet another shop.

'I'll be going, Anthony. I am so glad to have met you.'

'Me, too, saar. I've often thought of coming to your house. But your mother passed away, and I didn't visit you then. I felt awkward about visiting you after.'

'You knew that my mother passed away?'

'Yes, saar. I knew.'

'These days, we do not set up our kolu grandly or anything like that.'

'Is that so, saar?'

'But I often think about it, the times you used to come home and put up the decorations. How did you select colour paper like that?'

'Like what, saar?'

'You remember your Navaratri decorations?'

'Yes, saar.'

'Do you always use those colours?'

'No, saar. I worked out what colours to use in your house before I bought the paper.'

'Do these colours differ from house to house?'

'Yes, saar. Colours for one house won't be right for another.'

'What do you mean by "not right"?'

'Yes, saar. No good at all.'

'Why?'

Anthony paused for half a second. Then he asked me, 'Shall I tell you why, saar?'

'That's why I'm asking, can't you see?'

'There are ghosts even in your house, saar.'

Now I stood silent for a while. All kinds of memories and thoughts exploded within me; they soared, collided against one another and got tangled up. What Anthony said just might be true. I too had a weapon in my armoury. I used it.

'Anthony, have you ever seen a ghost?'

Anthony gave me a wonderful smile.

'Have you actually seen a ghost?'

He gave no reply, evading my question, just as he had done the last time.

From the original Vannangal (1985)

Evolution

'You didn't know about Suguna's concert, did you? She sang yesterday,' Thyagarajan told me in Hindi.

'Where?'

'In Indiranagar, at the Guptas'. I went there expecting to meet you.'

Thyagarajan's interest in me wasn't founded solely on my musical prowess. My brother, Harikrishnan, is a commission agent. Thyagarajan bought cut-piece pant lengths through him at a heavy discount in Godown Street, and sold them to customers on an instalment purchase plan. He earned some five or six rupees per piece.

When I finally managed to shake him off and came out, I felt the sting of the sun's heat on my face. At forty, I was still prone to acne-like eruptions. If even a handkerchief came into contact with these pimples it was sheer torture, an agony so extreme that it inspired hatred for life itself.

A similar feeling engulfed my heart when I thought about how I never got a chance to sing an attentive audience into raptures in spite of all that I knew of music. My students might show me great deference and respect, but the thrill of listening to them sing even a tiny piece of what I had taught them, and seeing an audience shake their heads in approbation—that experience eluded me. I don't usually dwell on disappointments, but then along comes someone like Suguna to give the lie to such delusions.

I went to a nearby shop to make a telephone call.

The shopkeeper reached under the cash box and put the instrument on the counter. 'Don't make it too long, seth,' he said.

I moved the telephone to one end of the counter. It was difficult to dial the number with my torso squeezed and neck extended into that cramped space. In an effort to distract myself, I fished out a one-rupee coin from my pocket and placed it on the counter. If you wanted to make a call from one of those shops, the shopkeeper would always admonish first: 'Don't touch the telephone unless you have a rupee in change!' If you handed over the coin to him right at the beginning though, he might even give you change for a ten-rupee note afterwards.

As usual, there was no ringtone the first time. I waited a little before I dialled again, carefully this time, my neck aching all the while. The telephone rang at the other end. Alert, ready, I waited to begin the conversation. I stayed that way for a long time, but the telephone just kept on ringing.

I took the coin back from the shopkeeper and stepped on to the street. The sun had grown harsher, but my anger at Suguna had subsided a little.

I boarded a crowded bus at the terminus; paid seventy paise for the ticket and travelled standing all the way. When I entered the bungalow, I asked the servant boy who came to the veranda if his mistress was at home. He went in, and within a couple of minutes, Annapurna emerged.

'Oh, Master! When did you come? Did I keep you waiting?' She must have come directly from the kitchen. There was a dusting of wheat flour on the back of her hand.

'I spent half an hour trying to get you on the phone and couldn't get through. So I thought I'd drop by.'

'Is that so? I don't think there were any calls this afternoon.'

'The phone kept ringing, but there was no answer.'

Annapurna remained silent, reluctant to leave any room for further argument. Perhaps the roti on the stove was burned by now.

'When can we have the class?'

Annapurna said clearly, 'Not today, Master. I have another half an hour's work to do. How can I possibly keep you waiting?'

'If it's only for half an hour, it doesn't really matter. I'll wait here. If we miss today's class, then we can't have one for another fortnight.'

'Are you going out of town?'

'Yes,' I lied.

She went inside to finish her cooking. I turned on the fan in the hall and leaned back comfortably on the sofa.

Annapurna's son and daughter emerged from within the house. Both were wearing jeans. The son walked past me as though I wasn't there; the daughter smiled weakly at me on her way out. When the son started his motorcycle, the racket sounded like a plane was taking off right next to me.

I closed my eyes, but sleep eluded me. My life was now reduced to running after middle-aged women and waiting endlessly in their living rooms. Not one of my disciples was on the right side of forty.

Each woman had a husband, children, a household, difficulties in finding a cook, elections at the Guild of Service, the marriage of her husband's niece, shooting pains on the left side of her lower abdomen . . . And in the face of all these obstacles, I had to teach them Hindustani classical music—which demanded absolute precision in every note—well enough for them to give a solo vocal concert. Each displayed a different degree of passion for this singing-on-the-stage business. Take Annapurna. She might have felt: 'Why all this singing-winging? Why in the name of god did I get myself into this?' She had floundered her way through two whole years; finally her voice was seasoned. She had a natural gift for music. If only she had

had the urge to develop, to grow, she could have given several concerts by now. But she was too lazy to learn. She had persevered at finding a cook. In the past four months she had asked everyone she knew—including me—to look out for one. She had once mentioned to me that she had won awards at the national level twice for excellence in calendar design. She was an expert in many other fields. And she was very meticulous about preparing lunch for her husband. In a short while, it would be sent to his office in a tiffin carrier. She was cooking now only for his sake.

The servant brought a glass of hot milk, placed on a china saucer. Annapurna had added a little milk masala to it. It didn't seem likely that she would be done with her work in thirty minutes.

This time I was determined to take a nap. If I closed my eyes and focused on the spot between my brows, I was sure I would soon feel the cool hands of slumber. A music teacher couldn't possibly avoid situations in which he had to wait for indefinite periods, and they occurred quite frequently. If he held classes in his own house, he could make his students wait. But even after twenty years in this profession, I did not have a place of my own. If I wished to continue living with my brother, his wife, her mother, and their three children without causing them further inconvenience, giving music lessons in their two-room flat was out of the question. I could spend a hundred or two hundred rupees to rent a classroom in a school or some such place. There were many teachers who did that, but then I would end up with a group of students who were heterogeneous in talent and interest. And my star pupils at the moment—Mrs Gupta, Annapurna, Suguna and Mrs Kartar—would never be able to imagine, even in their wildest dreams, that they could learn music from such lessons and actually give stage concerts. And where did Suguna fit in?

I knew that sleep was beyond me. Brooding about Suguna would keep me awake. I had known her since before she became my student. We were in college together. She was fat even in those days, but in spite of that, she had set many hearts aflutter. I didn't know then that I would become a music teacher, and all she knew about music was that it was a cinematic device that carried the hero's yodelling past hill and dale and all types of terrain to his lady love, and caused her immediately to yodel back.

Three or four years ago, we met unexpectedly in Madras. I recognized her first. Our second chance meeting was at the Guptas' where she discovered that Mrs Gupta was learning Hindustani music. If Mrs Gupta could sing, why couldn't she? Who was her teacher? 'Oh, it's you! You actually teach music? Since when?'

Like all affluent people, Suguna too had just two children. If all Indians were affluent, we would have no need for this family planning propaganda. She had two sons. The younger one took piano and guitar lessons, while the elder thought that music was for layabouts. One day he said so to his mother in my presence, no less. From that day, Suguna got into a frenzy. She asked me if I could give her lessons daily, but I could manage only twice a week at the most. There were moments when I detected a different style in her singing, but she always corrected herself. Within a year, she had attained a degree of mastery that normally took six years. It seemed as if she was trying to prove that even she was accomplished.

'Master, are you sleeping?' asked Annapurna. She was a Kannadiga. All manner of people in Madras spoke to me in Hindi, invariably mixing up gender and turning the singular into the plural. But Annapurna spoke only Tamil to me, of which she knew very little. If things got a little out of hand, she switched to English. With great ease she held on to rigid orthodoxy and extreme sophistication as though it were the most natural thing in the world.

I picked up the tanpura. It must have been at least ten days since she had last touched it. I laid it across my lap and tuned the strings. For a moment, I felt the sadistic urge to make Annapurna weep helpless tears of rage. No one else could make a woman weep as easily as her music teacher could, not even her husband. You well-fed fat cow, see what I'll do to you today!

I felt a little frightened at this rage and hatred that seethed inside me. These middle-aged women, empowered by the vast experience of their years, had conspired to play volleyball with me. Three punches from this team. Three from their opponents. Then, three more from this team. Again, three from the other. I had become a plaything for them, to push around as they pleased! I stopped strumming the tanpura and glowered at Annapurna. She gave me a bewildered look.

'How did you like Suguna's concert?' I asked her.

'Which concert, Master?'

'Does she sing that often?'

'You're asking *me*, Master? You would know, surely?'

'All right, how was yesterday's concert?'

'Where, Master?'

'At Mrs Gupta's house, obviously.'

'But there was no concert, Master!'

'Suguna didn't sing there? But Thyagarajan told me!'

'Which Thyagarajan, Master? I don't know anybody by that name! Mrs Gupta gave a small dinner because she got elected president this year. There were just ten or twelve of us.'

'But does Suguna's singing call for more than a dozen in the audience?'

'No, it was no concert, Master. She sang. I sang too. Mrs Gupta sang. If you really think about it, it was your concert, Master. Only your students sang.'

'Who played the tabla?'

'Mr Gupta himself, Master. It was all very comic. That man can't keep a beat.'

If I had told her that even if it happened exactly as she had described it, it still didn't mean what she thought it did, she wouldn't understand. She didn't know Suguna like I did. Her goals were of one kind; and Suguna's, quite another.

I lay the tanpura aside. 'Let's not have the class today,' I said.

'Why, Master?' Annapurna's question was close to a plea.

'I'm giving up teaching and going away.'

Here was this formidable woman, who managed investments worth lakhs and occupied positions of power which decided the fate of many people, *waiting* to listen to my next bout of ranting and raving. Consider the range and variety of her life, its intricacies, its power to affect the lives of other people! That she was giving so much time and attention to this music class was totally puzzling. How grateful I ought to have felt! For all she knew, music would bring her no special distinction.

I stood up to leave. She rose too, reluctant to insist any further. Poor thing, how she must have rushed through her chores in the kitchen for my sake!

'So, when can we have the next class, Master? When do you leave on your trip?'

'Oh, I'm not going anywhere. Well . . . yes, I am . . . I am going away forever.'

She fell silent again.

'Forgive me, Annapurna. I am not feeling well today.'

'But why, Master? I knew it. You can't let a thing like this affect you.'

'You don't know how badly I've been betrayed.'

'Nobody has betrayed you, Master. You are always present in our minds when we sing. You are the inspiration, the source of all our knowledge. We owe you everything, Master.'

'You don't know, Annapurna . . .'

'Master, if I see tears in your eyes, I am going to break down.'

I regained my composure. Annapurna led me by the hand and sat me down on a sofa. She had guessed that my legs were too weak to allow me to stand for a long time.

A shadow moved across the doorway. Annapurna left me and went in the direction of the kitchen. I wiped my face with my handkerchief and came to the front hall. There was a uniformed man standing in a corner. One could have photographed us together—me in my faded, crumpled kurta admiring his dazzling white uniform, like in a soap advertisement with the caption: Lightning Bright! He looked at me and offered a small, defensive smile. I raised my hand to indicate that he could rest easy, and went to the veranda. A little while later the man in uniform went out with a tiffin carrier in his hand. Annapurna followed him. 'Oh, here you are, Master! I was looking for you inside,' she said.

'I'll come here next Monday. Is that okay?' I asked her.

She hesitated for a moment, then said, 'Yes, Master.'

I had already taken a step on my way out, when Annapurna said, 'Master, no one will ever betray you.'

'You are good-hearted, Annapurna, that's why you think no one will betray me. But from time immemorial, students have always betrayed their masters. Perhaps talent does not evolve and attain greatness unless the guru is betrayed. Perhaps they seek to atone for this sin by offering constant worship, praise and obeisance to the guru. I didn't betray my guru; that's why I have to wander around like this in the heat and rain, just to make a living.'

It was clear to me that although Annapurna was listening, she was not prepared to accept a word of what I was saying. Suddenly my respect for her went up a notch. If only she showed a little more interest in her music, she could sing at the national festivals of music in a couple of years from now. But her superior imagination did not lean even slightly in the direction of her talent.

'Suguna didn't sing for nothing, Annapurna. She probably sang only for fifteen minutes yesterday, but it was a rehearsal for something else. This Sahadev will not have anything to do with that concert.'

Annapurna stood in silence, apparently exasperated with me.

'You made me wait because you were cooking a meal for your husband. No, I shouldn't say that; I chose to wait.

Suguna invited me home one day and kept me waiting for a long time. When she came finally, she said she had a headache and an upset stomach, so I left. I walked down the street and stood on the main road for my bus. I was there for a long time. Then she passed by in her car; I thought she might have been visiting the doctor; I suspected nothing. But I learned the very next day that she had gone to a recording theatre, and from there to a shooting. Her headache and upset stomach had vanished. Do you want to know how? That Sanjeevi—you know, that violinist?—had promised her that he would recommend her to Poornachandra Rao and arrange for her to sing in films. Someone must have told her that Sahadev Master was no good if she wanted to sing in films. Now Violin Sanjeevi is her master.'

The impassive look on Annapurna's face seemed to say, 'But I know this already, you silly ass!'

How tough these women were!

For some reason, I thought of my brother's wife. From the unending nagging of an eighty-year-old hag to the ceaseless bawling of a three-year-old, she coped with everything; she toiled hard without reprieve in a dark room among seven or eight people. How tough she was. Has she ever once made a single remark about anyone, I wondered. And what a fine voice she has! Could she find the time to sing even for five minutes at a stretch? Was she ever free to do that? Didn't she have desires, too? Did she know that she was growing old . . . running out of time? How did these people spend all their lives doing these mundane, thankless chores with such amazing resilience and dedication?

Then with a great noise that seemed to shake the whole neighbourhood, that monstrous motorcycle bearing Annapurna's son and daughter entered the street and stopped in front of the gate. Annapurna ran to let them in. Their hair was in complete disarray.

It amazed me that Annapurna, through simply opening the gate and letting the children in, was able to create so much liveliness. They spoke no more than five or six words. The mother laughed once, the children also laughed with her. The place instantly assumed a radiance that excluded all possibilities of anxiety, rancour or rage.

This time too the son looked through me, but the daughter gave me a hint of a smile. It seemed to me that this young lady's smile was no less extraordinary than the enigmatic silence with which Annapurna had met my outburst.

From the original Virutti (1985)

Waiting in the Dark

He stumbled his way to the pot, drank a little water and went back to his chair. As the water trickled down his throat his load seemed to grow a little lighter. He even felt like having a bite, but all he had in the house was the pot of water. If he wanted to eat, he would have to venture out.

The urge to eat passed, and he continued to sit there. He wondered if keeping the house completely dark with all the lights off would actually make it invisible. Even when the street lights had been turned out and none of the lights in any of the neighbouring houses were on, you could still recognize the houses. Rather vividly, he thought. Then why did he bother with a self-imposed blackout? What purpose did it serve?

Unable to find a convincing reason, he got up, intending to turn on the lights. But such lucidity left him, and he sat down again. Light would certainly betray his isolation; he had not turned off the lights because he believed it would make his house invisible. Darkness, with its opaque, almost solid presence, was like an ally. Inside the envelope of darkness, he would not appear to his enemies as merely himself: alone, without friends, bereft of strength, fearful, and entirely incapable of averting the imminent calamity of defeat; instead, he would seem to them (he thought) as someone dangerous, fearsome, and in possession of unpredictable tactical possibilities for sudden and swift retaliation. Of course, he was none of these things in reality, but because the situation made it possible for him to appear as such, he should do nothing to change it.

He was waiting. Even from a hundred yards away, he could hear the sounds of ordinary life, which seemed to be going on as usual. Car horns, the sounds of bicycle bells, warning clangs of metal against metal at a railway crossing, the sound of big buses slowing to take a sharp turn and then revving their engines, the clatter of an unloaded pushcart, the steady drone of scooters and autorickshaws, the hoof-taps of a cow let loose for the night. If it was a cow, it must have been pregnant; a battened beast if it was a bull. From just listening to the sounds, he was able to tell the front hooves from the hind ones—even after the animal had passed his house. The street was plunged in darkness and silence yet again.

In that vast ocean of a city, where small, feeble sounds reached him across an ineffable distance, his own street floated like a hermetic bubble. Unable to bear the silence that had engulfed the outside world any longer, he wondered if he should let out a loud scream.

He had been able to scream and shout: he had screamed till his vocal chords were inflamed, shouted for hours on end. Innumerable loudspeakers across town had amplified the sound of his screams many times over and the noise had dulled everyone's hearing. Even tonight, sitting in the dark, he could hear the sounds coming from a few loudspeakers. Film songs were being played at a higher rpm, and the resultant high-pitched squeals, when amplified into the air, made the wind blow even colder.

When poor people hired a sound system and a few records for a day of celebration, perhaps a wedding, they played the same songs over and over again. If the person handling the sound system had a favourite song, it was repeated endlessly, bringing on an unrelieved sense of tedium. But this was not a wedding day; this was a day to celebrate victory. He was not a participant in that revelry; he had been left to sit here, alone in the dark, in the hushed silence, with his house blacked out, his throat parched, and his hungry stomach fed continually with the consolation of idle rumination.

Yesterday had also been a day of jubilation: garlands, processions, wall posters, loudspeakers and records, and the distribution of sweets. Yesterday, too, he had remained a non-participant in these goings-on. Yesterday, he had been a man who could despise these vulgar shows of triumph, who could give voice to his hostility; he was out in the open, out where there was light. The speeches he had delivered; the pamphlets he had penned; the favours he had sought from voters; the hopes he had nurtured in his heart; the efforts he had put into building a cadre of propaganda workers who could confidently enter bungalows and huts to plead their point of view forcefully, a view that he had created in them through relentless tutoring in slogans, appeals, arguments and counter-arguments (he had taken money for expenses occasionally, but more often than not he had spent money out of his own pocket to assemble his cadre for these classes) . . . After all that effort had suddenly become superfluous and meaningless, every little sound was terribly jarring; the open air made him gasp for breath, and all the things of this world stung his eyes with their radiance and made him squint.

Even after such profound changes had occurred in him, when he had stepped out—having trimmed the ends of his moustache as usual and put on a thick, white, cotton veshti and a shirt with a towel thrown over his shoulder—on to familiar streets, streets which had grown even more familiar in the recent past, streets where people he had met only last week—not just met but had smiled at, talked to and pleaded with—were still going about, he too felt that nothing had really changed anywhere.

After deliberately avoiding the morning's newspapers, he had reached a stage where he could not bear it any more, and so he set out to buy one. Since not a single copy was left unsold in any of the news-stands, he looked everywhere desperately, as if reading the newspaper was the only thing that would ensure his survival into the next moment, and reached a public reading room. There, he gathered the loose, out-of-sequence pages of newspapers—which had been taken apart to satisfy many readers at the same time—and read them line by line before returning home. His wife, her brother, and his four little children had nothing to say to him—they went about in a kind of drowsy wakefulness while he, out of sheer habit, sat down on the kitchen floor and quietly ate what his wife served him. He went off to sleep immediately after eating, without a thought in his head, without a vestige of hope. Sleeping on his side with his head resting on his right elbow caused a lot of perspiration on his face and neck. When the sweating became profuse enough to disturb even deep slumber, he woke up. His right hand was numb. He got up, washed his face and sat down in his chair. His wife's manner had not changed: she was silent. Her brother, who thought he was something of a grown-up because he was in his late teens, also did not say anything. But the children had already started chattering and playing about. They even came over to him, wanting to be cuddled. He could not stand it, nor could he bring himself to scold them for disturbing him. So he put on his shirt and went out. Outside, the revelries and celebrations were building up on a grand scale. It was clear that they would continue for the next few days.

Everyone on the street was full of joy. Even two days ago, there had been no sign that this result would cause such jubilation among the people. No, it was only that he hadn't read any of the signs correctly, and this made him angry with himself. Today was the outcome of yesterday, as tomorrow would be today's. He could not quite understand yesterday, so today surprised him. He wondered whether the things he saw, including himself, were real. He wasn't so much annoyed by reality as by his failure to see it for what it was. This made him bitter.

On the streets, the crowds were larger than usual. They were much more voluble today than they had ever been. Visibly less intent on listening to what others had to say, they were all trying to participate through their talk in the significance of the day. He had no one to talk to, so he made his own path and reached the thatched shed where, even as recently as yesterday, he had collected people, met and talked to them, made decisions, read books and journals, taken his meals and quenched his thirst. It stood on one side of the road, unclaimed by anyone, like an orphan. All the slogans, names, appeals and angry tirades—some written, some pasted and others hung on the sides and over the roof of the thatched shed—seemed meaningless today. In fact, they seemed to mock him as a deaf and blind fool for having based his passions and actions on those very words, an utterly meaningless exercise. Somebody had carried the bench away. He was a little surprised, and consoled, that they hadn't torn down the whole shed yet. He felt like drinking another cup of tea, although he had just had one at home. So he walked into a tea shop. That cramped little establishment had four tables squeezed into it, with four chairs around each table. He felt relieved for a moment when he saw no one familiar.

But as though he needed to be reminded of reality once again, one of the customers called out, 'Thondar is here, da. Have a look at him.'

He was startled, but without letting it show, he said, 'A cup of tea.'

'What's the matter, thondarey? He didn't pour you some tea today?'

He simply sat there, ignoring this taunt.

'That scoundrel, all holy with his streaks of ash, the one who kept stuffing you with biryani . . . what happened to him today, eh? He couldn't pour a little tea for you?'

A fellow who appeared to be the owner of the tea shop protested; 'Look, let's not talk politics here!'

'What a hassle! Even when you go to the barber shop, the fellow there tells you not to talk politics. What's so special about your tea shop, da? Why not here? Don't politicians drink tea?'

The boy brought tea in a cup and saucer and placed it in front of him. The owner came to him and said in a low whisper, 'Why don't you drink up quickly and leave, please? You could have sent for it, the boy would have brought it to you.'

'What, man? What does our thondar say?'

He got up to leave; he hadn't had even a sip.

'What, man? A fellow is asking you something with respect, and you're so arrogant you ignore him and walk away?'

He had started on his way out; he even had one foot on the doorstep when the fellow who had been taunting him rushed out to face him, yelling insults. He abused his tormentor in turn. In the five-minute fisticuffs that ensued, no one was really hurt. Fists which had intended to deliver mean punches never connected with their targets, crashing instead into various other objects in various other spots.

Other men at the tea shop broke up the fight. He walked home at a brisk pace. His wife was upset when she saw his torn shirt and dishevelled hair. 'Look, why don't you lie low for the next couple of days at least,' she begged. He cursed his attackers. 'Bloody rogues! They had to come in a gang to beat me up. Come on, da! Come one by one, if you dare. I'll break your limbs and hand them back to you!' he shouted. His wife's brother stood there looking bewildered. His wife tried to cover his mouth with her hands, pleading all the while, 'No, please. Don't.' His children, who had been playing outside, came home then, along with two or three other children from the neighbourhood. To the children, it had seemed at first like a routine quarrel between their parents; they clutched their mother's sari and stood there gaping. Once they sensed it was something else they moved away and stood silently. He wanted most of all to chase those neighbourhood children away, but some impulse kept him from bullying them out of his house.

Though he stayed at home, he could feel the mood of jubilation growing. Evening had turned into night. Lamps were lit. The street lamp in front of his small house, together with the lights from neighbouring mansions, lit up the street. His wife gave him a pointed look as she prepared to feed the children. Then, without calling him to eat, she served her brother and the children their evening meal. Afterwards, the children played, singing out the slogans they had heard and read for weeks—vazhga, veezhga, annachi, ennachi, and so on—and then the chugging of a railway engine in motion, and then film songs. After whiling away their time in these noisy capers, they curled up, each child in a different corner of the coir mat, and went to sleep. As soon as the sound of the news in English started drifting in from a radio set somewhere, his wife called him to eat. He sat down in front of his plate; then he remembered how, earlier that evening, he had walked away from his cup of tea without taking a single sip.

He was ravenously hungry. Though he knew for certain that there would be nothing left for his wife after he was through, he asked for more rice and gulped it down. He found that his fatigue was gone; his head had cleared and he felt a new strength. He could hear people talking in the street. Even at eleven o'clock at night, people were known to walk on that street, mostly on their way to or from a film. They normally talked to one another as they walked, but because the town was usually asleep by then, they always seemed to be talking too loudly. Tonight, however, the sounds were different.

'Dei! Come on out!' a voice rang out, calling out to him by his caste name. Following that, there was the sound of furious banging on his front door. Something landed on the thatched roof with a thud, perhaps a stone.

His wife stood paralysed, gripped by an extreme sense of panic. One of the children woke up and screamed. She knelt down immediately and covered the child's mouth with her palm.

'Come on out, you coward!' the voice demanded again.

He turned to his brother-in-law, who was standing there with a long wooden staff in his hand. He took the staff from him.

His wife begged him in a hushed whisper: 'Don't, please. Don't go out now.' She gathered her children from the mat and held them close. He went to the door at the back. 'Don't go out. Please,' she begged again. 'Stop him,' she ordered her brother. As the boy came towards him, he glared at him—that was enough to stop the boy in his tracks. They became aware of the lights in the neighbouring houses being turned off suddenly. He opened the back door and tiptoed away in the shadowy region along the wall. The area was dark except for his house and the street lamp. Then the light in his house went off.

He crept along the wall and came to the front of the house. Three people stood there: one of them was a boy who could not have been fifteen yet; he was smoking a bidi. Another one of the men held a casuarina stick in his hand. He leapt on them with a blood-curdling yell. With his first wild swing, he knocked away the casuarina stick.

They too let out answering war cries. His brother-in-law also entered the fray, twirling a stick menacingly with his wrist. The three assailants ran howling to the end of the street; they stopped there and threw stones.

He and his brother-in-law sped down the street, swinging their sticks ferociously and growling at their enemies. He screamed: 'Give me the knife, da. If any fellow dares to come forward, I'll chop his head off.' They stood at one end of the street while their attackers lingered at the other, blocking the street. The houses lining both sides of the street seemed uninhabited, lifeless in the night. There wasn't even the sound of a radio.

He kept shouting, 'Come on, da! You bunch of hired thugs! Come on, da!' His assailants howled from the other end of the street and hurled stones at them constantly, even though the distance was too great for the missiles to reach their target. Suddenly they ran away. He dropped his stick and ran after them. The reason for the attackers' flight was immediately obvious: two policemen on bicycles were approaching the street.

He and his brother-in-law remained in the middle of the street. One policeman asked him, 'What, man? What is this noise about?'

'They were trying to break into my house and attack me, saar,' he said.

'Who are those fellows, man?'

'Who came to your house? Who is this boy? What's that in his hand?

'My machaan, saar. These fellows came to finish me off, that too in my own house!'

'What's that in his hand, man? Sami! Drag these fellows off to the station. This is a big nuisance nowadays.'

'But we didn't do anything,' saar. Those fellows came to my house to beat me up.'

'Then why is there a stick in *his* hand? You, get them to the station, quick!'

Only when they started out for the police station did he notice that the street lamp in front of his house had been put out.

He did not sleep a wink till his wife came to the police station the next morning. Her face was swollen from weeping and fright; she couldn't have slept at all. Her brother had managed somehow to curl up in a corner and catch some sleep.

They let him go. But his brother-in-law was held back. He took his wife and children to a relative's house and left them there. She wept and pleaded with him to stay with them in the safety of the house. She begged him to go and see this person and that. To go and see the big leader he had worked for, and tell all the leaders about the attack. Even though she could see from his face that he would not do any of this, she still kept entreating him. He left her there, came straight home and locked himself in. That people on the street were still going about their usual jobs seemed to belie the bizarre incident that had occurred right there only a few hours ago. There was no trace of the fracas, nor did any of them stop him to inquire about it.

Even at that late hour, he could hear a film song blaring away somewhere. Before, it had been a medley of songs from five or six different loudspeakers in the locality, combined and distorted into an amorphous cacophony; now he heard just a lone song playing. A woman's voice bragged: 'I am a man to match any man.' He was famished and his throat was parched. He listened to each word keenly. Suddenly he felt the urge to sit among the audience in some movie house where a Tamil film was playing.

He could probably slip away and get to a theatre without anyone knowing about it. Should he? What if he did?

He could, certainly. But what would that solve? Here was this boy, not yet twenty years old, locked up in a cell, probably curled up in a corner there. And to think that he had never treated the boy right, never spoken to him as though he mattered. Poor boy. Had he ever thought of taking him out to a film?

Again he felt the urge to scream out loud. If he did, people would certainly hear him. But who would bother to answer his call for help at this hour? The people who should have come to his aid had not come at all. His wife had implored him to go and see everyone he knew. 'You worked day and night for that man . . . go and see him now,' she had pleaded. 'Go to him and he will arrange bail for my brother,' she had said. Still he couldn't bring himself to call on that man. By then, he must surely have heard the news. He could have got into his car and come over, but he hadn't. So what if he had lost the election? He could have come over to see him anyway, but he hadn't. He too was probably lying low. Lying all beaten down in his easy chair, hardly talking to anyone and not at all inclined—no, not *brave* enough—to read the newspapers. So vexed that he was snapping at the children playing about in his house. Betraying his impatience with those who came to offer their sympathies and with those who came only to use the telephone, and ending the misery of their company with a few curt words of dismissal as though he was lying on a bed of thorns. Perhaps a few journalists turned up to interview him. Would they? Now? Yes, one or two obscure ones at least. He would tell them: 'A great injustice has been done.' Injustice, where *he* was concerned. And what was this great injustice? He must have spent a few thousand rupees without a second thought in the past two or three weeks; if he had won, he would have got those few thousands back many times over. For him, this was the only real difference between victory and defeat. He didn't have to sit alone in the dark, expecting his head to be smashed in at any moment, his bones to be broken, his children to be attacked, to lose his very life. If something untoward happened, he could call the police. The police were bound to turn up, at least for the sake of appearances.

Even if they did not do anything by way of help or protection, the very sight of a police helmet near the house signified something else altogether. 'Go to the police station and explain everything,' his wife had told him. Her father had said the same thing. Fie on her face, her father's face, and the wretched face of that whole stupid crowd. Did they think the police would come readily, just like that, to protect someone like him? What had happened last night? *Those men* had had sticks, *they* were screaming and shouting, but it was *he*, along with his brother-in-law, who had to flop down for the night on that cold cement floor! Her bloody face. Useless bloody face. Fifteen years she had lived with him, but she couldn't understand this simple situation for what it was! She knew enough to crawl over to him late at night on her hands and knees, without disturbing the sleeping children who lay between them, once every four days, but did that mean she knew everything? Idiot-face. Damn fool. Clay head!

No, that wasn't fair. Poor thing, how could she have known anything about this? After all, he had never shared anything with her, had never explained things, never asked her opinion on anything. She in her own way understood what she took to be his actions, his hopes and his aspirations in the context of her limited world, and acted accordingly. He had never truly shared anything with her, except for that business, once every four days.

His hand shook with the urge to turn on the light. Were all his hopes and aspirations to be reduced to this . . . this waiting in the dark? Such great hopes, principles, aspirations! We are going to change the face of the world: equality in life and opportunity, and justice for all! He felt like laughing out aloud. He had not managed to treat his wife as an equal but he would establish equality in this vast world! He couldn't count on four people to stand by him at a time like this, yet he was going to change the world!

But was this something that could be faced with four others by his side? Could he summon them saying,

'They are going to beat me up. Why don't you join me and get beaten up too?' Yesterday, three of them had come to attack him. Today, there could be seven or eight. Yesterday, because he'd had the boy with him, he could chase them away. Today, if he had even one or two men fighting with him, together they could hit back. But those six or seven today might grow to ten or twelve tomorrow.

It soothed him to analyse other things instead of thinking about his wife. He was able to think of those things with a cool mind, without unnecessarily losing his grip on himself, without getting emotional. The men who had come yesterday would probably turn up with another four today. Yesterday, only one of them had brandished a stick. Today, all of them might be armed with sticks. They would attack him for his ideas, his hopes, his principles, and for the insult they imagined he was heaping on them through these ideas.

He stumbled again in the dark for a drink of water. Even the sound of the film songs had ceased. It was probably past eleven. Why were there no visitors yet? Perhaps they were not going to come tonight. Yesterday, they had come and gone before the neighbourhood cinema had begun. The show must be close to the intermission right now. Perhaps they planned to come here afterwards. If the matter had been concluded yesterday, he might have got off lightly—a broken hand, a leg or a rib, at the most. They never hit anyone on the head. Generally these hired goons only broke a limb or two. There'd been just three men, one of them no more than a boy. With a bidi in his hand, the boy couldn't have done much damage. They had even managed to hit those goons once or twice. Even if the blows had not been heavy, they would have been enough to bring on a frenzied desire for revenge. Perhaps, if his brother-in-law had not joined in, he wouldn't have had to wait like this. But he hadn't summoned his brother-in-law; the boy had come to his aid on his own. Perhaps today, no one else was as angry as the boy had been. Perhaps he wasn't enough of a man to bring on that kind of rage. Aiyo! Was that really true?

'Come on, you thugs, come! Hurry up!' he screamed aloud. At that moment it seemed far more preferable to fight like an animal, trading murderous blows, than to keep pondering on all manner of things in order to arrive at fresh discoveries about the world. 'Come on, come on, come on,' he chanted without pausing for breath, steeling his heart for whatever lay ahead. Since his mind had never before experienced such coercion, he fell asleep despite himself, still sitting. Not ten minutes passed before the first stone landed on his thatched roof.

From the original Kattiruttal (1971)

Deliverance

When they reached home, only the street lights were still awake. Saraswathi involuntarily felt around her waist for the door key. Only then did she realize that she was carrying the baby. Fast asleep, the child was clutching her blouse tightly with her fingers. She didn't find the key in its usual place, tucked into the waist fold of her sari.

She adjusted the baby's head on her shoulder and groped in her carry bag for the key. Her fingers found a jumble of random objects: a cheap towel, several wet rags, a stainless steel tumbler and a spoon. She also found a small paper pouch; she had wrapped the prasadam given after the puja a short while ago in a scrap of paper. The key was missing.

Her husband spat out the tobacco in his mouth and asked her, 'Where is the key, di?' If the key was not found in the next few seconds, he would certainly start shouting at her.

Saraswathi searched for the key with mounting anxiety. The child was about to slide off her shoulder and fall down; so she straightened up abruptly. There was a clinking sound, as though there was something inside the tumbler. She felt inside it; the key was in it.

As soon as they entered the house, Saraswathi looked for the matchbox and lit the lantern. After laying the baby on the floor, she set down the plate for her husband's dinner. Leftovers from the morning meal—rice and kuzhambu—had remained intact in their containers. Where could all the rats have disappeared to suddenly, she wondered.

Her husband rinsed his mouth and sat down to eat. Saraswathi carefully served the rice on his plate and poured two ladles of kuzhambu over it. A minute later, her husband looked up and scowled at her. 'The appalams finished this morning,' she told him.

After her husband finished eating, Saraswathi sat down to eat. The kuzhambu had a sediment of chickpeas, along with a few stones. When she was done, she cleaned the floor, and washed, dried and put away the vessels. While taking water from the metal container, she took extra care not to bang the tumbler against its narrow neck. The landlady had shouted at her once for handling her vessels noisily at night.

Her husband was already asleep, his mouth open and snoring loudly. The baby was also asleep. She couldn't feed the baby the milk she normally did at bedtime. She had last given the baby some milk at around half past seven or eight in the house where they had gone for the puja. Now the baby was fast asleep. She could wake the child, but it invariably cried while drinking milk. Then her husband would wake up too.

Saraswathi covered the milk sombu with a small plate and secured it further by inverting a large vessel over it. She then folded an old sari into four, spread it on the floor and lay down beside the sleeping child. The wick in the earthen lamp had been lowered as much as possible, but even that dim light dazzled her eyes.

She shut her eyes and began to silently recite the few slokams she knew by heart. '*Apasarba sarba badhramde dhooram kacha mahayachaha,*' she mouthed. According to her aunt, chanting this slokam protected a person from snakes. Saraswathi had never ever seen a snake, then why did she recite it? Perhaps it was her constant chanting that had kept the snakes at bay.

Thinking of snakes made her recall the prasadam she had brought home from the puja. As soon as they had arrived, she had emptied the bag of its contents, washed both dirty nappies and hung them out to dry. She had kept the packet of prasadam on top of the vessel in which she had set the curd. She and her husband had gone to attend a community puja in someone's house. Her husband was not given to pujas and prayers. His life comprised little else besides betel leaf, nut and tobacco, his monthly salary of one hundred and thirty-five rupees, cough and fever once a fortnight, one elder sister and two younger ones, testiness and anger, occasional bouts of physical violence, reading all the serials in the Tamil pulp magazines, the monthly rent of twenty-two rupees, being cordial and quarrelsome by turns with the landlord, going to the cinema once a week.

Returning earlier than usual from the office that evening, he had told her abruptly, 'We are going for a puja. Get ready, quickly!' He had spent one rupee and thirty paise on puja materials such as coconut and flowers, and fifty-two paise for the bus fare. After they got married and set up house on their own, he had never taken Saraswathi to the temple or to pujas. In the house where the puja was being held, everyone paid obeisance to an old, venerable man. His face exuded a kind of radiance. They said that he was a man of divine gifts, a mahaan who knew the past, present and future, and there was no human predicament he couldn't resolve with his blessing. Saraswathi had touched the mahaan's feet and then sat down in a corner in the women's section of the audience. Just looking at the man's face made her blissfully happy. Every now and then, someone went up to him and said a few words. The way he listened to them attentively and replied in one or two words seemed beautiful to her. The puja was being performed in the next room. When the ceremony with lighted lamps was over, they distributed vibhuti, kungumam and prasadam. Saraswathi wrapped them up in a packet. It did occur to her that she was putting them away along with the baby's soiled rags, but she couldn't help it. With the baby on one shoulder and a bag in her other hand, how could she carry a packet separately?

The lamp's small flame sputtered once and then dimmed. Saraswathi looked at her sleeping husband. His mouth was still open. Lying spreadeagled on his stomach, he looked as though he was flying off somewhere. His jamakkalam and blanket were pushed to a corner in the violent disorder of his sleep. Instantly, compassion and pity for him flowed inside her. How could this man, who now slept so unaware of himself, have abused her in front of ten or fifteen people for not running after the bus when she was burdened with the baby and the bag? When they had left for home after the puja, it was already close to ten. They were barely fifty yards from the bus stop when their bus arrived. Hitching up his veshti, her husband had sprinted and managed to get on to the bus. Saraswathi had walked as fast she could, but the bag had extra-long handles, so it hung low to the ground and kept bumping on the road and against her shins. The street was badly lit. There was a large crowd at the bus stop. Not even half of them had clambered aboard when the conductor shouted, 'No room!' and blew his whistle. The bus began to move. Saraswathi scarcely knew how she had run after it. The bus, which had taken off at great speed, stopped abruptly a short distance ahead, and her husband jumped out after a frantic struggle through the milling crowd. The corner of his veshti got caught under someone's toes. The conductor on his part let loose choice abuses. It was only then that Saraswathi had reached the bus stop. Her husband shouted at her so vilely that her ears stung. If there hadn't been people about, he might have even hit her. The next bus followed soon enough; this one wasn't so crowded. After she got on to the bus, Saraswathi became aware of the growing dampness around her toes. She looked down and realized that she had stubbed her big toe; and that her injured foot was trailing blood.

Saraswathi woke with a start. She had dropped off to sleep. Thank god the child had not woken up. As soon as it made the slightest sound, she had to give it milk. But where was the feeding bottle?

Saraswathi shook off her somnolent state and hurried to the kitchen with the lamp. The feeding bottle wasn't in the alcove where it was normally kept. She ransacked the bag she had taken along that evening. She had emptied it right after they reached home. Where was the bottle? She must have left it behind at the puja. She felt a sharp pang of fear. The child was only used to the bottle. Saraswathi had bought it for one and a half rupees, and now she had left it behind. How could anyone forget a baby's feeding bottle? Soon the child would wake up hungry and cry. What was she going to do?

She turned a big brass pot upside down and stood on it, trying to reach a packing crate in the loft. It was rather big and out of her reach. Among the worthless junk in that crate was an old-fashioned silver conch for feeding the baby. Since the box was made of planks nailed together, she was sure to find plenty of cockroaches and moths. The conch would smell, and she wouldn't be able to get rid of the odour easily.

Saraswathi couldn't even budge the crate. Her foot slipped and she fell as the brass pot tumbled and rolled noisily along the floor. Along with it came her husband's voice with a kind of tremor: 'Who is that? What's that noise?' The child woke up as well.

'It's nothing! Just me,' Saraswathi replied quickly. She stood the pot upright and straightened her sari. The child called out, 'Amma!' She removed the wet cloth from under the baby and after spreading another sheet on her lap, she laid the child on it. The child began to cry. Saraswathi picked up the tumbler of milk and pinched the baby's nostrils between her two fingers. The child opened its mouth wide in order to breathe and she poured the milk into its mouth. The child choked, spluttered and wailed even louder.

Her husband called out, 'Ei, what's all this?'

'The baby is drinking milk,' she replied.

'Stop that racket!'

'She's almost finished.'

'Useless bitch can't even *feed* the child, let alone stop its crying! Ei, stop that!'

'Just one minute, there's only half the tumbler left.' But the child screamed and wailed really loudly this time as it choked on the milk again.

Seeing the ferocity with which her husband leapt up from his bed, Saraswathi bowed her head. The first blow fell on the back of her head. Even though it caught her only on the tip of her ear, a sharp pain shot through her earlobe. The next blow was on her jaw. Then the next. Then, another. And another. Yet another. And another after that. Finally, he dragged her by the hair towards the door. She fell to the floor. Milk spilled all over the floor.

'Get out! Get out right now!' he shouted.

Suddenly, Saraswathi stood up and said, 'Hm . . .' Startled, her husband drew back. She widened her eyes and said, 'Hm . . . be careful!' He stood completely stunned. She too was still. The baby had stopped crying. For a few seconds, there was a deafening silence in that room. Saraswathi quickly went into the kitchen and fetched a rag to mop up the spilled milk. Then she laid the child on her lap and began patting it to sleep. Her husband stood like a statue for a long time. Then he slowly went and lay down. Saraswathi couldn't imagine how such intensity of feeling had flared up inside her in just a second. When he had stood there, shocked at her outburst, it seemed even a light breeze would blow him away.

The day dawned.

Her husband didn't drink his morning coffee. He took a long time reading the neighbour's copy of the Tamil daily. When the child tottered its way to him, he was neither loving nor annoyed. He bathed and got ready to leave as early as half past eight. Saraswathi came to him anxiously and said, 'I've finished cooking. Why don't you eat something?' There was neither a vegetable dish nor any appalams that morning. Not even a few mustard seeds to add flavour to the meal. He put on his coat and left without looking back. She waited till eleven, hoping he would return. Once, when he had left early, he came back home to eat. But that day he didn't come at eleven. Not even at one. Saraswathi finished her meal listlessly. She had put a lot of leftover rice from the previous day to soak in water. She didn't have to cook that night. There was nothing at home to cook anyway. She didn't have any money either. There were a few stained coins in the tin that served as a savings box; if totalled they would add up to a rupee . . . perhaps. That was all.

When dusk fell, Saraswathi gave the child a little milk. Even though the baby was slightly cranky, she was able to cope because her husband was not at home. He returned at seven. This time he sat down to eat. Just rasam and curd rice. She had borrowed four appalams from her neighbour, promising to return them the next day. Her husband slept with his mouth open as usual and his limbs akimbo, as though he was flying off somewhere. The child woke up several times during the night and wailed. But he didn't get up, didn't yell at her.

Another day dawned. Saraswathi prepared a cup of coffee with the little coffee powder that was left. Her husband sat in the veranda and read the newspaper. He didn't say a word to her. She stood in the kitchen, unable to decide what to do. Then she made up her mind and went to the front door. Even at a rent of twenty-two rupees a month, their portion was walled in from the neighbours, giving them a modicum of privacy. It was only at the back, beyond the kitchen, that all the four tenants shared a courtyard, well and pump. Saraswathi hesitated for a moment, not knowing how to draw his attention.

Finally, she said, 'We have just enough rice for one meal.'

Startled, he raised his head and gave her a wide-eyed stare. Then he put his head down again and grunted, 'Hmm.'

'We are out of coffee powder too. And dal and mustard, we need at least a hundred grams of each.'

'Hmm.'

'We don't have appalams either. I have to return at least fifteen appalams to the lady in the opposite house.'

'Hmm.'

'Kerosene too. There is only a little left in the bottle.'

'Hmm.'

'Then . . . if we can manage it, we need to buy a feeding bottle for the baby.'

'Hmm.'

Saraswathi took a deep breath to prepare herself. Then she went to her husband, held his feet and began to wail.

He was stunned for a moment, then he turned his attention back to the newspaper as if nothing important had happened.

She stammered, a few words at a time, in between uncontrollable sobs: 'What did I do? Why are you like this? Why have you refused to talk to me for days? Who do I have in this world, except you?'

One or two neighbours peeked through their windows. The vegetable vendor stopped to watch them too.

'What have I done wrong? I keep out of your way as much as I can, yet you get annoyed at the very sight of me.'

'Hmm.'

He still pretended to be reading the daily with great concentration. But since she was still clutching his feet, he found it difficult to hold the newspaper in front of him. So he held it raised above his head. He would surely get a crick in the neck within a couple of minutes.

'Who do I have except you? How can I cook proper meals if you don't bring the provisions? What more can I say? You already know everything! Then why do you torment me by not speaking to me? Have I ever behaved contrary to your wishes, even for a day, for an hour?'

By now, a few people in the street had become spectators.

'When I borrow this and that from the neighbours, and when I can't return things as promised, do you know how I agonize over what they might think of you?'

Saraswathi's sorrow choked her throat. If only there was the tiniest bit of love in her husband, nothing would seem difficult. But she ended up saying something else and not what she had intended. She became incoherent.

The child crawled along the floor to the doorstep and bumped its head on it. Saraswathi rushed to the baby and rubbed its head so it wouldn't swell. The small crowd in the street began to disperse. Her husband sat there for a while as though he was thinking of something; then he went inside and got ready for work. Saraswathi went and stood behind him. 'Hit me. Hit me till you break my bones. You are behaving like this because I resisted your hitting me, isn't it? Here, hit me. Beat me all you want.'

'All right. Leave me alone,' he said. At that moment, she would have done and said anything he asked of her. She let go of his hand and stood aside. He put on his slippers and left.

She remained standing there. She couldn't understand the situation. Something had gone wrong with her life, and it was marking her whole existence with grief and turmoil. There was not even a moment of peace and trust and mutual caring between husband and wife. What a vast rift there was between them! Would this ever be bridged? What would it lead to? She had to look after the child. But the child could hardly be expected to understand her despair. If it weren't for the baby, she wouldn't have the faintest desire to go on.

Saraswathi didn't cook that day. Nor did her husband return home for lunch. A boy came and dropped a handbill. It announced the inauguration of a new furniture shop in their street. Tables, chairs and cupboards made of genuine teak and rosewood were for sale at easy prices with a guarantee on quality, it said. The child played about happily—it had hardly given any trouble these last two days: no indigestion or constipation. It was noon. The sari she had washed that morning lay in a wet pile in the kitchen. Saraswathi picked it up and slowly spread it on the clothes line. Her weary mind lay curled up in a corner, barely able to feel even hunger and thirst. She could hear the hard sound of batter being ground on a stone mortar in the neighbouring house. Voices from the street, the drone of a radio set somewhere, the kerosene vendor's cries—all these sounds were immersed in a vast ocean of silence. They rose now and again to the surface and sank back into its depths. A procession of ants crawled busily along one wall, ending in the alcove on the opposite wall. She had kept the packet of prasadam from the Kanda Sashti puja there. Had she remembered last night, she could have served it to her husband at dinner. She took the packet, removed the ants by blowing on them and put away the sacred sweetmeat in a safe place. Why had they gone to the puja, if this was all the benediction they were to get? Had they offered worship only to end up a broken family, and for her heart to wither and die from the weight of all the buried grief she could never express to anyone? Perhaps one should expect nothing but punishment from God. For a moment, Saraswathi had a vision of the mahaan's face at the puja.

Her despondency vanished when she thought of him. She now saw an end to all her sorrows. If she surrendered at the feet of the mahaan whose countenance had been radiant with serenity and compassion, all her troubles would cease. He would grant her deliverance. She couldn't be of service to him every day. Nor could she spend a lot of money and organize grand pujas. She couldn't even manage the bus fare to go and listen to him speak two days in a row. But he would know all this about her. All she had to do was surrender at his feet and cry out, 'Swami, you are the sole refuge for this poor woman.' Then everything would be all right.

The child was asleep. Saraswathi took fifty paise in small change from the little box in which she saved money for offerings to God. She gently picked up the baby and the small container of hot milk, and went to the neighbour's house. Everyone in that house knew of her husband's cruelty; even so, they often treated her without the slightest consideration. Sometimes, though, they came to her of their own accord and bemoaned her fate. The old lady of the family was resting in the front room. Saraswathi called out, 'Mami!'

The lady turned around to look and asked, 'Is that you, Saraswathi?'

'Could I leave the child with you? I'll be away for just an hour.'

'What was that?' the lady asked again.

'I've just received word that my aunt is seriously ill. I must rush and find out how she is now. Please mind the child for a little while. There is milk here. If she gets up, please give her the milk. I will run along and be right back.'

'But your child will cry all the time without you.'

'Just for a little while. I'll be right back.'

'Mm, all right. Just leave her there.'

'Here you are.'

'Have you kept two or three rags for the child? She will dirty the house.'

'I have. They are right here.'

'When a woman visits her aunt, can't she take her child along? Call themselves women!'

Saraswathi hesitated for a moment. Then she told the lady, 'I'll lock up the house and give you the key. If he comes home in the meantime, give it to him.'

'Hm.'

'I am sure I'll return before the milkman comes. But if he should come earlier, please buy and keep one ollock.'

'Now I have to post someone in front of your door to look out for the milkman as well?'

'No, Mami. After all, the same milkman comes to both our houses. I'll be back before that. Please look after the baby till then.'

Saraswathi took a bus and reached the locality, but couldn't recognize the house where they had seen the mahaan. The area was not familiar to her. Her husband had not told her whose house it was, nor had she asked him. Most people at the puja had come with their families, but she had not known any of them. She had not participated in any conversations there. Only the lady of the house had asked Saraswathi her name, where she was from, how old her child was, and so on. And this was just before they gave away the prasadam. At that time, there had been no opportunity to get acquainted with anyone.

The rickshaw-wallahs in the locality, and even the two domestic servants she asked, did not know the house where a newly arrived mahaan was staying. After wandering about here and there for more than half an hour, Saraswathi suddenly remembered something. There had been many old ladies at the puja, two of whom in particular had kept up a ceaseless banter. Since Saraswathi had been sitting close to them, she couldn't help overhearing snatches of their conversation. In the middle of their wide-ranging discussion covering sundry topics, one of them had said, 'Endi, this cinema star Thangamani, doesn't she stay right next to this house? Her father was a mere driver in my father-in-law's brother's house ten years ago. Now he is flourishing. Spends in lakhs, I believe.' Saraswathi inquired where cinema star Thangamani lived. She was surprised that even someone like her, numb with despair as she was, was able to think resourcefully just when she needed to. She found the house in a matter of minutes.

The lady of the house noticed her as she came up the stairs. She welcomed her at the door and invited her in. Even at that hour of the afternoon there were many people about. The mahaan sat on a swing in the large hall. A young man was singing bhajans to the accompaniment of a tanpura. Saraswathi touched the mahaan's feet and went to the back of the house to wash. The lady of the house took her to the kitchen and gave her a little sweet pongal. She asked her where she was from and how many children she had. Saraswathi told the lady of her earlier visit two days ago. Despite herself, she also mentioned the feeding bottle she had left behind then. The lady of the house said, 'Oho, it is yours then.' The bottle had been cleaned till it sparkled. Saraswathi suddenly felt full of strength and hope.

The singing continued in the hall.

There was a telephone in one corner of the room. Somebody had lifted the handset and placed it next to the instrument. Saraswathi sat down inconspicuously against a wall. The mahaan would be able to see her only if he turned around, but it was the only place she could find. The singing was melodious. Once or twice, the mahaan closed his eyes and sat still, listening intently. The rest of the time, his gaze fell on the people in the room, one by one. Most of them were familiar to him, and he smiled kindly at them. Saraswathi waited, looking up at him with rapt attention. He never turned and looked her way.

Someone emerged from inside carrying a large plate heaped with flowers and headed towards the puja room. Inexplicably, just as he was walking past Saraswathi, the plate slipped and fell noisily to the floor, and the flowers scattered. Even the singer suspended his singing for a moment. The mahaan turned around. The man who had dropped the plate stood quaking. 'Forgive me, Swami,' he blabbered. Saraswathi became aware that the mahaan's eyes were now on her. Her skin broke out in gooseflesh. The flowers were gathered back on to the plate and taken away. Saraswathi waited there, not even blinking. The mahaan looked at her again with immense compassion. A great sob heaved out of her. She saw that he had noticed it.

When the mahaan looked at her for the third time, it seemed to her as though he wanted to ask her something. Saraswathi put the feeding bottle down on the floor, and went near him. She did another namaskaram and stood up. When she saw the boundless sympathy that glowed

362

in his face, her eyes welled up with tears. He did not say a word. But his look seemed to ask her with great concern, 'What is your sorrow, my child?' She began, 'Swami . . .' but couldn't speak further. What, of everything, would she name as her sorrow, and how would she describe it?

The mahaan waited, smiling, with an expression that said, 'You can tell me everything, my child.'

'Swami . . .' she began again. By now, two or three people had come up to the mahaan. One of them was the man of the house. He introduced his friends to the holy man. She stood aside. Then the singing came to an end. The man of the house called the singer to the mahaan and whispered something. The mahaan distributed vibhuti to everyone present. Someone brought a gold necklace and showed it to him. Then the mahaan rose and went inside. Saraswathi remained standing near the swing. The people in the room chatted with one another. In a little while, the crowd dispersed. No one seemed to notice her standing there.

The sun had begun to set. Her child would certainly have woken up by now. The neighbour would have given the milk. Even her husband might have returned

Saraswathi crossed the room with the swing and went further into the house. There were a lot of people there, having snacks and coffee. They all seemed to know one another. She went from one room to another. No one stopped her. Finally she came upon the lady of the house who was talking to several people; she was busy giving instructions to someone who looked like he was in charge of the kitchen. She called softly, 'Mami.'

The lady of the house said, 'Yes?'

'Where has Swami gone? Can't I meet him now?'

'Oh, he has already left for japam.'

From the way she said this, it was obvious to Saraswathi that she wouldn't be able to meet the mahaan for quite some time. She gasped, blacking out momentarily. The people around her watched silently.

Saraswathi said, 'Then I will take leave of you, Mami.'

'All right.' The lady called someone to offer turmeric, vermilion, fruit and betel leaves to Saraswathi.

Saraswathi walked away reluctantly, and everyone instantly resumed talking.

She walked briskly to the bus stop. There was no point in staying back. For a moment she thought she would burst into tears. And then her mind became completely empty, void of all feeling.

When she reached home the child was awake. But her husband had not come home yet.

He never returned.

From the original Vimochanam (1961)

Glossary

'pa, 'ma	Terms of respectful familiarity for men and women respectively, often used with friends, acquaintances and strangers in public spaces
Akka	elder sister
Angavastram	An ornamental piece of cloth, worn formally over the shoulder by men
Annachi	Informal address for elder brother
Appalam	Flat round chips made of rice or lintels; eaten fried or roasted, sometimes in lieu of vegetables
Athimber	Brother-in-law—elder sister's husband
Ayya, 'ya	Term of respect for an older man, demonstrating subservience
Badmaash	Villain
Besh	Term of approbation

Bhagavathar	An accomplished singer
Chittappa	Father's younger brother
Darsanam	Divine spectacle, considered a boon to the devotee
Ek Din Ka Sultan	King for a Day
Ennachi	What happened?
Jamakkalam	Thick rug
Japam	Silent meditation and prayer
Kanakadara	Shower of Gold
Karagam, Kavadi	Dance from the Tamil folk tradition, usually in propitiation of native deities
Kolam	Decorative designs drawn on the front courtyard, floor, etc., with rice flour or flour-paste
Kolu	Arrangement of decorative dolls at home, during Navaratri
Kotwal	Head policeman
Kungumam	Vermilion powder, worn by women on their foreheads as an auspicious mark
Kuzhambu	Thick lintel gravy on a tamarind base; usually eaten with rice
Maadiveedu	House with an upper storey

Maapillai	Son-in-law
Machaan	Brother-in-law—wife's younger brother
Mahaan	Great sage
Maistry	Supervisor, usually of construction workers
Namaskaram	Showing respect with folded hands, or by prostrating
Mrichakatika	The Clay Cart
Navaratri	Annual festival of nine nights in worship of Goddess Durga
Ollock	A traditional measure of volume. One ollock is equal to one-sixth of a litre.
Paati	Grandmother
Prasadam	Votive offering of food, distributed to devotees at the end of a puja
Rahukaalam	The period each weekday—lasting one-and-a-half hours—that is considered inauspicious
Ramar Pattabhishekam	The coronation of Lord Rama as the king of Ayodhya
Sastrigal	One who is well-versed in the Shastras, often a title for a priest who conducts religious rites

Sattakkaris	Literally, shirt-wearing girls
Seth	Widely used form of address for north Indians in Chennai
Sombu	A small metal container with a narrow neck
TC	Transfer certificate
Thambi	Literally younger brother, but also used to address a youngster
Thondar	Party worker
Vaazhga	Long live!
Veezhga	Down, down
Veshti	Ankle-length lower garment, worn by men
Vibhuti	Sacred ash, used in ritual worship of Shaivite gods, worn by devotees on their foreheads as a mark of piety